RY

LAUREN CHILD

FORT

LOOK INTO MY EYES

CANDLEWICK PRESS

 W9-BYA-198

This is a work of fiction. Names, characters, places, and incidents are either products of the author's imagination or, if real, are used fictitiously.

Copyright © 2011 by Lauren Child
Series design by David Mackintosh

All rights reserved. No part of this book may be reproduced, transmitted, or stored in an information retrieval system in any form or by any means, graphic, electronic, or mechanical, including photocopying, taping, and recording, without prior written permission from the publisher.

First published in Great Britain by HarperCollins Children's Books, a division of HarperCollinsPublishers Ltd

First U.S. edition 2012

Library of Congress Cataloging-in-Publication Data is available.

Library of Congress Catalog Card Number pending

ISBN 978-0-7636-5120-6

12 13 14 15 16 17 BVG 10 9 8 7 6 5 4 3 2 1

Printed in Berryville, VA, U.S.A.

This book was typeset in Eames Century Modern.

Candlewick Press
99 Dover Street
Somerville, Massachusetts 02144

visit us at www.candlewick.com

For **A. D.**

"If the eyes truly are the window to the soul, then some people would be wise to install blinds."

ANYA PAMPLEMOUS, from her book
The Puzzles That Lie Within

There Was a Girl Named Ruby

IT WAS A CRISP OCTOBER DAY on Cedarwood Drive, and a two-year-old girl was standing on a high stool in front of a huge picture window. She was watching the leaves fall, studying the patterns they made as they whirled their way through the air. Her eyes followed them until her gaze was caught by a single yellow leaf almost exactly the shape of a hand. She watched as it swooped down into the yard and then sailed up high over the fence and across the street. She watched as it danced up and down in the breeze and then slapped flat onto the windshield of a passing truck.

The truck pulled up in front of old Mr. Pinkerton's gray clapboard house. The driver climbed out, walked up the path, and knocked on the door. Mr. Pinkerton stepped out onto the porch, and the driver produced a map. The two men struck up a conversation.

Exactly one minute later an elegant woman turned the corner, carrying a large green picnic basket. With a glance to the house and the slightest nod from the driver, the woman slipped out of her heels, scooped them up, and nimbly scaled Mr. Pinkerton's fence. Mr. Pinkerton was busy studying the map and noticed nothing; the child saw everything. Forty-five seconds passed and the woman reappeared: she was carrying the same basket but it looked much heavier than before and its contents seemed to be moving.

The little girl attempted to grab her parents' attention, but since her use of language was still limited she could not get them to understand. She watched as the woman pushed her feet back into her black shoes, walked to the rear of the truck, and disappeared out of view. Mr. Pinkerton chatted on. The girl jumped up and down, pointing at the window. Her parents, sensing she might be eager for a walk, went to put on their coats.

The child drew a truck on her chalkboard.

Her father smiled and patted her on the head.

Meanwhile, the driver folded his map, thanked Mr. Pinkerton, and returned to his vehicle, waving to him as he drove off. The yellow hand-shaped leaf fluttered to the ground. The woman, now minus the picnic basket, walked on by. She had a fresh scarlet scratch on her left cheek.

The child spelled out the truck's license plate with her alphabet blocks.

Her mother put them away and dressed her in a red woolen pom-pom hat and matching mittens.

The family left the house and strolled down Cedarwood Drive. When they reached the gray clapboard house, the little girl paused to pick up the yellow leaf, and there underneath it, found a small tin button embossed with an image of something. What was it?

A sudden cry shook the stillness of Cedarwood Drive. A cry that cut right through the heart of the child. She gripped the button tightly and felt the pin dig into her palm. The neighbors came spilling out onto the street to find the kindly Mr. Pinkerton doubled up with grief. Despite the best efforts of the Twinford Crime Investigation Squad — a search which continued for sixteen weeks — Mr. Pinkerton's prize-winning Pekinese dog was never seen again.

It was on that October day that the little girl resolved to dispense with the toddler talk and brush up on her language skills. More important, that was the day she set her sights on becoming a detective.

The little girl was Ruby Redfort.

An Ordinary Kid

WHEN RUBY REDFORT WAS SEVEN YEARS OLD she won the Junior Code-Cracker Championships — solving the famous Eisenhauser conundrum in just seventeen days and forty-seven minutes. The following year she entered the Junior Code-Creator Contest and stunned the judges when they found her code impossible to break. In the end it was sent to Harvard University professors, who eventually managed to solve it two weeks later. She was immediately offered a place for the following semester but declined. She had no interest in becoming, as she put it, "some kind of geek freak."

Some several years later . . .

CHAPTER 1
You Can Never Be Completely Sure What Might Happen Next

RUBY REDFORT WAS PERCHED ON a high stool in front of the bathroom window, her binoculars trained on a cake delivery truck that had been parked on Cedarwood Drive for precisely twenty-one minutes. So far no one had emerged from the truck with so much as a blueberry muffin. Ruby gurgled down the last dregs of her banana milk and made a note in the little yellow notebook that lay in her lap. She had six hundred and twenty-two of these yellow notebooks; all but one were stashed under her bedroom floorboards. Though she had taken up this hobby nine years ago, no one, not even her best friend, Clancy, had read a single word she had written. Much of what Ruby observed seemed pretty mundane, but **EVEN THE MUNDANE CAN TELL A STORY {RULE 16}.**

Ruby also kept a vivid pink notebook, dog-eared and smelling of bubble gum, and it was in this that she listed her Ruby rules — there were seventy-nine so far.

RULE 1: YOU CAN NEVER BE COMPLETELY SURE WHAT MIGHT HAPPEN NEXT. A truth no one could argue with.

Ruby was a petite girl, small for her years — at first glance a very ordinary-looking kid. There was nothing particular to mark her out — nothing, that is, until you looked a little longer. Then you would begin to see that her eyes were ever so slightly different shades of green. When they looked at you, it was somehow hard to remember the point you were arguing. And when she smiled she revealed small doll-like teeth, which somehow made it impossible to consider her anything *other* than a cute kid. But the most striking thing about Ruby Redfort was that when you met her you felt a strong need for her to like you.

The bathroom phone rang. Lazily, Ruby reached out and groped for the receiver.

"Brandy's Wig Salon. Hair today, gone tomorrow."

"Hi, Rube," replied the voice on the other end. It was Clancy Crew.

"So, Clance, what gives?"

"Not a whole lot actually."

"So to what do I owe the pleasure of this call?"

"Boredom," yawned Clancy.

"So why don't you get yourself over here, bozo?"

"Well, I would, you know, Rube, but my dad wants me home.

He's got some kinda embassy-type function and he wants us all smiling, you know what I mean?"

Clancy Crew's father was an ambassador, and there was always some function or other in progress. Ambassador Crew liked to have his children scrubbed and serving canapés to prove what a great family guy he was — though truth to tell he was usually too busy to even remember their birthdays.

"Some people have all the fun," drawled Ruby.

"Yeah, my life stinks," said Clancy.

"So cheer yourself up, why don'tcha. Scoot yourself over, watch a few toons, and you'll still be home in time to smile for the cameras."

"OK, Rube, you've talked me into it. See you in ten."

Ruby put down the phone. It lived on a shelf with two others: one was in the shape of a conch shell, the other disguised as a bar of soap. She had a whole lot more of them in her bedroom. She had been collecting telephones since she was about five years old, all in different shapes and colors. The donut phone was her first — the latest, a cartoon squirrel sporting a tuxedo. Just about all of them had come from yard sales.

She was about to continue her bathroom-based surveillance when the intercom buzzed. Ruby's parents had sensibly fitted them on each floor to keep shouting to a minimum.

She pressed the *Speak* button.

"Hello, how may I be of assistance?"

"Howdy," came the voice from the other end of the intercom. "This is Mrs. Digby, your housekeeper. May I please remind you that your parents will be home from Switzerland in two and a quarter hours."

"I know, Mrs. Digby, you told me that a half hour ago."

"Glad you remembered. May I also point out that they may be a little grief stricken to see the state of your bedroom."

"It's my style, Mrs. Digby — 'layered.' It's very in vogue."

"Well, may I continue to remind you that some magazine folks are coming to photograph this very house tomorrow, and if your mother sees it in its 'layered' state, you will be in what's commonly referred to as 'the dog house.'"

"OK, OK," Ruby sighed. "I'll take care of it."

The Redfort house, dubbed the Green-Wood house on account of its environmental features, had been designed in 1961 by famous architect Arno Fredricksonn. Even now, a decade or so later, it was still considered state of the art and was regularly featured in architectural journals.

Ruby returned to the bathroom, sat back down on her stool, and continued to stare out of the window. The truck was still there but now there was a raccoon sitting on its roof. The bathroom door opened, and in ambled a large husky dog, which sniffed around before settling down to chew the bathmat.

"Bored, huh?" said Ruby, slipping off her stool. She padded into her bedroom and surveyed the wreckage. It was not a pretty sight. Ruby wasn't so much untidy as she was a spreader — she had a lot of stuff, and when she was busy working on something the *stuff* had a habit of creeping from one surface to another, and this was what her mother did not like.

"Darn it!" muttered Ruby. If the magazine people were coming, her mom would just about freak if this was what they saw. She could almost hear her father saying, *"For the sake of your mother's sanity — do something, Ruby."* So she set about slipping records back into their sleeves and pushing books onto shelves. Ruby had a lot of books; they were arranged floor-to-ceiling across one end of her room.

A FICTION SECTION: both English and foreign titles.

FACTUAL: comprising anything.

GRAPHIC NOVELS AND COMICS: subject — largely crime and mystery.

Ruby and Mrs. Digby had a shared enthusiasm for crime and thrillers: fact or fiction, whether in book form or on the screen. They would often sit down with a large bowl of blue corn chips and watch the quiz show *What's Your Poison?* When Ruby was several years younger, Mrs. Digby would settle Ruby to sleep by reading one of her favorite crime thrillers, *The Claw at the Window.*

PUZZ1 ES: Puzzles were Ruby's passion. Any kind of puzzle: crossword, anagrams, riddles, even jigsaws — anything that needed to be solved by finding the "pattern," the "trick," or the "key." This had led Ruby to . . .

CODES: She had read many books and essays on the subject. In fact she was a subscriber to *Master Code Monthly,* a little-known Chinese subscription-only magazine. Subscribers had to prove their code-cracking talent before they were permitted to sign up. 't was this journal that had led her to read the following:

* Garp F nholt's *The Theory of Code: Its Abstract Duality and Subtext* (to be honest, Ruby had found this overstated and not a little tedious).

* Sherman Tree's more vital *Unlock My Brain.*

* Anya Pamplemous's thirty year study of codes, *The Puzzles That Lie Within,* which she also very much enjoyed.

But her personal handbooks were both written many centuries ago: one by the Greek philosopher Euclid with the simple title of *X;* the other a tiny indigo book (origin unknown) that was filled with all manner of codes. It explained riddles and poems and equations — patterns, symbols, and sounds. It was a code-breaker's bible.

Having dealt with the books, records, and papers, Ruby began the more complex task of sorting through clothes; all of which seemed to be on the floor of her closet. It was here, underneath a pile of striped knee-high socks, that she unearthed her glasses.

Boy, am I glad to see you!

Although Ruby would on occasion wear contact lenses, she didn't much care for them; they had a habit of falling out at exactly the wrong moment. If Ruby Redfort had an Achilles' heel, it was her eyes; without some sort of visual aid, life was just a blur.

There was another buzz from the intercom. "Yuh huh?"

"What are you doing?"

"I'm un-messing. Why?"

"Just checking."

"Mrs. Digby, you are one suspicious woman."

Having put away as many of her clothes as she could be bothered to put away, Ruby grabbed all the remaining garments and stuffed them down the laundry chute. She was in the habit of tipping all sorts of things down the laundry chute — even, on occasion, herself. It saved time.

Judging her work finished, Ruby's finger hovered over the TV's *On* switch, but her attention was caught by what sounded like activity in the kitchen. Seven years ago she had a rigged up a reverse periscope device so that she could see what was occurring in the kitchen below. Today she saw Mrs. Digby taking a fresh batch of cookies out of the oven.

Nice work, Mrs. Digby.

She slid her notebook carefully inside the hollowed out door frame, and went downstairs.

RULE 2: IF YOU WANT TO KEEP SOMETHING SECRET, DON'T LEAVE IT LYING AROUND.

CHAPTER 2
There's a Lot of Truth in Fiction

WHEN RUBY ENTERED THE STYLISH, modern kitchen, she was automatically handed a vile-smelling green drink. Ruby glared at Mrs. Digby, bearer of the unfortunate liquid.

Mrs. Digby shrugged. "Don't look at me, it's your mother's orders — she wants you to grow." Sabina was always trying to get Ruby to eat foods that might promote growth. "Personally I don't see what's so wrong with being short," Mrs. Digby added. "I've always been short, and it's never stopped me from getting by in the world."

This was true. Mrs. Digby was probably one of the smallest and most determined people one could meet. She had been with the Redforts long before Ruby was born, and before that she was housekeeper to Ruby's mother's parents. Her face resembled an autumn leaf — dry and covered in lines. When she applied lipstick, it bled along the tiny cracks around her mouth, creating miniature rivulets. She was getting on in years, but no one was exactly sure of her age. If asked she usually answered, "Sixty, seventy, eighty . . . who's counting? Not me, that's for darn sure."

Mrs. Digby spoiled Ruby whenever possible but never, ever, went against Mrs. Redfort's dietary instructions. Sabina Redfort was always putting her household under one health regime or another, and Ruby and her father dreaded them *all*.

Ruby took the drink without arguing, brought it to her lips and said, "Mrs. Digby, could I have just one cookie, just to take the taste away?"

Mrs. Digby considered the request for a mere moment. "Well, your mother didn't say you couldn't — so I guess it would be all right." She turned her back for a second, maybe two, and in this tiny moment Ruby poured the drink down the sink, having been careful to first make sure she got some of the green liquid on her upper lip.

"Yuck!" said Ruby.

"There's a miserable kid," said the housekeeper, wiping Ruby's face as if she were still just a toddler. Mrs. Digby looked at Ruby's T-shirt, which bore the statement *some days stink* and muttered, "Well, who can argue with that."

She paused.

"On second thought, your mother will. If I were you I might avoid the trouble by changing into something, you know — frilly."

Ruby made a face. "Frilly" was neither in her vocabulary nor her wardrobe. As far as her attire went, she was more often than not dressed in jeans, sneakers, a T-shirt printed with either a somewhat hostile word: *bozo;* an interesting number: *1729;* or some less than agreeable statement: *bored beyond belief.* But she knew what Mrs. Digby meant, and she knew she had a point.

The backstairs door opened, and in walked a young woman followed by three large boxes of heirloom tomatoes balanced on a pair of skinny legs.

"*Hola,* Ruby. How are you?" said the woman.

"*Bien, gracias,* Consuela," replied Ruby. "Hey, is that you under there, Clance?"

"I think so," muttered Clancy, struggling to heave the boxes onto the counter. He rolled his eyes. "I'll just go and fetch the others." Clancy was a good-natured person. Mostly he tended to like people, but he didn't much like Consuela. Too bossy. Mrs. Digby was no big fan either.

The trouble had begun when Sabina Redfort rather rashly decided that Mrs. Digby's cooking was too stodgy and that they should adopt a more olive-oil-and-tomato-based diet. This had led to the hiring of dietary expert Consuela Cruz. Consuela had been flown over from Seville, Spain, along with many suitcases and countless cooking utensils, and though her salary was eye-watering, Mrs. Redfort considered her to be worth every penny.

The new diet may have been helping maintain healthy hearts, but it certainly wasn't generating much love. Mrs. Digby made a muttering sound deep in her throat, Consuela clucked her tongue, and both women left the room by different doors. Ruby, now alone, piled several cookies (ten to be exact) on to a plate and went about making some more appealing drinks (two banana milks with strawberry ice cream). The banana milk was imported from Europe, for though Brant Redfort had tried, it seemed impossible to find anywhere inside the U.S.A.

Ruby popped straws in both drinks and carefully carried them out of the kitchen, sucking on one of the straws as she went. She was about to climb the stairs when she caught sight of the little light on the answering machine flashing to indicate a message. She pressed *Play*.

"Hey there, Redfort gang! It's the Humberts here. Freddie and I were just saying how much we would like it if you all came over. And Quent would just adore to see darling Ruby! Call us back, won't you! Bye bye bye!"

This voice belonged to Marjorie Humbert, a family friend, wife of Twinford City bank manager Freddie Humbert, and the mother of Quent, the dullest boy in town. Ruby automatically pressed *Erase* and continued on her way. She was followed by the large husky.

"Hey there, Bug," cooed Ruby. "Wanna watch some TV?"

When she entered her room she caught sight of herself in the mirror. Mrs. Digby was right: if she wanted to avoid a whole lot of grief she might want to put on a dress. She rummaged through her closet until she found an interesting red and white number she had picked up at a thrift store — if Ruby wore anything other than jeans and T-shirts, then it was usually secondhand. She was one of those girls who people talked about as "having her own style," which was sometimes meant as a compliment and sometimes not. The hem of the dress was secured with sticky-tape, but it was hardly noticeable if you weren't looking too closely.

Ruby pulled on some black over-the-knee socks and a pair of Yellow Stripe sneakers. The dress still retained its thrift store odor, so Ruby sprayed herself with some expensive perfume. (Oriental Rose: she had a sizable collection of beautifully bottled fragrances which, when worn, mingled with the odor of the bubble gum she so often chewed, creating a unique Ruby Redfort fragrance.)

Clancy had not yet reappeared, so Ruby carried the tray of

snacks up the open-tread staircase that connected her room to the rooftop. She liked to sit up here on warm evenings looking at the stars, writing in her notebook, reading, and, more than occasionally, watching the portable TV. She settled down in the beanbag, in one hand a cookie and in the other a large green apple. She believed that the healthy attributes of the apple might counteract the bad effects of the cookie. (Ruby Redfort had a lot of theories like this one.)

She looked up when Clancy popped his head through the trapdoor. Clancy was a shortish, scrawny-looking boy — not exactly your "yearbook kid" but certainly one of the most engaging characters you were likely to talk to, if of course you bothered to *talk* to him, which most people didn't.

"Oh, boy! I had to make a dash for the stairs or she would have had me peeling tomatoes for the rest of my life. I wouldn't mind but tomatoes give me hives."

He slumped down next to Ruby, who was busy flipping through the channels. Ruby was a keen watcher of TV — she watched *a lot*. She loved sitcoms, dramas, news shows, quiz shows, documentaries, but it was the detective shows that were her TV passion, and *Crazy Cops* in particular. *Crazy Cops* was a police drama that Ruby and Clancy were practically addicted to; it was very informative while at the same time being extremely entertaining. They had both picked up their knowledge about police investigations and human behavior from watching *Crazy Cops*. *"There's a lot of truth in fiction,"* was something Ruby was fond of reminding her parents whenever they complained about her "TV habit." Sunday night, however, was toon night, and they were just into a fourth episode of *Grime Girl of the Crime World*, when Ruby heard her parents' car pulling into the driveway.

Clancy looked at his watch and groaned. "I guess I gotta go. My dad won't exactly see the funny side if I'm late."

"That's too bad, Clance. But hey, don't forget to smile."

"Yeah, yeah, some friend you are. I'll call you later."

He left by climbing from the roof onto a branch of the large tree handily positioned right next to the house—from there he could shinny his way down to the yard. Ruby usually descended more conventionally, by way of the stairs.

Noticing that she had forgotten to tackle the large pile of shoes in the middle of the room, she fetched the beanbag and placed it on top. The room looked magazine-shoot tidy. She took one last look in the mirror, then adjusted the barrette securing her long dark hair in a firm side part, giving her a look of utter composure.

Satisfied, Ruby sort of half walked, half hopped downstairs, followed silently by Bug.

CHAPTER 3
Sounded Like Dessert

HEY HONEY, HOW'S MY GIRL?" said her father, lifting Ruby up over his shoulder and mussing her hair. It was a "welcome home" ritual Brant Redfort had never grown out of.

"Hey, Dad, do ya wanna cool it? You're messing with my look!" said Ruby in a somewhat strangled voice.

"Oh, Brant!" said Sabina Redfort, pretending to disapprove. "For an intelligent man you really can behave like a total nut." No one but Sabina would ever describe Brant Redfort as intelligent. Ruby had been born to parents who would never be giving Einstein a run for his money.

In many ways nature *had* been generous to Brant and Sabina. They had been given an easy charm and likeability, good looks, and generous personalities. But for all their fairy tale–like graces they had little going on upstairs in the smarts department. However, you would be hard-pressed to meet a more popular couple, and for this reason they headed up just about every committee or fundraising benefit in Twinford. They were what's known as "socialites."

The Redfort family walked upstairs to the living room and settled down on one of the large white couches.

"So how was Switzerland?" said Ruby.

"Oh, it was wonderful, just wonderful. If we hadn't had to get back for the museum launch we would have stayed longer," said Sabina wistfully.

"Oh, yeah? What museum launch is that?" said Ruby.

"Ruby, surely you haven't forgotten about the Jade Buddha of Khotan!" exclaimed her mother.

"Sabina honey, she's pulling your leg," said Brant, raising his eyes heavenward. "You have been talking about nothing but the museum launch for the last two months."

"Oh, very cute!" laughed Sabina as she pinched Ruby on the cheek.

Ruby's parents were both wildly excited about the Jade Buddha coming to Twinford. Stolen from the ancient kingdom of Khotan during the eighth century and missing for more than a thousand years, the Buddha had recently been rediscovered encased in a block of ice somewhere north of Alaska. The archaeologist who dug the artifact out of the glacier was the senior curator of the Twinford City Museum, Dr. Enrico Gonzales. In recognition of this monumental and heroic discovery, the people of Khotan had agreed to have the Buddha displayed at the museum for a limited period before it made its long journey home. Brant and Sabina were, of course, on the museum party committee.

"You guys sure do travel light," said Ruby, looking around for their suitcases.

"Oh, yes," said her mother. "The airline managed to lose every piece of our luggage. Can you believe it!"

"So I guess you lost all your vacation pictures too?" said Ruby, hopefully. Ruby had endured many tedious hours of her parents' vacation snapshots and would go to any reasonable lengths to avoid the misery of a family slide show.

"No," said her father. "Luckily I kept all the film in my carry-on luggage. I can't wait to get them developed. You'll see I got some beautiful shots." Ruby considered this unlikely; Brant was a horrible photographer.

After an effusive welcome from a very excited Mrs. Digby — "Good to have you back at last, you've been away too long!" — and a good deal more fussing — "You've lost weight, Mrs. R., you need feeding up" — supper was ready and the family sat down to eat. Mrs. Digby had gone to a lot of trouble with the table, and there was a huge floral display that was very difficult to see over or, indeed, around.

During dinner, Ruby's parents burbled on about the wonderful hotel and the delicious schnitzel and the beautiful Alps. And the conversation went something like this:

SABINA: *Quite the tastiest schnitzel I have ever tasted.*
BRANT: *And what about those Alps! Talk about high.*

Until Ruby wished they would start talking about the Jade Buddha again. But then, of course, they did.

SABINA: *Speaking of Switzerland, Marjorie mentioned that the Buddha's glass display case has been expertly designed by a Swiss expert. No one's met him, no one. He's a complete recluse.*
BRANT: *Oh, yes, that's right. A fellow named . . . what's his name, honey?*
RUBY: *Klaus Gustav.*

Ruby hadn't exactly been *listening*, but she had been party to so many of these discussions that her brain had absorbed all the interesting and less-than-interesting details.

SABINA: *That's right, Ruby! Well, according to Marjorie, the glass display case will be the shape of a cylinder and is going to rise up through the museum floor at the stroke of midnight!*

BRANT: *How does he do it, do you think?*

SABINA: *Beats me! Must be some kind of magician. No one even knows how you get that glass cylinder open — it's top secret.*

BRANT: *Well, if their glass is as excellent as their schnitzel we are going to be in for a treat!*

. . . and they were back to talking about schnitzel again.

Ruby wished hard for some kind of distraction before her brain froze over. And her wish was granted by a loud thud and a high-pitched shriek.

"Whatever in the world was that?" exclaimed Mrs. Redfort.

"Sounded like dessert," said Ruby.

"What?" said her mother.

"I must say having Consuela around is great if you are looking to lose weight, but I am afraid our friend Bug has been pounding it on."

"Bug's been putting on weight? What do you mean? Why would Bug put on weight?" asked Mrs. Redfort.

"On account of all the low-flying food in there," replied Ruby. "Mrs. Digby and Consuela throw ingredients at each other nearly every night. Most of it ends up on the floor and Bug is only too happy to clean up, if you know what I mean."

"What!" said Brant, who was very much against pets eating their owners' food.

There was a crashing sound followed by a yelp.

"Yeah, I've pretty much gotten used to it but you may get complaints from the neighbors any day soon."

"Oh, we don't want that," said Brant, looking over toward where Mr. Parker lived. Mr. Parker was a very difficult man.

"Get used to what?" said Sabina.

"Kitchen friction." replied Ruby. "Mrs. Digby can't stand Consuela, and Consuela can't stand Mrs. Digby. It's been like this ever since you guys went away."

"Really?" said Sabina.

"Oh, yeah," said Ruby, raising her voice a little to make herself heard over what sounded like the smashing of a cut-glass tulip vase. "It's been terrible. I must say this fish is very good though."

Sabina slammed down her napkin, stood up, and strode over to the kitchen door.

"I wouldn't do that if I were you, Mom," warned Ruby through a mouthful of mackerel. But Sabina was not to be deterred. She opened the door just as Mrs. Digby took aim with a pitcher of tomato juice. Consuela ducked, and Sabina found herself covered in red gloop.

"Mrs. Digby! What has gotten into you!"

Mrs. Digby quickly reached for a dishcloth, put it down, and picked up a large towel.

"That's the second time today that someone has thrown a drink over my Oscar Birdet suit!" exclaimed Sabina.

"Really? Who was the first?" inquired Ruby, who was by now standing in the doorway and chewing on a carrot.

"Some frantic little man at the airport spills my martini all down my front, and now this! Boy, this tomato juice is never going to come out."

"Let me clean it up, Mrs. R.," said Mrs. Digby, who was looking rather pale in the face.

"I'll thank you not to touch it, Mrs. Digby, it's dry-clean only!" replied Sabina, these last words coming out rather more sharply and with more volume than she had intended.

"Is never gonna be clean again, Mrs. Redfort. No way José," said Consuela, giving Mrs. Digby a smug look. Sabina was about to try and calm things down when Mrs. Digby got in first.

"Well, I can see whose side you are taking in all this, and

me a person you've known your whole entire life. I see thirty-six years of service and loyalty count for very little around these parts. Maybe I'll just go and pack the few sorry possessions I own and get out of here for good! No doubt Cousin Emily will take me in."

"Oh, Mrs. Digby! Please don't . . ." pleaded Sabina, but it was no use. Mrs. Digby was already making her way downstairs to her housekeeper's apartment. There would be no pancakes for breakfast, that was for sure.

Ruby was relieved when the telephone rang.

"Redfort high-drama society. You want drama, we got it."

She hoped it would be Clancy Crew. He would certainly lighten the atmosphere. But it was Marjorie Humbert.

The following words were delivered by Ruby at super high speed to avoid conversation.

"Hello Mrs. Humbert yes I'm weller than you could begin to imagine I would love to chat but I know my mother is on the edge of her seat at the prospect of talking to you — bye, bye, bye!"

Ruby handed the phone to Sabina. "Gotta walk Bug," she said, and whistled to the dog.

Jeepers, could I use some air.

Ruby and Bug left by the back door and made their way down

Cedarwood Drive, turning right on Amster Street. Ruby decided to stop by the tree on Amster Green; a large oak in the middle of a triangle of grass. It stood there surrounded by blossoming trees; a wooden bench sat directly under it. The oak tree was old, with branches that twisted toward the ground and swept up again. It was perfect for climbing. Ruby and Clancy liked to sit in this tree and watch the people down below; when the tree was in leaf it provided perfect cover.

Ruby jumped onto the bench, swung herself onto the lowest branch, and from there made her way quickly up to the highest climbable limb. Finding the hole in the bark, she felt around with her hand and pulled out a piece of elaborately folded paper: a perfectly formed origami turtle. Ruby and Clancy had gotten into the habit of leaving each other tree notes, written in code and usually folded in this complicated way as it meant they would be sure to know if someone had gotten there first; origami was impossible to re-fold without knowing how, and *very* few people knew how. Clancy had obviously written the note on his way back home because it said,

```
Wvitp xrauuziv vuwp eofyboc
    efivrlw ay va mq vcwpw.*
```

*THIS IS A VIGENERE CIPHER. IF YOU WANT TO CRACK IT YOU WILL NEED TO FIND THE KEY. CLUE 1: THE EYES HAVE IT.

Ruby smiled, scribbled something on a bubble-gum wrapper,

Nsyq ltszsjyk wvy ptrwayoe!

pushed it into the hole in the tree, and climbed back down.

When she got home, she found her parents were still discussing the tomato gloop incident. Her mother was saying, "I hate for Mrs. Digby to be unhappy but we can't lose Consuela, she is a dietary genius."

"Why don't I call that house-management agency?" said her father. "See if they can't send someone to sort of keep control."

"I guess it's worth a shot," replied her mother.

The telephone began to ring.

"I'll get it!" called Ruby. She was sure this time it would be Clancy complaining about all the smiling he had had to do at his dad's dinner, but disappointingly there was no one on the end of the line.

CHAPTER 4
Full of Nothing

THE NEXT MORNING RUBY WAS JUST fixing her barrette the way she always fixed her barrette, when the phone in her bathroom rang.

It will be Clancy, she thought. *I'll bet he's calling to complain about his hives.*

She picked up the receiver.

"Twinford sewage plant, how may we assist?"

But there was no reply.

"Weird," muttered Ruby, replacing the handset.

There was no sign of Mrs. Digby—no doubt she was still smarting about the tomato-juice incident. So Ruby swallowed a large glass of orange juice in a single gulp, grabbed her schoolbag with one hand and a chocolate peanut cookie with the other, and shouted good-bye to her parents, who didn't hear because they were engaged in a fascinating discussion about which dry cleaner might best remove a tomato juice stain from a silk jacket.

BRANT: *Honey, take it to Quick Clean. Then you'll have it back in no time.*

SABINA: *Are you kidding, Brant? This is an Oscar Birdet jacket! Do you even know what that means? I'll take it to Grosvenors.*

RUBY: *Oh, brother.*

Ruby's bike had a flat, so she was taking the school bus this morning.

Twinford Junior High School was two buildings really. One old, grand and in some ways beautiful—a little run-down on the inside but somehow comfortable. The other starkly modern, stylish, and sterile. Ruby sauntered into class just before Mrs. Drisco, her homeroom teacher, called out her name. Mrs. Drisco made the same comment she always made when Ruby was late, and Ruby made the usual faces behind her back.

The truth was, Mrs. Drisco found Ruby Redfort *"Rather full of herself, utterly unmanageable, and impossible to teach."* Ruby Redfort found Mrs. Drisco *"A royal pain in the derriere."*

They were both right.

When it came to teaching the smartest student in the history of Twinford Junior High, Mrs. Drisco was out of her depth. On the other hand, it was a little pathetic for a grown-up teacher to be so snarky.

Once this little pupil-teacher exchange was over, Ruby went and sat down next to Clancy.

"So was last night fun?" whispered Ruby.

"Well, that depends on what you call fun. My sister Nancy accidentally sat on the Spanish ambassador's dessert," replied Clancy.

"Oh, well at least she *got* dessert — some of us weren't so lucky," said Ruby.

"What?" said Clancy.

"Never mind, I'll tell you later," whispered Ruby.

It was the usual Twinford Junior High day, nothing in any way out of the ordinary. Ruby had the usual interaction with her archenemy, Vapona Begwell, which went something like this:

VAPONA: *Hey, Ruby, can you see outta those glasses because my suggestion would be, don't look in the mirror if you don't wanna give yourself a fright.*

RUBY: *Why, you gonna be standing behind me?*

❋ ❋ ❋

There was a mildly interesting geography lesson followed by a mind-numbingly dreary French class (Ruby's French was already so good that she spent the lesson reading *War and Peace* in the original Russian). History had Mrs. Schneiderman promising in the next week or so to give a lecture on the Jade Buddha of Khotan. "My, it's the most fascinating story," she said. "I could talk about it forever."

"Meet my folks and you probably will," muttered Ruby.

At lunchtime Ruby got into an altercation with Mrs. Arthur over the **let them eat cake** T-shirt she was wearing. Ruby was protesting about Mrs. Arthur's strict guidelines about cake — or, more accurately, no cake. Mrs. Arthur had banned cake.

MRS. ARTHUR: *Cake is in no way essential and should not be present in any child's diet.*
RUBY: *Cake is one of life's great wonders and who would deny wonder to a child?*

All the pupils with the exception of Denning Minkle, who had a sugar allergy, supported Ruby. However, Ruby was requested to turn her T-shirt inside out or risk a month of detention.

Ruby said good-bye to Clancy, who was being kept behind

so he could retake his French vocab test. He was nervous; French made him feel queasy, and Madame Loup gave him the shivers.

"You'll be fine, Clance," said Ruby, as she slipped him an index card. "Copy this list onto your arm and you'll have no problem."

The piece of paper had all the test answers written in code — the code they had devised a couple of years ago and perfect for a situation like this. To the regular human on the street it just looked like gobbledygook.

Then it was time to catch the bus back to Cedarwood Drive.

Yes, everything was pretty normal. Things only began to get strange when Ruby arrived home.

She swung open the gate and saw that the front door to the house was standing open and a police car was parked in the drive. As she walked up the stairs to the kitchen, she could hear the voice of Sheriff Bridges.

Now what is he doing here?

It didn't take Ruby long to find out. She stood there in the living room, openmouthed.

Everything had gone. Well, almost everything. The telephone was still plugged into its socket and was sitting on the floor. Apart from that the house was as empty as a house could be. Even the dust was gone. It was obvious to anyone, even someone who had never visited the Redforts before, that they had been robbed.

"Yes," said her mother, guessing her daughter's thoughts, "Every room is full of nothing."

CHAPTER 5
More of Nothing

RUBY TURNED AND RAN UPSTAIRS, right to the top of the house. She went into her empty bedroom and set about pulling at the wobbly floorboards. As she lifted them up she was met by the yellow glow of her six hundred and twenty-one yellow notebooks.

Thank goodness, it seemed everything was in order. Next she checked the doorjamb and was reassured to see that, yes, the six hundred and twenty-second notebook was also safe. She checked her other eleven hiding places before breathing a huge sigh of relief.

As Ruby turned to leave the room, she caught sight of her donut phone tucked underneath the bookcase. It was the only remaining phone from her collection and the only remaining *visible* object in the room. She picked it up and dialed Clancy's number. He wasn't home yet, so she left a message. "Call me, OK?" Then she went back downstairs. As she walked into the kitchen she adopted an expression of quiet distress.

"I'm sorry, sweetheart," said her mother kindly.

"Don't worry, Ruby, we're going to track this yo-yo down," said the sheriff, patting her on the shoulder. "I'll see myself out, Mrs. R."

"Good-bye, Nat," called Sabina.

Two minutes later the doorbell rang.

"Oh, Ruby honey, would you get that?" asked her mother. "It's probably Nat, he's forgotten his notepad."

But when Ruby answered the door she was surprised to see a remarkably handsome, rather tall, formally dressed man. He was neither particularly young nor would he ever be considered in any way old — in fact it was impossible to really put any accurate age on him.

"You are inside out," said the man, extending his hand.

"Huh?" said Ruby.

"Let me guess, the so-called authority figures didn't like your silent demands?" he was pointing at her T-shirt, which was of course inside out, the *let them eat cake* slogan no longer visible.

"Oh, yeah," she said. "Something like that . . ."

How did he know about the school cake protest? she wondered. *Who is this guy?*

Her mother by now had made her way downstairs. "Can I help you?" she asked uncertainly.

"Hitch," said the man, looking into the house. "I see you go in for the minimalist look."

"Pardon me? Oh, yes, I see what you mean. We've been robbed," stammered Sabina. "I'm afraid there's nothing to photograph."

"Well, luckily I didn't bring my camera."

"Why ever not?" Sabina said, shaking his hand. Ruby noticed the man wince as if the action had caused him a sudden flash of pain.

"Because I take terrible photographs — always getting my thumb in front of the lens."

Sabina looked blank. "But aren't you the photographer from *Living Luxury* magazine?"

"I'm a household manager — from Zen Home management. You called this morning?"

"Oh!" said Sabina brightly. "You're the butler?"

"I prefer household manager, but butler if you insist."

"But I only called the house-management agency a few hours ago, they said no one would be available for weeks, how did you . . ."

"I returned from London unexpectedly two hours ago. My previous employers, Lord and Lady Wellingford, suddenly decided to tour the palaces of India and no longer required my services."

"But surely they will be back in a few weeks?"

"Not for three years," he replied quickly.

"It takes three years to tour the palaces of India?" said Sabina.

"They are traveling by elephant."

A likely story, thought Ruby. *I'll bet he got fired.*

"So, do you want to see my references? I don't think you'll be disappointed." He winked at Sabina and she giggled.

"I'll bet I won't!" said Sabina cheerily.

Oh, brother! thought Ruby.

"I'm so glad you're here, Mr. Hitch."

"Just Hitch — that'll do fine."

"Oh, of course, that's a butler thing, isn't it, calling yourself by your last name."

"Well, in this instance it's more of a me thing. It's my only name — only my mother calls me anything else."

"Oh, and what does she call you?" asked Sabina.

"Darling, usually."

"Well, you can call me just Sabina — or darling — no, just kidding . . ."

Ruby looked at her mother. Something strange had happened. *Why was she giggling like an idiot?*

"Anyway, I don't mind telling you, Hitch," Sabina went on, "things have been none too pleasant around here lately, no siree

Bob. First the airline totally lost our luggage, and now look—
we have been cleaned out."

Sabina babbled on excitedly about the tomato incident and
Hitch listened. It was if she had fallen under some kind of spell.

What is this guy, some kind of hypnotist?

Sabina was interrupted by the ring of the telephone.

"At least we still have the telephone!" cried Sabina, delighted
that one small possession had escaped the burglar's grasp. "I
expect that'll be the airline! Get that would you, Ruby?"

Ruby walked over to the phone and picked up the receiver.
"Chuck's Cheesery, you want cheese, we aim to please."

But for the third time there was absolutely no one on the end
of the line. She hung up and was about to dial Clancy's number
when the phone rang again.

"Look, buster, if you ain't gonna talk, why call?"

"I'm sorry?" said a low, gravelly voice.

"What's with all the heavy breathing and hanging up? It *is*
considered *rude* you know," snapped Ruby.

"I have no idea what you are talking about—I am not in
the habit of calling people with whom I have no intention of
conversing," replied the voice.

So who called me those other times? Ruby wondered.

"I am looking for Ruby Redfort," said the voice.

"Well, you found her," replied Ruby.

"Good. So now that I've found you, all you've got to do is find me."

"Excuse me?" said Ruby. "What is this, a quiz?"

"Well," the voice said, "a little bird told me that you notice everything — but do you notice everything Ruby Red?"

"The name's Ruby Red*fort*." Ruby didn't like her name to be messed with.

"As I was saying," continued the voice, "I hear that you are quite the code cracker, that you are capable of noticing the smallest things, the tiny details and how they connect. I bet *you* can see when something is plumb square in the wrong place, while everyone else just walks on by. You can see that something ordinary might mean something extraordinary once it's put in context. Am I right?"

"I can crack a code," said Ruby struggling to sound more confident than she felt.

"Good," said the voice, and the line went dead.

"So what's the code, buster?" said Ruby to no one but herself. She slowly put down the receiver.

Now what?

Hitch meanwhile, true to his job description, had been managing the Redfort household. By the time Brant Redfort walked in the door Hitch had brought in some of the lawn furniture, conjured camp beds from nowhere, and ordered sushi for dinner. Sabina was leaning on the countertop and chatting as if she had known him a good deal longer than one hour and forty-two minutes. Though Ruby observed that the conversation was not exactly scintillating.

"So would you believe it, Hitch, I take my little Oscar Birdet jacket to the dry cleaners — you know, Grosvenors on Harling Street? And what do they say? *'Sorry, Mrs. Redfort, but we won't be able to fix this, it's too delicate.'* Can you believe it? What kind of dry-cleaning service are they?"

"Well, it *is* an Oscar Birdet, so maybe they felt a little out of their depth."

"You *know* Oscar Birdet?"

"Sure I do."

"Aren't his designs exquisite?"

"Divine. Look, leave it with me. I'll take it to my dry cleaner tomorrow, he knows what he's doing," said Hitch. "And if he can't fix it, he'll send it to someone who can."

"Boy, I can't wait for Mrs. Digby to meet you."

"Mrs. Digby?" he asked.

"Our housekeeper. We had a misunderstanding. I expect she's still at her cousin Emily's cooling off — she's going to just love you."

Ruby wasn't so sure. Mrs. Digby 'couldn't abide fools,' and as far as Ruby was concerned this guy struck her as a prize turkey.

He was busy unpacking something from one of his bags.

"Hey, how cute—you travel with your own toaster," exclaimed Sabina.

"Well," said Hitch, placing it on the countertop. "It's a good one, and who doesn't love toast?"

There it was again, the little flash of pain, vivid just for a second when he lifted his right arm.

"I can't argue with you there," Sabina said, nodding.

"That's some butler," said Ruby's father, impressed.

Ruby made a face. *Because he carries a little toaster every place he goes? Had the body snatchers broken in and removed her parents' brains?*

She went up to her room and pulled out her yellow notebook—she was thinking about what Hitch had said about his previous employers. *Who are these people who can just up and tour India for several years on elephants? And why at such short notice?* Ruby couldn't help feeling this Hitch guy wasn't telling the whole truth about the Wellingfords, if indeed the Wellingfords even existed. And what if they did?

He'd probably cast them adrift in the middle of the North Sea and stolen all their money. No, there was something about the timing of his arrival which made the hairs stand up on the back of Ruby's neck. It reminded her of Mary Poppins — the way he had just arrived out of thin air.

Only thing was, Hitch was no Mary Poppins.

Ruby thought about **RULE 29: JUST BECAUSE A LION SAYS IT'S A MOUSE DOESN'T MAKE IT A MOUSE.**

All evening Ruby waited to hear again from the mystery caller — but the phone didn't ring and that night Ruby lay on her makeshift bed running over the conversation again and again in her mind.

Why did the caller hang up? You want a person to crack a code — why not give them the code? Geez! There were some strange folks out there.

But then, when the hands of her watch reached 4:43 a.m., Ruby sat bolt upright.

Of course! How could she have been so dumb — the mystery caller *had* given her the code! The whole conversation was a code!

CHAPTER 6
Fifteen Dollars and Forty-nine Cents

DESPITE THE UNPLEASANT PROSPECT OF having to wear yesterday's socks, Ruby was in a good mood and eager to get up and dressed long before her school day began. She was surprised to see her morning drink (one-third grapefruit, one-third cranberry, one-third peach — with a straw) sitting waiting for her. How did that Hitch guy know what she drank for breakfast? What's more, where did he get the straws from?

So mind reading is what they teach them in butler school.

The morning paper was lying on the countertop, and Ruby glanced at the headlines.

MAYOR WAGES WAR ON GARBAGE: "LITTERBUGS ARE TRASH" SAYS MAYOR ABRAHAMS.

GOOD AS GOLD: FIVE TONS OF GOLD BULLION TO BE DEPOSITED IN TWINFORD CITY BANK VAULTS.

HEAVEN SCENT: TWINFORD NATIONAL BLOSSOM DAY SET
TO BE THE MOST SPECTACULAR SINCE RECORDS BEGAN.

Hitch had obviously been to some twenty-four-hour supermarket because the countertop was covered in a vast array of breakfast possibilities.

"That's some butler," muttered Ruby, as she set about pouring Choco Puffles into a paper bowl. Out of habit she rummaged in the pack to find the free gift: it was a brain-teaser puzzle consisting of five shapes which, when arranged correctly, would make a perfect square. Ruby did it in six-and-a-half seconds. She threw the paper bowl into the trash and stood listening for sounds of life. There was no sign of Hitch, and her parents weren't up yet, so she gave Bug his breakfast and went out to patch her bike tire — but miraculously it was already fixed.

"Boy! That's some butler," muttered Ruby again.

"Thanks."

Ruby looked up to see the amused face of Hitch. He looked kind of pleased with himself, which irritated her.

"So what's wrong with your arm?" said Ruby.

"I'm sorry?"

"What's wrong with your arm?"

"I'm surprised you noticed."

And he was surprised too; he thought he had concealed his arm injury well.

"I notice things; I'm good at that," she said.

"I guess you are," he said.

"So what happened?"

"Just a touch of housemaid's elbow. I need to lay off the dusting."

"Oh yeah, housemaid's elbow, that well-known complaint."

Stuffing her notebook into her bag, Ruby whistled to Bug, got on her bike, and rode off toward the center of Twinford, her dog running alongside. All the way there she tried to remember exactly what the mystery caller had said.

"Do you notice everything, Ruby Red?"

"A little bird told me. . . that you are capable of noticing the smallest things, the tiny details . . . I bet you can see when something is plumb square in the wrong place, while everyone else just walks on by."

Bug had no trouble keeping up with her, and in no time they had reached Chatter-Bird Square. She was pretty sure she was right about Chatter-Bird Square. There wasn't a Plum Square in Twinford, at least not one that Ruby knew about, and in any case Chatter-Bird fitted with the clue "a little bird told me." She looked around her. There was nothing obvious to be noticed—but then that was the point wasn't it?

"The smallest things . . ."

Look for something tiny, Ruby. That could take all day. The square, in fact a park, was big and would soon be teeming with people on their way to work.

"People walking on by . . ."

Bug had wandered off. He was busy going from tree to tree sniffing and doing what dogs do. Ruby watched him sniffing along the ground, making his way over to the tree in the middle where the footpaths met. He had spotted a brown paper bag on the ground under the tree and was busy trying to get whatever was inside it out.

"Geez, Bug, do you have to eat everything? You just had breakfast a half hour ago."

Ruby went over and picked up the bag, and out fell three squishy plums.

"Kinda weird to find plums at this time of year," thought Ruby. And then she looked up at the tree and down at the fruit and she remembered what the voice had said. This was a plum tree and it was in the middle of the square.

"Plum in the middle of the square . . ."

"Where . . . everyone just walks on by . . ."

She walked right up to the tree and then walked around the trunk and then she saw it, something red.

"Do you notice everything ruby red?"

The voice had not been saying her *name*, it had been telling her to *look* for something red. The something red was a price sticker — it had Joe's Supermart printed across the top and a price, $15:49, printed in the middle.

Is this the clue or is this just a price sticker?

She looked at it some more.

If it's a clue then I guess I'm meant to go to Joe's Supermart — but fifteen dollars and forty-nine cents? I'm meant to go in there and find something for fifteen dollars and forty-nine cents? I bet there's nothing in Joe's Supermart for fifteen dollars and forty-nine cents. No one who had fifteen dollars and forty-nine cents would shop there.

The dog looked at her stupidly — he didn't know what was going on but he wouldn't mind doing something else. Ruby was taking no notice though—she was just staring at the little sticker. After a couple of minutes of silent staring she got back on her bike and headed off toward school.

When she got to the crossroads in the middle of Bird Street she called over her shoulder, "OK, Bug, time to go home." The dog looked at her, disappointed, but he knew what to do and he took a left and Ruby cycled on up the hill. She would be early for once.

As soon as she arrived at Twinford Junior High she went to look for Clancy. He was there already of course—overly punctual was his style.

"Hey, what happened to you?" he asked. "You sorta look like a truck ran over you and then decided to reverse."

"Yeah well, I didn't get too much sleep on account of someone stole my bed," replied Ruby.

"Someone stole your bed?" said Clancy, his mouth open like a fish.

"Yeah, and that wasn't all they took."

"What do you mean?" said Clancy, flapping his arms.

"We don't have a *single* piece of furniture left," said Ruby dramatically.

"You got robbed?" mouthed Clancy.

"I guess you could call it that — though it looks more like we moved but no one bothered to tell us where we were moving *to*."

"They took everything?" said Clancy, his eyes widening.

"Everything except the phones," said Ruby. "By the way thanks for your call, buster."

"What call? I didn't call," said Clancy. "My dad grounded me on account of me having to re-take that French test, wouldn't let me call, so I didn't."

"No, I noticed," said Ruby. "But someone did. I tell you I got some super strange telephonic activity last night."

"You did?" said Clancy. "What kinda super strange — weird strange or creepy strange?"

"It's hard to say," said Ruby. "One was a hang-up and the other was this gravelly voiced woman."

"Like the woman in *A Date with Fate*?" asked Clancy.

"Sorta," said Ruby. *A Date with Fate* was a show that had been running for years; each week some mildly creepy ghost story was introduced by this old actress with this raspy voice — the stories tended to be a little lame.

"What did she say?"

"It's hard to explain exactly — some kinda code."

"You crack it?"

"Not yet, but listen—before that, this kinda chiseled guy turns up at our house and says he's the house manager my mom requested, only of course my mom being my mom is calling him a butler."

"You got a butler! Wow," said Clancy, impressed, even though *his* family had never been without one his whole entire life. "What's he like?"

"A total airhead," said Ruby.

"That doesn't sound good," said Clancy. "You don't want an airhead butler."

"Well, technically he's not a butler, he's a household manager—whatever that means."

Clancy whistled. "Mrs. Digby's not gonna like that!"

"Yeah, well, luckily she's with her cousin Emily right now, but you're right. She's bound to notice there's something a little off about this guy."

"How do ya mean—off?"

Ruby paused for effect. "I think there's something sorta strange about him."

"Like what, for example?" said Clancy, unable to keep the thrill out of his voice.

"He seems to know too much. Things he couldn't know— well, not unless he was psychic or something."

"So where did he come from?" asked Clancy. He was on the edge of his seat, or at least would have been had he been sitting down.

"London, supposedly. But who really knows," replied Ruby.

"He's English?"

"No, he was just living there — the people he used to work for have 'suddenly' gone off riding elephants for three years." Ruby loved getting Clancy all wired about the possibility of some dark mystery.

"Perhaps he stole their money and did away with them," he said earnestly.

"Well that *might* explain the flashy car — he's got this silver convertible — but I am not sure it explains the *arm* injury."

"The arm injury? You've got an injured butler? You don't want an injured butler. He's really injured?"

"Oh, yes," said Ruby, nodding. "He looks like he was involved in some kinda accident."

"Or shoot-out!" whispered Clancy conspiratorially. "You know what, Rube? I'll bet he's not even a butler. He's almost certainly a hit man or something."

"You've got some imagination, Clance my old pal!"

But she didn't tell him the thought *had* crossed her mind.

Ruby wasn't one to get in trouble unnecessarily, but she was finding it hard to concentrate and several times during class it was noted that she wasn't paying attention. The thing was she just couldn't put it together—what was the significance of fifteen dollars and forty-nine cents?

After lunch it came to her—she couldn't believe she had been so stupid—it was the most simple kind of clue, the staring you in the face kind. So obvious you missed it. As Ruby all too often remarked, **PEOPLE OFTEN MISS THE DOWNRIGHT OBVIOUS {RULE 18}.**

It was Mr. Walford who got her to see it. He used to be in the military and liked to be precise about things. He was a stickler for using the twenty-four-hour clock.

"Redfort, Ruby," he barked. "It is precisely thirteen thirty-one, recess is no longer in progress, march your way swiftly to class please."

Ruby stopped in her tracks, paused, and then suddenly turned to Mr. Walford. "Three forty-nine p.m.! Of course! Not fifteen dollars and forty-nine cents but fifteen hundred hours and forty-nine minutes—or put another way, eleven minutes to four."

The price sticker is telling me to be at Joe's Supermart at 3:49 p.m.

Mr. Walford looked at her as if she was a complete crazy but that didn't matter. Nothing mattered . . . oh, except for the school basketball tournament, scheduled to begin at sixteen hundred hours.

Darn it, Del is going to kill me.

Ruby would be sorely missed if she didn't show. Del's team, the Deliverers, was playing Vapona Begwell's team, known as the Vaporizers, and there was always a lot of rivalry. Del Lasco would not forgive her unless she had a good excuse, and even then, she still might not.

Inspiration came during Phys Ed when Ruby dramatically faked a foot injury—everyone saw as she tripped down the outside steps. A stuntman couldn't have done a better job.

"Jeepers! My toe, I think I just broke my little toe."

Ruby knew that toes get broken all the time and that they don't necessarily require a trip to the emergency room. More often than not you just need to ice it. She had no trouble convincing anyone that she wasn't going to be playing basketball anytime soon—Ruby was an accomplished actress.

"Too bad Ruby, we're really gonna miss you," said Del, kicking furiously at a weed. This was no lie, Ruby Redfort *would* be missed because what she might lack in height she made up for in skill. She had the amazing knack of distracting the opposition and scoring before they knew that they had even lost possession of the ball.

"Yeah, Del, I know. I'm sorry," said Ruby, wincing as she hobbled toward the nurse's office.

Mrs. Greenford, the school nurse, couldn't get either of Ruby's parents on the phone, which was unsurprising since some time ago Ruby had changed their contact details in the school files. The numbers now sent any member of the staff to an answering machine with the reassuring message, *"If Ruby should need to come home early today, I am around, please put her in a cab."* (Ruby could do a flawless impression of her mother.) This way, if ever she wanted to pull a stunt like this, her parents would not be informed.

Ruby limped off to the taxi.

"So I'm to take you to Cedarwood Drive?" said the cab driver.

"Nah, change of plan — Joe's Supermart on Amster," said Ruby.

The driver gave her a knowing look and nodded. "Yeah I was a kid once — don't worry, my lips are sealed, sweetheart."

CHAPTER 7
Don't Call Us
We'll Call You

WHEN RUBY ENTERED THE SUPERMART her ears were assaulted by the tinny sound of the worst kind of Muzak. Ruby caught sight of old Mrs. Beesman, who was busy filling her cart with what looked like two hundred cans of cat food. It was rumored that she had somewhere approaching seventy-four cats, but as far as Ruby knew no one had ever been in Mrs. Beesman's house to count them. She noticed Mrs. Beesman was wearing earmuffs.

Smart lady, this music could damage your brain.

Ruby walked slowly around the aisles, studying the shelves carefully until she saw what she was looking for. In the middle of a shelf displaying unnaturally vivid cookies and cakes, she saw an item that just didn't belong. A box of very cardboard-looking Real Health Crackers. They claimed to be *Delicious nutritious yummy snacks — no sugar no eggs no wheat no additives,* but the truth was the packaging looked tastier than the contents.

Something wholesome in Joe's Supermart, now that is unusual.

Ruby looked at the price sticker and sure enough, across the top it said, ORGANIC UNIVERSE. The words of the mystery voice came back to her.

"You can see when something is plumb square in the wrong place."

With the box of crackers under her arm, Ruby left the store and made her way across the street to Organic Universe. The wooden chimes jangled as she entered, and the smell of sensible food hit her. She headed straight for the cookie aisle, and there, right next to two boxes of Health Crackers, sat a telephone directory. She replaced the box of Health Crackers she was holding, picked up the directory, and carried it over to the phone booth by the door.

Now what? she thought.

Above the phone were hundreds of cards advertising all kinds of different health-giving treatments, from color therapy to water therapy, and then . . . a card which simply said, DON'T CALL US WE'LL CALL YOU.

Ruby took the card down from the board and looked at it closely, but apart from a decorative pattern around its edge, there was no other information. She sat down on the wooden stool by the phone booth and waited. After twenty-five minutes the man behind the counter was eyeing her suspiciously.

DON'T CALL US
WE'LL CALL YOU

"Can I help you?" he asked in an extremely unhelpful tone. He was a young guy, nervous-looking, with a nose that seemed too big for his head. It made his face look awkward.

"No, I'm just fine thanks," replied Ruby, doing her best to sound casual. "I'll let you know if I need anything."

The big-nosed guy obviously didn't want to get into an argument with a schoolkid but he wasn't about to let her out of his sight.

Ruby silently watched the minute hand tick slowly around the clock face, while the big-nosed guy walked around the store, eyeing her furtively. If someone was trying to test Ruby Redfort's patience, they were doing a good job, though patience was not a quality that Ruby was lacking.

However, she was relieved when at exactly two minutes

to five, the phone rang. She jumped and almost knocked the receiver off its cradle. "Hi, hello," blustered Ruby.

"Am I talking to Ruby Redfort?" asked that same gravelly voice.

"Yuh huh, yes," confirmed Ruby.

"Good, glad you made it this far. I have a job offer for you — let's make a date . . . how about tomorrow night at eight for eight not a minute sooner not a minute later. And keep it zipped."

"Anything else you wanna tell me?" asked Ruby.

"Yes," said the voice. "Be lucky."

No good-bye, just the dial tone.

I guess directions would be too much to ask for, thought Ruby as she left the store.

On her way back home Ruby stopped off at the green. Up in the tree she found a neatly folded origami cuckoo. She knew what that meant without even reading the note.

THE CUCKOO: a parasitic bird who takes over the nest of another by pushing the host's eggs out and laying its own in their place. If necessary the cuckoo will devour the host-bird's young.

In other words,

THE CUCKOO: a ruthless killer and imposter.

The cuckoo was of course Hitch. It was classic Clancy Crew — he was joking but kind of serious at the same time. He had a sixth sense for trouble. He was often saying, "The thing is Rube, I got a hunch about this," or "Trust me, I got a feeling I'm right about that." He could never explain why he had a hunch or where it had come from but the remarkable thing was, he was almost always right. Ruby unfolded the bird and read the note.

Vc spf jdyye I fucefy xrs. C ussxubu ds!

Ruby smiled. It wasn't easy to fool Clancy Crew. Ruby tore a piece of paper from her notebook, wrote Zvuu lvh miv, dsps mpcxd zcf oiwswuzv?, folded it, and pushed it into the knot.

When Ruby got home she saw the same police car once again parked in the driveway, and as she walked up the stairs she heard the familiar voice of Sheriff Bridges and also another voice, which turned out to be a police detective.

"So you didn't notice she was gone, Mrs. R.?" asked Sheriff Bridges.

"Well, to be honest, Nat, what with everything else disappearing I just didn't get around to noticing. I wasn't surprised *not* to see her yesterday — she said she was going to stay with Emily — but Emily says she hasn't seen her for two weeks."

"Emily?" inquired the detective.

"Her cousin Emily — lives in North Twinford. You see the thing is she was offended. She shouldn't have been, but that's Mrs. Digby all over, she gets offended at the drop of a hat."

"Offended? By what, Mrs. Redfort?"

"You know, anything really. It can be the smallest criticism. I have to be so careful, the slightest thing can set her off; I ask her to dust, she thinks I'm criticizing, I ask her not to, she thinks I don't trust her with a duster . . ."

"No, Mrs. Redfort," said the detective, who seemed to be trying hard to hold on to his temper. "I meant to say how did you offend her *this time*?"

"Well, look, it's like this, Detective," interrupted Brant Redfort. "Sabina stepped into an argument between Consuela, our talented new chef, and Mrs. Digby, our much-loved housekeeper — some tomato juice was thrown and Sabina was understandably rather upset."

"It went all over my new Oscar Birdet jacket. It's most probably ruined — tomato juice is stubborn to get out," said Sabina.

"The thing is," continued Brant, trying to keep the conversation on track, "Mrs. Digby felt Sabina was taking Consuela's side — she's very high-strung."

Ruby was by now standing in the doorway quietly observing. The detective was writing something in his notepad, obviously thinking very hard.

"What is it?" asked Sabina.

"Could just be that your Mrs. Digby is somehow involved in all this — have you thought of that?" He waved his arm to indicate the now furnitureless house.

"Oh, now, come on, Detective! Nat, you've seen Mrs. Digby — you really think a little old lady is capable of stealing every stick of our furniture?" Brant was appalled by this suggestion.

"Well, as it happens, I don't. But as the detective says, we have to follow up every lead."

"Maybe she wasn't acting alone," said the detective.

"Oh, you must be out of your mind — Mrs. Digby practically raised me!" exclaimed Sabina. "That's an awful thing to say."

"Maybe I am, and maybe it is, but you have to admit it's quite a coincidence her disappearing at the same time that you lose all your million-dollar stuff, wouldn't you agree, Mrs. Redfort?"

"Well yes, but—but—"

"I'm just saying, we need to look into it," said the detective, closing his notepad. "Thanks for your time."

He left by the back door.

"Sorry not to come with better news," said the sheriff.

Just then his radio crackled. *"Nat, you there? We got a problem at the City Bank."*

The sheriff sighed and spoke into the radio. "Not again. OK, I'll get over there right away."

He looked up at the Redforts. "Darn it, this gold delivery's causing mayhem. The new alarm system keeps triggering. It better be fixed before that shipment arrives." He smiled reassuringly. "Look, I'll let you know if I get any more leads. You take care. Remember, get those locks changed!"

"What's left to steal?" said Sabina, closing the door.

Ruby glanced over at Hitch. He looked far from the suspicious character Clancy wanted him to be; he was busy making cocktails and seemed not the slightest bit interested in this latest development. Was he listening? It was hard to be sure. He seemed a lot more concerned about squeezing limes than he did about a little old lady who was missing and presumed a felon. Maybe there was nothing sinister about him at all. Maybe he was just a bit dumb.

Handsome but probably not a lot going on upstairs, thought Ruby.

Brant caught sight of his daughter. "Hey, Ruby honey, what happened at basketball?"

"Oh, you know, bounced a ball, shot some hoops, came home. What's going on?"

"Well that . . . *detective* fellow wanted to interview Mrs. Digby about the robbery, but no one can find her."

Ruby took a breath. "Do you think it's possible . . ." her voice was hushed so her mother wouldn't hear. "Do you think it's possible that Mrs. Digby was stolen, you know, along with all our stuff?"

Brant Redfort smiled, "That's a good one, Rube!"

But Ruby wasn't joking.

"I'm serious, Dad. Perhaps she was kidnapped?"

"If she was kidnapped then we would know about it," said Brant.

"Not necessarily, the kidnappers might be waiting a while before they make contact—you know, to build up the tension."

"You know what?" said Brant conspiratorially.

"What?" said Ruby.

"You watch too much TV." He laughed, patted his daughter on the head, and walked into the living room. Ruby sighed as she straightened the barrette in her hair.

"*And you guys probably don't watch enough,*" she muttered under her breath. This kind of situation was always coming up in *Crazy Cops*. Ruby had learned a lot about the workings of the criminal mind from watching this show. It was on tonight, and if Mrs. Digby were here they would be watching it together — side by side on the couch. Except there *was* no couch. Wherever Mrs. Digby was now, Ruby wondered, was she watching Crime Night?

Ruby's sleep was fitful that night. She had a hard time dozing off, and when she did, she dreamed dreams that gave her no rest. Dreams where the telephone rang and the voice on the other end spoke in riddles. Dreams where her mother was taken hostage by a dangerous toast-eating butler and her father was shot at by crazy furniture thieves, and all the while the voice of Mrs. Digby called out to her from some faraway prison cell. She was woken by her own voice calling, "*Where are you, Mrs. Digby?*"

She sat up and rubbed her eyes. Mrs. Digby a criminal? That detective was a prize bozo. Mrs. Digby would never commit a crime — well, not a crime against the Redforts anyway. Ruby's mind began sifting through worries, exploring solutions, hitting dead ends, and doubling back to square one. She consoled herself with **RULE 33: MORE OFTEN THAN NOT THERE IS A VERY ORDINARY EXPLANATION FOR THE "EXTRAORDINARY" HAPPENING.**

But it was no use, she was wide awake.

She got up, pulled on a sweatshirt, and quietly made her way downstairs — she didn't want to wake Bug. But Bug was already awake and staring intently at the man sitting in the kitchen. Ruby froze: from her vantage point she could see Hitch, perched on a stool, his right shirtsleeve rolled up high to reveal a bandage at the top of his arm, which he slowly began to unwind.

She held her breath and became as still as the walls.

She watched as gradually all the gauze was removed to reveal what could only be a gunshot wound.

Meanwhile,
somewhere in the
middle of nowhere . . .

Mrs. Digby was crawling out of a flotation tank. She emerged in a polka-dot bathing suit, somewhat dazed and disoriented, finding herself not quite in the Redforts' spa gym. Certainly most things were familiar, but at the same time everything was very, very unfamiliar. All the furniture was the same, all the objects were the same, all the art was the same, what was odd was that there was no house.

"Where in all heaven have the darned walls gone?" she exclaimed.

She appeared to be in an enormous aircraft hangar containing just about everything the Redforts had ever owned.

The last thing Mrs. Digby had been aware of was climbing into the flotation tank at three o'clock the previous day — she had been suffering from angry thoughts concerning her rival in the kitchen, Consuela, and thought she could do with some isolation time — or who knew what she might do.

Sabina Redfort had had the flotation tank installed only the other month, having taken advice from her personal healer, who had persuaded her that she needed more time with herself.

Mrs. R. always finds it very calming — what harm could it do? I guess it prunes the skin a little but at my age what's a little pruning?

Mrs. Digby had thought these thoughts as she climbed in, lay down, pulled the door shut, and instantly fell into a heavy sleep.

Boy, had she slept!

What *was* the day, she wondered? *Better not be Tuesday*, she thought, catching sight of the Redforts' kitchen clock. *If it is, I'm missing Crime Night, and I never miss Crime Night.*

CHAPTER 8
Getting Lucky

BY DAYBREAK RUBY WAS UP, showered, and pulling on her clothes despite the fact that there was no one to nag her. Ruby was no early bird, everyone knew that. In desperation her parents had given her an alarm clock which showed a bird pecking at a worm. It made a pleasant tweeting sound if set for any time before 7 a.m.—later than that and it made a sort of strangled squawking noise. Ruby walked into the bathroom and was surprised to see, laid out in neat piles, jeans, T-shirts, over-the-knee socks, and other essentials. On closer inspection she saw that these garments were more than acceptable; in fact, they were exactly the clothes she might have chosen herself. There was even a T-shirt printed with the words, *keep it zipped.*

This could not be the work of her mother.

She spotted a typed note next to a pair of size 5 Yellow Stripe sneakers.

Hope you approve. Had my stylist friend Billie pick these things out for you — she's good at that kind of thing. Hitch.

Airhead he might be, but he was certainly good at his job. Ruby moseyed downstairs to say thanks and found Hitch examining a piece of toast very closely, almost as if he were reading it.

He looked up, startled, and immediately began to spread it with peanut butter.

"Toast?" he said.

Not just an airhead but a weirdo too, thought Ruby.

Today, Ruby felt like taking the bus. She made it to the stop in plenty of time, clambered aboard, and sat down, barely acknowledging her friends Del and Mouse. The two girls tried to get her attention.

"Hey, Rube," called Del.

Ruby didn't even look up.

Del looked at Mouse. "Was it something I said?"

Ruby was staring at the card she'd picked up in Organic Universe and chewing furiously on her pencil — what was it she wasn't seeing? What was there to see? Just the words *Don't call us we'll call you* and the simple decorative border — nothing to give any indication as to where the meeting would take place.

"Tomorrow night at eight for eight" was all the voice on the telephone had said.

What am I missing?

"So Ruby, I see your toe is all mended," said Del.

Ruby looked down at her foot — she had forgotten all about her fake injury. "Oh, yeah," she answered.

Mouse looked at Del and sort of widened her mouth and rolled her eyes — this was her silent way of suggesting that all was not right with Ruby Redfort. Even Clancy Crew couldn't get any sense out of her — and when Vapona Begwell dared to suggest that Ruby's "recovered" broken toe was either a miracle or she was some cowardly faker who had chickened her way out of the basketball game, she barely even blinked.

"Hey, Redfort," sneered Vapona. "Did those burglars steal your guts along with the furniture?"

Clancy couldn't believe it. "You gonna let her get away with that, Rube?"

"Look, my mind's got bigger concerns than Bugwart right now."

"Has something else happened?" said Clancy eagerly. "More burglars? Something else go missing?"

"As a matter of fact, yes."

"What?" said Clancy.

"Mrs. Digby," replied Ruby

"Mrs. Digby?" mouthed Clancy.

Ruby nodded. "She isn't at cousin Emily's and she isn't back home. We don't know where she is."

Clancy's eyes were saucers. "Do you know what I think? I think the butler who isn't a butler took her."

"And why would he do that, Clance?"

"So he could get her job — get her outta the way."

"My mom didn't *give* him the job because Mrs. Digby had *gone* — she didn't even *know* Mrs. Digby had gone when she hired him."

"Yeah, well, I still think he's bad news," Clancy said firmly.

"Yeah, well, maybe you're right 'cause guess what? I saw his injured arm — he doesn't know I saw it but I did and I am telling you. Clance, that's no housemaid's elbow he is suffering from — more like gangster's shoulder."

"So I was right," marveled Clancy. "He *was* in a shoot-out." His face lit up. "You know he's probably on the run, hiding out at your house, stealing your stuff and selling it."

"Clance, that brain of yours never ceases to amaze."

But she couldn't help thinking he might not be so far from the truth.

Ruby pretty much sleepwalked through her morning classes, so distracted was she by the puzzle she needed to solve. And then at 2:30, during History, she suddenly saw what it was she couldn't see before.

Mrs. Schneiderman was giving a very tedious lecture about the ancient Greeks, and those students who weren't staring out of the window were busy painting their fingernails with Wite-Out and generally working hard to keep from falling asleep. It wasn't that anyone didn't *want* to be interested, it was just that Mrs. Schneiderman was one of those people who managed to make even the most interesting things sound very dull indeed. It was something to do with her delivery; she tended to ramble. Ruby was brought out of her thoughts and back into the classroom by the sound of one hundred thumbtacks falling to the floor. Ruby looked across the room and saw the ever accident-prone Red Monroe frantically trying to scoop them back into their container.

"Sorry, Mrs. Schneiderman," she said. "They just sorta fell off my desk."

The tacks had rolled right across the room, and a few had ended up under Clancy's chair. As he stood up to help, a couple of them lodged themselves in the sole of his left sneaker. Mrs. Schneiderman was trying to regain the attention of her students and rapped her ruler on the wall. Ruby looked up and saw, projected on the screen, a slide showing a simple repeat pattern, the famous Greek key pattern used on pottery, mosaics, and it seemed, almost everything ancient Greek.

"This is a decorative border called *meander,* first used in the Greek Geometric period," said Mrs. Schneiderman loudly. "The name *meander* conjures up the twisting and turning of the Maeander River. 'Greek key' is a modern term used to describe the pattern. It is always useful to remember that, in history, decoration is very rarely purely decorative, it is usually there to symbolize something or convey a message."

Ruby was suddenly very alert. She reached behind her and felt for the jacket hanging on the back of her chair. Locating the left pocket, she pulled out her notebook containing the little white card — the one from Organic Universe. On it were the six words, *don't call us we'll call you,* but it wasn't the *words* that Ruby was interested in. The thing that got her attention today was the pattern decorating the edge of the card. She had previously overlooked this, considering it to be simply decorative — thus forgetting one of her own rules, **RULE 13** in fact, **THERE IS MORE TO MOST THINGS THAN MEETS THE EYE.**

Now she studied the decorative border carefully. It was made up of interlocking figure eights which repeated all the way around the edge of the card.

"Tomorrow night at eight for eight . . ."

Ruby knew the time was set for eight but what if the destination was also eight? *"Be lucky,"* the voice had said. Why? Why did she need to be lucky?

After school, Clancy and Ruby picked up Bug and biked out to the ocean. Ruby found that watching the husky racing in and out of the waves helped her mind relax, but still she had no answer. It wasn't until they started off for home that something clicked. Ruby was riding very slowly along the sidewalk. Clancy was on foot; his bike chain had broken and he was telling her about how this oil sheik had been on the way to meet with Clancy's dad when he ran out of gas.

"Imagine the scene. He is an actual oil baron and he runs out of gas!"

"That's pretty funny," said Ruby.

"But that's not all, his chauffeur flags down this old truck and who does it belong to?" Clancy didn't wait for her to guess. "Only old Mr. Berris who owns the local gas station, that one that's closing down due to lack of business. Old Mr. Berris has a spare can, fills up the sheik's car, and the sheik makes it to dinner on time!"

"That's really something," smiled Ruby.

Clancy couldn't get over the irony of the situation. "Here is a guy with all the fuel he could ever want but he has to borrow a can from some little old guy who is about to close down due to no one buying his gas!"

"He certainly got lucky," said Ruby, and then she stopped — she had stumbled on the final piece.

"What's up? What did I say?" asked a bewildered Clancy.

"Sorry, Clance, gotta split. I promise I'll tell you tomorrow!" she said, steering herself off the curb and back on to the street. "Drop Bug off, would ya," Ruby called as she turned in the direction of Mountain Road and pedaled like crazy up the hill.

"What?" shouted Clance. "What just happened?"

"I think I just got lucky!" she shouted back.

CHAPTER 9
A Small, Dark Space

RUBY PULLED UP AT EXACTLY THE SPOT where she was sure she was meant to be. It was just out of town on Mountain Road, at a place where the road bent around to the left. It was the site of the old gas station. The only thing remaining of it was the faded sign that still pronounced, BE LUCKY, TREAT YOUR AUTOMOBILE TO SOME LUCKY EIGHT GAS.

It had been an unusually sunny afternoon, and the road still felt warm under her feet. She took a look around.

Am I meant to be meeting someone?

There was nothing in any direction, nothing at all. Ruby was about to admit to herself that she had made a mistake when she noticed a manhole cover. She walked slowly over to it and brushed the dust from the cover with her hand. The manhole cover had a company logo on it—a picture of a fly with the words *Bluebottle and Lava* underneath it. Around the edge was the same repeating pattern as on the card, and there was a number in the middle: 848.

Eight for eight.

She waited, only taking her eyes off the manhole to check her watch. At precisely eight o'clock she began working on getting the cover open.

There was a trick to it, and after only a few minutes she had worked it out: eight turns clockwise, four counterclockwise, and another eight clockwise — bingo. With some effort she lifted the lid and peered down into complete blackness.

Ruby Redfort's one real fear was a small confined space. Not cupboards or tiny rooms, or tunnels she knew her way out of — no, it was a small dark space she had never before encountered . . . a small dark space with no way out . . . with no oxygen . . . *that's* what she was scared of.

She stared into the void for five minutes, thirty-two seconds before she got a grip on herself.

Was she really going to come this far and no further? Her instinct told her it would be OK, but her body wasn't so sure. Very slowly she eased herself down into the drain and jerkily pulled the manhole cover over her head. She merged with the dark; no more hands, no more feet — it was as if she had dissolved into black. The panic rose up through her body and started to play its usual tricks on her mind. Her breathing became short and rapid; she felt dizzy and sick.

"Get a grip, Ruby," she hissed. There was something reassuring about hearing her own voice spilling out into the darkness. She thought of Mrs. Digby. All her life, Mrs. Digby had been there to squash her fears and prop up her spirits. If she were here now she would say,

"Don't tell me you're troubled by a little darkness, Ruby? Good gracious! You don't want to waste your time being scared of the dark when there are so many other bigger things to be frightened of — like for example getting to my age and losing your marbles or being run down by one of those city buses with their maniac drivers. Those are fears — the dark's the least of your worries, kid."

Just thinking about Mrs. Digby made Ruby breathe more easily. "Mind over matter," that's what Mrs. Digby always said and she was right. Ruby had made it **RULE 12: ADJUST YOUR THINKING AND YOUR CHANCES IMPROVE.**

Actually, it was probably the best rule there was.

Never panic!

RULE 19: PANIC WILL FREEZE YOUR BRAIN. Panic will get you nowhere. Panic can get you killed.

She began to edge forward through the nothingness, and as she moved her senses got sharper. She felt the tunnel getting steadily bigger, and realized that the surfaces were smooth—not gritty as she might expect them to be. It didn't smell dank; in fact it didn't really smell of anything. She could feel twists and turns and before long was standing not crawling—yet still there was no light. All sense of time melted away until she could not accurately say how long she had been down there.

She was hot and tired when she stumbled into what amounted to a brick wall. She felt around her, stretching up and reaching across in all directions but there was no way forward, only back. It seemed the tunnel led nowhere—it had all been for nothing.

Ruby sank to the ground, put her head in her hands, and wondered how she was ever going to summon the energy to get herself out of there. How long she sat there she did not know.

A sudden deep shuddering sound, as if the earth were on the move.

A blinding light—light as white as the dark was black.

Ruby was jolted to her feet, eyes squinting, heart racing.

And then the voice.

"So you made it, Ruby Redfort."

CHAPTER 10
The Voice

RUBY KNEW THAT VOICE. It was the voice of the telephone, the voice of the codes and the riddles, but she could not see where it came from.

Slowly her eyes began to adjust, and she found that the wall was no longer a wall. She stumbled forward into an entirely white room.

It was a big room, huge, at its center sat an enormous desk. Behind the desk sat a woman; the owner of the gravelly voice. The woman was older than Sabina but not "old." Dressed completely in white, she was elegant and strikingly beautiful, immaculately groomed — although in no way "dolled-up," as Mrs. Digby would put it.

Under the white desk Ruby could see the woman's feet — she wore no shoes and her toenails were painted cherry red, the only visible color in the room. She was studying some papers that were spread out across the desk; engrossed in these, she was too busy to bother looking up.

A fly buzzed aimlessly around the room.

Ruby wasn't bad at physics, in fact she was pretty good, but even she couldn't work out how a space this big could fit into a space this small — it was like she'd crawled through a drain and ended up in a ballroom.

"Wow," said Ruby. "Your decorators really know how to make a place feel roomy."

The woman reached for her glasses, then, showing only the merest hint of curiosity, she peered across the desk. She paused before asking in a far from joking tone, "Do you know why you are here?"

"Because you called me up and got me crawling down a tunnel?" said Ruby.

The woman paused again. "Do you know who I am?"

Ruby looked at the desk, then above it at the all-white painting, and then at the carpet on the floor. After some close looking she began to see a pattern in the white mat and gloss paint, and another in the pile of the carpet. The patterns were all made up of the same letters, two letters.

"LB?" she said.

The woman nodded, *almost* smiling. "LB is correct. I am in charge here."

"And where exactly is here?" asked Ruby.

"The hub of it all, the hub of intelligence."

"Come again?" said Ruby.

"Well, if you must have a label — Spectrum."

"Nope," said Ruby. "Still means nothing to me."

"And nor should it," said the woman. "Spectrum is a secret agency — a very secret agency."

"Well, nice going," said Ruby, " 'cause I never heard of you. So who do you work for, the government?"

"To put it simply, we work outside the government but not against the government, if you know what I mean."

"So what you're saying is, you're the good guys."

"We like to think we are the *good* good guys, but good guys will do."

"Everyone *always* thinks they're the good guys," said Ruby.

"Yes they do," said LB. "But happily for us, *we are*."

"Well, *you* might know that, but how do I?"

LB took a deep breath. "As I understand it, part of your 'intelligence' lies in your almost impeccable instincts. Ask yourself one thing: something led you here, but was it your good instincts or just simple curiosity? Would you take the risk of crawling through a suffocating black tunnel if you thought we were the bad guys?"

It was a good point.

"So what does LB stand for?" asked Ruby.

"None of your beeswax, as someone your age might say," replied LB.

"No one my age would say that — not unless they were pretending to be someone your age."

LB didn't seem bothered by this remark, but instead opened a drawer and selected a shiny red file. "Are you curious to know why we had you crawl through a tunnel?"

"Pretty eager," Ruby drawled, as if she couldn't care less.

LB opened the file. "We first became aware of you five years ago. We took a look at that code you created for the Junior Code-Creator Competition, and we heard about the Harvard offer. I imagine you remember?"

"Yeah, I remember," Ruby mumbled. It was an experience she had tried hard to live down. She had not relished the attention.

"We were interested, but when we discovered exactly how old you were, that you were just some little kid, we thought again."

"So, what? You don't think I'm 'just some little kid' now?"

"Well, since you're asking, yes, but now we're desperate," replied LB.

"Wow, you sure know how to pump up a person's ego."

LB gave her a hard stare. "We've been watching you for

a number of years. Since you appeared on our radar we have had access to your grades and school assignments. You're not normal."

"That's you paying a compliment, right?"

"I wouldn't take it that way."

Ruby shrugged. "So why'd ya call?"

"I need to know if you are willing to work for us — just the one job, you understand."

"Doing what?" asked Ruby.

"We'll get to the details in due course but I need to know, are you in or are you out?"

"You must have a lot of confidence in me."

"That, or I'm crazy," said LB, shuffling her papers.

"But can I be trusted?" said Ruby.

LB stopped shuffling and looked up. "We think so. One thing you seem good at is keeping your mouth shut."

"And if you're wrong?" said Ruby.

"And if we're wrong," said LB, leaning forward. "And you do turn out to be a blabbermouth, then who's going to believe you?"

It was true, a schoolgirl was going to have a hard time convincing anyone but Clancy Crew that there was a secret agency situated beneath the street if you only took the trouble to lift the manhole cover just underneath the sign for Lucky Eight gas.

"So, are you willing to take the assignment?"

"I have no idea what it is."

"You'll be briefed once you have taken *and passed* the required Spectrum test and been cleared by security." LB paused. "I should make clear that this will be a desk job: there will be no car chases, no jumping out of airplanes in black turtleneck sweaters, and it will not make you *one of us,* you will *not* become an agent, you will simply be carrying out this one task, and when it's over you will go back to your boring humdrum schoolgirl life."

"Gee, lady," Ruby exhaled. "It's on the tip of my tongue to say yes."

"Oh, I forgot," said LB. "There is a small fee."

"Do I pay you or do you pay me?"

LB ignored this last comment. "Your decision?"

"But you haven't told me what I have to do."

"This is a once-in-a-lifetime offer. Yes or no?"

"Well, I don't know," said Ruby, chewing on her fingernail. "There *is* this biology assignment I'm working on. You see I have to imagine my life as a plankton, and I reckon thinking like a plankton is going to take time. I mean, gee, I'm not sure I can spare the hours."

"Look, plankton girl," drawled LB. "Cut the baloney and let's get things straight, are you in or are you out?"

Ruby gave LB one of her sideways stares before answering. "I guess the plankton can wait."

"Good, glad to have that sorted out. We will arrange for you to be excused from class. Other than that, don't call us we'll call you."

"Anything I need to know?" said Ruby.

"Uh-huh. **RULE ONE: KEEP IT ZIPPED.**"

Ruby lifted the drain cover and felt a large hand grab her by her jacket collar.

She shrieked in a most un-Ruby-Redfort-like way.

"Take it easy kid. I thought you might like to throw your bike in the trunk and get a ride home." Ruby looked up to see the tan face of the Redfort household manager.

"How'd you know I was here?"

"I guess you just struck me as the kind of girl who likes to spend her evenings crawling down drains."

Ruby looked at him hard. "Who exactly *are* you?"

"Spectrum sent me to babysit you," said Hitch, wiping dust from his hands.

"Well, sorry to put you out of a job," said Ruby. "But I've been putting myself to bed since I could climb into my cradle."

"Well, Ms. All-grown-up, what you've got to understand is that this isn't just any job, they're trusting you, kid — trusting you with things no one gets trusted with."

"So what you are saying is, you work for them?"

"Yeah, I work for them."

"Don't tell me you're a spy too," said Ruby.

"Agent," corrected Hitch.

"Right, so you're not even *slightly* an actual household manager?"

"No, I am just looking out for you while my arm heals. I needed an assignment without the action — though you can't deny I keep a pretty clean kitchen."

"Should I believe you?" asked Ruby. "The truth isn't exactly your strong point — how's your housemaid's elbow, by the way?"

"Getting better, thank you."

"Good. So what actually happened?"

"I got shot."

"Who by?"

"Someone."

"I had no idea butlering could be so dangerous. What did you do, break one of the Wellingfords' Ming vases?"

"There are no Wellingfords."

"I didn't think so. Who shot you, then?"

"Trust me, kid, you don't want to know."

"And why would I trust you?"

"I've got an honest face."

"A pretty one maybe, but I wouldn't call *pretending* to be a butler honest."

"Well, I can assure you it doesn't feel like pretending to *me* — feels like hard work. Your parents are kind of persnickety."

"Maybe you aren't as good as you think you are. Clancy had a hunch that there was more to you than the whole butler thing."

"I'll take that as a compliment."

"I wouldn't. I thought you were a bozo. What normal person travels with his own toaster?"

"Communication device actually — it sends and receives written messages."

"That figures," said Ruby, recalling the image of Hitch examining his toast. "So how does this whole undercover thing work?"

"Well, your parents must never suspect a thing; *no one* must ever suspect a thing — and that includes your pal Clancy Crew. That's **RULE NUMBER ONE: KEEP IT ZIPPED.**"

"So I heard," said Ruby dryly.

"So you're clear on this?"

"Yeah, don't blab — sounds pretty simple to me."

"No, kid, that's where you're wrong — that's the difficult part. Code breaking and all that other stuff — that's easy compared to keeping a secret like this."

**Mrs. Digby
was beginning
to make herself
at home. . . .**

She had investigated her surroundings and discovered that although she was trapped — *nothin's gonna budge these locks* — in what amounted to a giant warehouse, she was at least very comfortable.

So this is how it feels to be a Redfort, she said to herself as she stretched out in Brant Redfort's designer lounge chair. She was by now attired in one of Sabina Redfort's evening gowns — it was a full-length silver sequined affair and rather dressy for kicking about an old warehouse, but Mrs. Digby had always wanted to try it and besides, who was ever going to know?

Mrs. Digby, ever practical — *my ancestors were pioneers, they panned for gold, survived eating boiled raccoons and raw berries, sometimes boiled berries and raw raccoons* — had managed to find a long extension cord and had powered up the well-stocked refrigerator. She wasn't going to starve anytime soon, that was something.

The Digbys have always survived and always will because we're not afraid of a little hard work and a little discomfort, said Mrs. Digby to herself as she arranged Mrs. Redfort's faux mink stole around her shoulders.

Now, if I could just find a way of getting reception on this TV.

CHAPTER 11
The Eyes Followed the Hands

SHE WILL BE IN MIAMI," said Brant Redfort.

"Who will be in Miami?" repeated Sabina.

"Mrs. Digby," said Brant. "Remember that time she got so mad at you for putting us all on that pickle diet? Said it would pickle us from the inside out."

"Uh-huh."

"Well, what did she do? She took off for Miami, stayed there till you saw sense." Brant folded his arms like a man who had just successfully completed the cryptic crossword.

"You know what, Brant? You're a genius!" She turned to Ruby. "Your father's a genius, Ruby!"

Ruby thought this unlikely but said nothing.

"Miami! That's exactly where she is," continued Sabina. "Playing poker, I'll bet. Thank goodness for that." She poured herself another tomato-celery health juice. "She loves to gamble!" Sabina picked up her magazine, *Faces of the Absurdly Rich.*

"Well, this is going to make old Freddie happy. It says here that security has been stepped up to record levels. Twinford City Bank now has the safest bank vaults in the whole of the country."

"Well, I'm relieved to hear it," said Brant. "I just deposited my latest paycheck! I certainly don't want to gamble with that!"

Sabina laughed like he had just cracked the joke of the century.

Ruby, who despite appearances had actually been paying attention to this conversation, thought about what her father had said — not about the gold, but about Mrs. Digby. Gambling in Miami — it was certainly a possibility.

She was roused from her thoughts by a piece of toast freshly delivered to her plate. It was telling her something:

Be ready in ten. Wear your sneakers.

Mrs. Bexenheath, the school secretary, looked up to see what at first glance she imagined must be some Hollywood film star. It was as if he had accidentally strayed off the Walk of Fame and wandered unwittingly into the shabby halls of Twinford Junior High — so entirely out of place was he. However, this handsome man struck up an easy conversation with her, and before a minute had passed Mrs. Bexenheath had found herself agreeing to excuse Ruby Redfort from all lessons for the foreseeable future. She had concentrated carefully, all the while staring into his Hollywood eyes, wondering if they were brown or hazel. And although after he had left she couldn't exactly remember *why* she had excused Ruby from classes, she did find herself very sympathetic.

"Of course! Of course, she must take all the time she needs," she had gushed.

"Just remember, Mrs. Bexenheath, keep it hush-hush — oh, and don't bother Mr. and Mrs. Redfort, if you need to ask anything then be sure to bother me."

"Oh, I will, I will," said Mrs. Bexenheath sincerely.

Hitch thanked the school secretary for her warmth and kindheartedness, and promised that *yes,* he would make a point of visiting the school again soon. Then he said good-bye and returned to the car where Ruby was waiting.

"So?" said Ruby when Hitch got back into the driver's seat.

"Mrs. Bexenheath sends her warmest wishes and insists you take all the time you need."

"Really? What did you tell the old crab apple?" asked Ruby.

"Well, it seems that your grandmother has contracted a rare but not infectious virus while bird-watching in the Australian

Alps — condition, serious," Hitch said, turning the key in the ignition.

"There *are* no Australian Alps," said Ruby.

"Well, someone should have told your grandmother that because now look at her."

"I can't, she's in New York — probably all tucked up in her penthouse apartment," said Ruby.

"Let's not tell Mrs. Bexenheath that, or she might get *really* upset."

"You know what, man, you're some butler."

"I prefer household manager, but thanks, kid. Now, I think we should pay our friends at Spectrum a little visit."

"Why is it called Spectrum?" asked Ruby

"You'll see," said Hitch as he sped out of the parking lot.

Ruby sat back. Maybe this guy wasn't so bad. He certainly knew how to concoct total nonsense. Perhaps they were going to get along after all.

When they entered HQ it wasn't via the manhole cover that Ruby had previously used. No, this time they had to climb along the side of the Twinford Bridge. She now understood why the toast had recommended sneakers.

They stopped when they found a tiny rusted metal doorway

covered in graffiti — nonsensical words and sprayed-on images, including one of a fly. Different from the one on the manhole cover but a fly nonetheless.

"How come we're not going down through that old drain?" she said.

Hitch smiled. "There's a saying at Spectrum: 'If you want to lead the enemy straight to your door, just keep using the same one.' That's why there are many ways to enter Spectrum. We are always sealing one up and opening another. We have to. We can't risk anyone finding our true location."

"But how do they construct all of this?" said Ruby, peering into the gloomy passageway. "All these passages and corridors? And how do they link up? I don't get it."

"And nor should you, kid," replied Hitch with a wink.

Hitch and Ruby were greeted by a dowdily dressed woman who introduced herself simply as Buzz. She was the least buzzy person Ruby had ever seen.

"Buzz?" repeated Ruby.

"It's a nickname," said Buzz, by way of explanation. It was clear she wasn't the chatty type. The reception area was light and glossy, spacious in a way that made you wonder where they got all the space *from*.

"Give us a minute, will you, kid?" said Hitch.

Ruby wandered across the hall-like room, her eyes darting from object to object, her brain trying to make sense of the place. Buzz and Hitch were talking way over on the other side of the room. Ruby could make out every other sentence, or just about — most of it was pretty dull but one thing she heard intrigued her.

"How do you think she measures up to you know who?"

"Bradley Baker? Your guess is as good as mine."

"Well, if she even comes close I'll be amazed."

"Perhaps she'll surprise us all."

Ruby had no idea what they were talking about. Bradley Baker? Who was he and why did she have to measure up to him?

"Ready, kid?" called Hitch.

She stopped pretending not to listen and walked over to where they were standing. "What now?"

"You need to be security cleared and then you can take the ninety-nine-second test."

"What's the ninety-nine-second test?" asked Ruby. "And why do I need to take it? I thought I already passed."

"Kid, everyone who walks through the Spectrum door has to take the agency test — it's protocol."

Before Ruby could argue further, they were interrupted by

a middle-aged man with wild-looking hair and a slightly stupid grin.

"Come on, Ms. Redfort, time for your close-up," he said. "Just got to get all your security details: a nice mug shot, a couple of paw prints, footprints, height, weight, hair color, eye color, teeth color, nail color, you name it, I need it."

A comedian, thought Ruby, but it turned out he wasn't joking.

After all the checks had been made and every hair on Ruby's head had been counted—at least that's what it felt like—there was some time to kill before she had to take the Spectrum test.

"Buzz, give the kid a little tour of the gadget room," said Hitch. "That'll keep her out of trouble."

He was wrong about that.

Buzz matter-of-factly acted as tour guide, pointing out this and that as they walked. Corridors peeled off in every direction and staircases wound up through various rooms. It wasn't like any spy agency Ruby had seen on TV—it was *much* more interesting. For a start, with the exception of LB's office, everything was in color. Ruby had imagined the whole of HQ would be black, white, and chrome—that was how a spy agency was meant to look. But this was unexpected—each department was painted in shades of a different color; corridors gradually melted from blue to indigo to violet.

"Oh, I get it," said Ruby. "That's why you guys call this place Spectrum — it's the colors, right?"

"Uh-huh," said Buzz, nodding.

When they got to the gadget room, Ruby's pulse started to race. Ever since she was tiny she had always dreamed of having special powers. What had attracted her to the *Agent Deliberately Dangerous* graphic novels were the gadgets. There was always a gadget which Agent Deliberately would pull out in the nick of time — thus saving his life and often the lives of many others.

Buzz pointed out a small, silver object.

```
THE BREATHING BUCKLE.
To be used underwater. Slip buckle off belt, place
between teeth, and breathe comfortably for twenty-
seven minutes, two seconds.
WARNING! NO RESERVE AIR CANISTER.


GETAWAY SHOES.
Depress green button on base of left shoe to
convert to "roller shoes."
```

Big deal, thought Ruby, *a kid at my school has those.* But then she read on.

```
Depress red button on base of right shoe to
activate power jets. Maximum speed ninety-one
miles per hour for a distance of approximately
seven miles.
WARNING! CAN CAUSE FEET TO OVERHEAT. AVOID USE ON
RUGGED TERRAIN.
```

Kinda small, aren't they? mused Ruby. *Must be for some woman with feet like a kid.*

She moved to the next cabinet: displayed inside was an elegant, cropped cape-jacket. It was white with a fur-edged hood, and had one large, shiny glass button.

```
LADIES' PARACHUTE CAPE.
Push button to activate chute.
WARNING! TO AVOID EARACHE, ENSURE HOOD IS UP
BEFORE EMBARKING ON AIRBORNE DESCENT.
```

"We don't use that anymore," said Buzz, glancing over her

shoulder. "None of our female agents will be seen dead in it. Apparently it's out of style."

Ruby didn't agree at all. What did Buzz know about fashion anyway? The woman looked like a walking mushroom. As far as Ruby was concerned, this was one cool-looking cape.

Buzz moved on, pointing out various tiny lifesaving survival gadgets and deadly lifesaving weapons — all disguised as ballpoint pens, brooches, miniature radios, hats, umbrellas, sunglasses, car keys, and a thousand other things.

However, what really caught Ruby's eye was the watch. It was in a glass drawer contained in a special cabinet with a notice that said, *for display only — do not remove.* The watch face had cartoon eyes, and the eyes followed the hands. The second hand had a fly at the end of it that ticked steadily around the dial. *That fly again.* For a split second it triggered something in her memory. Autumn leaves whirled through her mind and a strange dark feeling lurked but she couldn't grasp hold of it. And then just like that it was gone.

The watch strap was brightly striped and fastened with an interesting clasp and the face was colored enamel with chrome surround. It was desirable simply because of the way it looked, but of course there was more to the watch than its appealing appearance. The label said, THE FLY, ESCAPE WATCH and in red letters underneath, it said, STRICTLY DO NOT TOUCH.

But how could Ruby resist? While Buzz was on the far side of the room, busy reading out the specifications of some much less interesting gadget, Ruby slipped the watch off its stand and popped it on to her wrist — it was a perfect fit.

She pressed the winder and out shot a titanium cable, barely visible to the naked eye — it had a hook on the end and was clearly designed as a sort of climbing device. Ruby could see that by twisting the dial you could make the cable longer or shorter depending on how much you needed. What she couldn't immediately see was a way of unhooking the hook and retracting the cable — which was unfortunate because seconds later the door opened and Ruby heard the sound of softly padding feet. *Bare* feet.

LB.

Ruby stood very still and smiled a big smile. She hoped LB wouldn't notice what had happened, and she hoped that if she did then the smile might go some way to softening LB's reaction.

This, it turned out, was a wrong assumption.

"Redfort, if you must grin like an idiot, please don't direct it at me," drawled LB. She clearly hadn't noticed Ruby's predicament, and launched into a conversation with Buzz. Ruby wrestled with the cable — she finally managed to unhook it and even managed to find the retracting device just before Buzz signaled to her that it was time to take the exam. Unfortunately there was no chance to replace the watch back in its drawer.

Buzz was in a hurry. "Just push that drawer shut," she said. "Once we leave the room everything locks automatically."

Ruby knew if she was caught with the watch then her agent assignment would certainly be over. There was nothing else for it but to stuff it deep into her jacket pocket. Maybe there would be a chance to return it later — after she took the test.

No one need ever know.

CHAPTER 12
The Silent *G*

THEY WERE MET IN THE CORRIDOR by an uptight-looking man in a self-conscious sort of suit.

"Ruby . . . Redfort?" he said, reading from his clipboard as if there was a whole group of schoolchildren waiting to take a secret agency test.

Ruby looked around. "Well, I'm pretty sure she's called Buzz," she said, nodding at Buzz. "So I guess that would be me."

The man sniffed. "Follow me, would you." He was *very* uptight. He could only be about twenty-three and was dressed in a pathetically showy way. All hair product and bleached teeth but no style.

Ruby caught sight of his identification badge. "Miles Froghorn?"

"That's Frohorn," corrected the man. "The *G* is silent."

He led her down a series of orange through yellow through ochre corridors. Ruby trailed her fingers on the shiny gloss paint and the man snapped his head around. "Please don't touch." Ruby opened her mouth to speak but the man held up his hand. "No questions please."

Boy, is this guy a prize potato head.

They continued in silence until he stopped, opened a door of uncertain color — commonly described as sludge — and pointed to a desk in the middle of an empty room. He then placed a pile of papers on the table. "Here's a pencil. You have one hour and one minute. You are required to give only *one* answer, any erasing, any changes of mind, will be seen as a *wrong* answer. If you have an urgent need to go to the bathroom, suppress it. Any questions? Good, I didn't think so."

"Yep, Mr. Froghorn, just one actually." (She ignored the silent *G* thing.) "Have you ever considered moving into the hospitality industry because boy, I really think you might be wasting those great people skills."

Froghorn looked at her, all beady eyes and defensive — like a cobra. Or was it a jackal?

"Do your test, little girl, fail it, and then I'm sure an adult will drive you home. *A few* people here might rate you, but you need to be aware that you are no Bradley Baker and you never will be."

"Just who is this Bradley Baker?"

*TO TAKE THE 99-SECOND TEST, GO TO WWW.RUBYREDFORT.COM

But Froghorn wasn't about to explain. When he exited the room he slammed the door so hard the sound echoed down the corridor.

I must remember that silent G, said Ruby to herself.

Ruby picked up her pencil and took a look at the papers in front of her. There were thirty-seven problems and one hour and one minute to solve them in. That meant just ninety-nine seconds on each one. She glanced at the clock and began reading.

`Spectrum Agency Test—37 problems—Time 61 minutes.`

`(1) You have to take three criminals back to the County Jail: Alexei Asimov, Carlo Carlucci, and Walter Trunch. You have to cross a river on the way, and the boat only takes two people at a time. The trouble is that if you leave the criminals together, Asimov will kill Trunch, and Trunch will kill Carlucci. How can you get them safely across the river?`

She smiled. *Geez, that was easy — just thirty-six to go.*

`(2) You have seven gold bars. However, one of them is a counterfeit and weighs less than the others. You have a`

set of balance scales but you may only use them twice.
How do you identify the counterfeit gold bar?

Boy, if all the questions were going to be this simple the time was really going to drag.

(3)

$$9! \prod_{p \text{ prime}} \left\{ \left(1 - \frac{1}{p}\right)^4 \left(1 + \frac{4}{p} + \frac{1}{p^2}\right) \right\}^{-1} \lim_{T \to \infty} \frac{1}{T \log^9 T} \int_1^T \left| \left(\sum_{n=1}^{\infty} n^{-(1/2+it)}\right) \right|^6 dt$$

Now, this was more like it — question three was one of those questions that keep highly respected mathematicians up all night. Ruby furrowed her brow — for about twenty-eight seconds, then she grinned.

Oh, I get it.

When Froghorn walked back into the room, he found Ruby hunched over the test papers, chewing her pencil.

"Oh, dear, you seem to be stuck — too hard?" asked Froghorn, barely able to contain his mirth.

"Well, it's just I'm sorta confused."

"Never mind, little girl, it *is* a very difficult test — tricky for children to make sense of."

"Oh, that's a relief because this question didn't make any sense at all."

He looked over her shoulder.

(25) Spectrum agents Bret and Emily and Chuck are all driving to a Clairvoyants concert. They set off an hour before the concert. Bret takes route A which is twice as long as Emily's route B but the average of their two routes is the same as Chuck's route C. Trouble is Bret gets lost and goes 10 miles out of his way, meaning he ends up traveling as much as the combined distance Chuck and Emily travel. Assuming they all drive at 40 miles an hour, how late is Bret for the concert?

"I have to admit, less able people do find that a tough one." He smiled meanly.

Ruby looked at him, all big-eyed innocence. "Oh, that's not the problem. I get that the answer is fifteen minutes — it's just I don't get why anyone would travel for over an hour to go see a lame band like the Clairvoyants."

Miles Froghorn's mouth twisted into a mean little O. He snatched up the papers and stormed out of the room. Ruby wished she could tell Clancy about this super sap. She could just see Clancy's expression, mouth wide, eyes blinking — boy, would she love to tell him all this.

While she waited, Ruby amused herself by doodling unflattering pictures of Froghorn in the back of her notebook — they were pretty good actually.

Twenty-five minutes later there were footsteps in the corridor and Ruby was relieved when it was Hitch who walked into the room and not the Silent G.

"Ready to go, kid?"

Ruby nodded.

Hitch motioned to the door. "Come on, then, let's get out of here before Froghorn sees those unpleasant little cartoons you did of him."

"Hey, how did you know about that?"

"I was watching you on the monitor. Not bad, you have a talent for caricature."

"Thanks," said Ruby. "Clancy and me are thinking of publishing our own comic book."

"Good for you," said Hitch.

They walked in silence for about fifteen seconds before Ruby blurted, "So?"

Hitch gave her a blank look.

"So, how did I do?" said Ruby.

"Oh, that," replied Hitch. "Yes, well done — thirty-six out of thirty-seven. Not bad."

"I got one *wrong*?" said Ruby, dumbfounded.

He winked. "Nah, kid. I'm just messing with you."

Ruby stopped walking. "So you're saying I passed? I musta passed, right? I mean thirty-seven out of thirty-seven, that has to be a pass."

Hitch looked at her. "Don't get your underwear in a twist kid. You passed."

She tried to keep her cool but still, she *had* just passed the ninety-nine-second test; anyone would find themselves smiling about that, *wouldn't* they?

When they stepped inside the elevator, Ruby asked, "So who is this mystery Bradley Baker guy?"

"Bradley Baker?" replied Hitch. "He's no one."

There were a lot of things Ruby didn't know about Spectrum but one thing she was already sure about was that Bradley Baker was not "no one."

CHAPTER 13
As Good as Gold

HITCH LED RUBY TO A RAINBOW-COLORED office where Buzz was sitting. Her desk was a circle and she sat in the middle surrounded by telephones — each one a different color.

"Now what?" said Ruby.

"Now you wait here, good as gold until someone tells you otherwise," said Hitch firmly.

"What am I waiting *for*?" asked Ruby.

"LB," he said. "She wants to brief you — so don't go wandering off, kid. Sit tight. That's a rule, remember?"

Ruby *did* sit tight — for all of twenty-nine seconds. And then she had an idea. This might just be her chance to return the watch before anyone knew it was missing.

She looked over at Buzz, who seemed to be waiting for one of the fifty-two phones to start ringing.

"So that's why you're called Buzz," said Ruby.

Buzz looked baffled.

"The phones, people always buzzing you?"

"No," said Buzz. "That's not why."

It didn't take long before one of the telephones *did* start to ring, the yellow one. Buzz picked it up and started talking in Japanese. That's when Ruby stood up and signaled that she urgently needed to take a trip to the restroom.

"It's OK," she mouthed silently. "I know where it is, I'll be fine."

Buzz bit her lip anxiously and pointed at her watch to indicate "Don't be long."

Ruby opened the door and walked speedily down the corridor until she got to the restroom. She went in, took off her sneakers, and placed them in one of the stalls. This way if anyone were to come in, what they would see would be Ruby's feet. She then silently slipped back out and ran softly up the corridor, remembering to turn right when she reached crimson, and left when it dissolved into cerise. The door, she remembered, was about halfway down. Now for the code. She recalled how Buzz had looked at her watch before she had punched in the numbers.

I'll bet that's it.

She pulled the Fly Escape Watch from her pocket, checked the dial, and punched in the exact time.

The door clicked open. *Too bad I gotta return this watch, it's coming in kinda handy.*

As she walked, the lights in the display cases popped on around her, the gadgets gleaming under the glass, like jewels at a jewelers. She went over to the drawer where the watch belonged and was about to open it when something caught her eye. It was a silver whistle — it looked like a dog whistle but the label was smudged. Maybe it was the ribbon, maybe it was the fact that she had always wanted a silver dog whistle, but Ruby found that she couldn't resist slipping it over her head and looking at her reflection in the glass.

She blew into it — no sound at all. Surely it wasn't *just* a dog whistle? She blew into it again and again, still nothing. In her frustration she started blowing and inhaling in the way that one might suck air in and out of a harmonica.

"Must be broken," said Ruby out loud, but her voice seemed to be coming from far, far away.

Wow, so it's a voice thrower. She inhaled again. "Hello," she said. This time her voice sounded as if it was coming from right behind her. She experimented some more — there were four little holes in the whistle, and whichever one her finger covered determined the direction her voice came from — north, east, south, or west of her. Point the whistle up — her voice was thrown above her.

It was precisely at the moment she called out the words, "I'm over here!" that someone else decided to enter the room.

Ruby quickly ducked down behind the cabinets.

"Did you hear that?" said a voice she didn't recognize.

"Hear what?" said a second voice.

"Hey, these lights shouldn't be on."

"Must be something wrong with the sensors."

"You think? Unless of course . . ."

"What? Someone set them off? Should I call security?"

Ruby froze.

Oh, boy, now I'm in trouble.

She was almost about to give herself up when the first voice said, "Well, either that or go get some bug spray — could be a large spider. You know how many spiders set off alarms and sensors? I'll tell you, *a lot.*"

"Really? Must have been a pretty elephant-sized spider."

"Don't tell me you're scared of spiders."

"Not scared," said the second voice, a little aggravated. "Just don't like 'em is all." Ruby could hear the footsteps moving toward her.

Darn it, she mouthed silently as she tucked the whistle inside her T-shirt. Now she had managed to steal *two* things. She made herself very flat and began to crawl forward on her stomach. She could just about squeeze her way under the cabinets and make it to the door. Once in the corridor she sprinted as fast as she could to the restroom and retrieved her sneakers.

When she returned to her seat in Buzz's office she was flushed and perspiring.

"You know, you don't look so good," said Buzz.

"Yeah, well, I don't *feel* so good," said Ruby sincerely. "But give me a few minutes and I'll be OK."

"So long as you're sure." Buzz looked concerned; she wasn't used to queasy kids. "Well, if you're really certain you're OK," she said warily, "LB wants to see you. I'll walk you to the waiting area outside her office. Don't go anywhere, don't touch anything. In fact, don't move until LB comes to get you."

"Sounds like fun," said Ruby.

No one was around, which gave her a good chance to snoop about. On the walls were big colorful paintings, all of them abstract. Some of them made your eyes ache to look at them.

LB must be a fan of op art, thought Ruby. Her mother sold a lot of this kind of work at her modern-art gallery, and Ruby knew that it was usually very expensive. One entire wall was painted with concentric circles in colors that seemed to buzz and vibrate. Ruby stared at it so hard that she eventually lost her balance and fell forward. Putting her hands out to save herself, she unwittingly pressed a hidden catch, and what had looked like a wall sort of became a door and swung open.

Oops.

There in front of her was a room completely empty but for hundreds of black-and-white photographs, which covered the walls from floor to ceiling. Photographs mainly of people: people and cars, people up mountains and in jungles, people on elephants, people canoeing down rapids. One picture particularly intrigued her. It was of a youngish boy, sitting at the controls of an airplane and smiling at the camera. She guessed he must be the son of one of the agents. There was another of him scuba diving.

Lucky kid, she thought. Up high on the far left was a picture of a man looking a huge crocodile in the eye. He was making a stupid face, his eyes were crossed and he appeared not even slightly bothered by the reptile. The man looked familiar but even with her glasses on Ruby couldn't quite make out who he was or where she had seen him before. Curiosity getting the better of her, she dragged a chair from the lobby and climbed up to take a closer look.

"Well, I'll be darned, he certainly is *some butler!*" she said out loud. Hitch could only have been about twenty in the picture, and out of a suit he looked quite different.

"So, you're a snoop, Ruby Redfort."

Ruby spun around, and losing her balance, she toppled off the chair and landed in an undignified sprawl on the cool rubber-coated floor.

She was eye level with a pair of bare feet—the toenails painted red.

"Oh, sorry, I didn't mean to, it was sort of an accident, the door kinda opened on its own," Ruby stammered.

"What next? It *wasn't me*?" LB's voice was chilly. She wasn't mad—she was furious.

"I'm not making excuses or anything—just saying it was an honest accident."

"You accidentally opened a concealed door? Accidentally dragged a chair into a private room? Accidentally stood on it and started accidentally examining my personal photographs? What complicated accidents you have."

"Well, when you put it like that it sounds kinda bad," said Ruby.

"Too much curiosity can be fatal," said LB. "Something it is wise to remember." This statement sounded a little sinister and Ruby quickly picked herself up off the floor. She noticed she had torn a hole in her jacket — a huge rip down the left sleeve — which only added to her humiliation.

"I'm sure I didn't see anything important — by the way, that's a very nice picture of you. When was it taken? You look kinda young, is that your boyfriend?" Ruby was pointing at a picture of a girlish looking LB, who was smiling warmly at a good-looking young man. However, the real life LB was not smiling, she was glaring. If Ruby thought she was going to distract LB with the old flattery and fast talk routine then it seemed she had a great deal to learn about LB.

"If it wasn't for your test results and what we already know about you, I might be sorely tempted to think again."

"Look, I'm sorry. I'm not a snoop, not normally anyway . . ."

"OK, cut the baloney, Redfort. You have one chance but use it carefully because right now I'm this close to telling you to take a walk." LB was holding her thumb and forefinger very close to represent the amount of slack she was prepared to give Ruby — it wasn't much, about a millimeter.

Ruby kept her mouth shut.

LB pointed at the chair and Ruby sat down, but before anything could be said, a light flashed on LB's desk intercom.

She sighed an exasperated sigh and said, "Now, I am going

to leave you for about three minutes, certainly no longer; try not to touch *anything*. Sit on your hands if you have to."

LB left the room. Ruby sat completely still for two minutes and fifteen seconds — not a twitch until she spotted a small, brightly colored object that had fallen under LB's desk. She couldn't help herself; she reached out and picked it up. It was a key ring, with a sort of puzzle attached. It had letter tiles you could slide around to form words, or perhaps *a* word.

The door opened — Ruby quickly palmed the key ring and tried to act normal.

LB sat down. "I'll cut to the chase. We need you to go through some files. We recently lost our code breaker, and we find ourselves one very valuable brain down."

"How did you lose him?"

"*Her*, actually — she died. She was on vacation, mountain climbing."

"She fell?" asked Ruby.

"Avalanche; by the time they dug her out it was too late. They never did find her climbing partner."

"I'm sorry to hear that," said Ruby, popping some bubble gum into her mouth.

"Could you *lose the gum*," said LB. It wasn't a question. Ruby lost it.

"She was unlucky, there was no warning, it took everyone by surprise." LB paused as if collecting herself. "Anyway, Lopez was working on a case, code name Fool's Gold. They uncovered a plot to rob the Twinford City Bank, though we still have no idea who is involved."

"The Twinford City Bank? The unrobbable bank?" said Ruby, astonished. "When is it planned for?"

"The evening the gold bullion arrives from Switzerland. It will be deposited in the Twinford bank on April twenty-second, and the robbery is set to take place twelve hours later."

"So, if you know all this, why do you need me?"

LB didn't say anything for a long moment; perhaps she was wondering if she could trust this short, green-eyed kid from Twinford. Then, taking a slow breath she said, "We got a call from Lopez. She was three days into her vacation when she left a message with Buzz. She said, 'Tell the boss I missed something first time around. Tell her I saw it in the mirror and it all made sense.'"

"That's it?" said Ruby, "Kinda cryptic isn't it? Who's the boss?"

"That would be me," said LB coolly. "Naturally she wouldn't have wanted to say anything obvious over an unsecured line. She said she would be in touch that evening when she got back from her climb. She had booked herself on the very next flight home. She was cutting her vacation short by ten days."

"Do you have any idea what she was talking about?" asked Ruby.

"We can be sure she was talking about a code — one she had missed. She must have figured it out while she was away."

"Did she have it with her?" said Ruby.

"Of course not. It is strictly forbidden to take classified information out of the Spectrum building. So we know that whatever she missed has to be in the Fool's Gold files. Which is why we want you to go through them in the same way she would have gone through them. See if you can't find what she didn't see first time around."

Ruby frowned. "What do you think she meant when she said she 'saw it in the mirror'?"

"She's referring to the local newspaper, the *Twinford Mirror* — that's where all the codes were hidden."

Ruby looked perplexed.

LB waved her hand impatiently; she needed to get on. "It will all be explained to you tomorrow. You will return here. Agent Blacker will take you to the file room where you can read through all Agent Lopez's papers and try to get a grip on this case. Understood?"

"Uh-huh."

"OK, so get out of here."

CHAPTER 14
Don't Erase Me

ON THE WAY BACK TO CEDARWOOD DRIVE, Ruby tried to work her Ruby Redfort powers of persuasion on Hitch.

"Don't you think it might be a good idea for me to have some kind of little radio device so I can radio in?"

"Radio in to where?"

"To HQ," said Ruby.

"No kid, you don't radio in to HQ. You always go via me."

"OK, so I should be able to radio in to you."

"And why would you need to do that?" said Hitch.

"Well, you know, in case I need to get hold of you super quick," said Ruby.

"And you can, by using that incredible gadget known as the telephone."

"But what if there is no telephone, or say someone was on it and I had to run all over looking for another one?"

"I imagine you are a pretty good runner." It was clear Hitch was unmoved by Ruby's argument.

"Oh, man, can't I have some little radio walkie-talkie gadget?" pleaded Ruby. "What's the big problem?"

"The 'big problem,'" said Hitch, "is *you* getting in over your head. Look, kid, this is a desk job, OK? You are being hired to go through files and decipher information. It is *not* a matter of life and death, and let's not make it one."

"But what if it is? What if I find something out—something kinda vital . . . to everything! And I need to follow it up on the double—get on someone's tail before they disappear; you know, step in before something bad happens."

"Kid, you do any 'stepping in' and you will be stepping out of Spectrum for good. You find something out, you sit tight. No drama, no heroics. Sitting tight is a rule—you got that?"

"Oh, man!" sighed Ruby. "Did anyone ever tell you that you can be a royal pain in the derriere?"

"All the time kid, so you'd be wise to remember this—you never act alone. That's another rule." Hitch looked her in the eye. "You hearing me kid?"

Ruby nodded. She was hearing, but it was hard to be sure if she was listening, and hearing and listening are two very different things.

❀ ❀ ❀

Back at the house, Ruby went straight to the living room and listened to the messages on the family answering machine. She just wanted to be sure that the school hadn't called and said something that would lead her parents to find out about her skipping.

Maybe Mrs. Digby will have phoned from Miami or wherever in tarnation she has gone.

There were several messages for her father from the detective, explaining that they had *"no more leads"*—several *from* her father for her mother, unusually bad-tempered, complaining about the airline and how there was *"still no sight nor sound of their luggage"*—one from the dry cleaner to say they were *"having trouble with the tomato stain and would have to send the jacket away for super cleaning."*

The final message was from Freddie Humbert and basically went on and on about his problems with the bank security system and how he was *"up to his ears in it"* and *"wouldn't be able to attend the museum meetings or indeed play golf for the foreseeable future."* Right at the end he said, *"Don't forget to tell that cute daughter of yours to give us a call. Quent would love to see her."*

Ruby made a face. A couple of hours with Quent Humbert was all she needed. She was about to erase the message when her father popped his head around the door. "Jeepers!" blurted Ruby. "What are you doing home?"

"Oh, I'm sorry. Got off work early. I didn't mean to make you jump. You checking the messages? Any good ones?"

Ruby pressed the playback button. "I don't know, I didn't listen." She headed upstairs to her room and checked her personal answering machine. There was a message. It was from Clancy.

"Hi, Rube, where were you today? You didn't say anything about skipping school. Are you sick? Whatever — give me a call, OK? Hey, don't erase me, don't erase me . . . aaaahhhh."

It was a classic Clancy Crew joke. Ruby smiled as she erased the message. Darn it, though, what *was* she going to tell Clancy? She hadn't thought about that when she had promised to keep it zipped. She couldn't lie to him — she never lied to him — but she had sworn she wouldn't talk. Hitch was right, code breaking was easy compared to keeping a secret like this. She needed to think. But all she *could* think was, *Darn it! Dad is sure to make me call Quent.*

She picked up her backpack and rummaged for the Spectrum Escape Watch, but it wasn't there. She was about to panic when she remembered she had stuffed it into her jacket pocket.

Now where is my jacket?

Then she heard her mother calling.

Geez, now what?

"It's time to eat!" called her mother.

The watch would have to wait — her mother was a stickler when it came to "dining time."

The meal seemed to drag on for just about ever. Ruby was finding her folks less than scintillating company. Most of what they said she had heard from her history teacher, Mrs. Schneiderman, and she certainly was in no hurry to hear it all again.

"Don't you just love the legend of the Jade Buddha, Brant?" cooed Sabina.

"Love it," replied Brant.

"It's kind of romantic, don't you think? To look the Buddha in the eye at the stroke of midnight — you know, as it rises up through the floor — and in that moment double your wisdom, and halve your age."

"Desperately romantic," agreed Brant through a mouthful of steak and tomato.

"I mean, imagine getting younger at the same time as you get wiser."

"*Never to decay or fade away* — wouldn't that be swell," enthused Brant.

They burbled on like this all through the main course and partway through dessert.

"Hey! How about we have some kind of lucky draw," said Sabina. "You know — put your name in the hat and you get the chance to look the Buddha in the eye on the stroke of midnight!"

"Like a lottery? Buy a ticket, win eternal youth?"

"You got it." Sabina could hardly contain herself.

"I think it's a swell idea," said Brant. "What do you think, Ruby honey? Swell idea or what?"

Ruby didn't answer; she was miles away.

"Ruby?"

"Huh? What?" said Ruby with a start.

"Your father and I were just wondering if there should be a Jade Buddha lottery with one lucky winner."

"Lucky winner of what?"

"One lucky winner to look the Jade Buddha in the eye at midnight!"

"Why would they want to do that?" asked Ruby, genuinely bewildered.

"Ruby, are you OK?" asked her mother. "You don't seem to have heard a word we have said."

"Sorry," said Ruby. "Just a bit distracted, I guess."

"I'll say," said her mother.

"Well," said her father. "I think I might just go and call Marjorie and Freddie—they're gonna love the idea."

"Oh yes, do, do, do!" said Sabina. She was quiet for one split second and then exclaimed, "I am wondering if it isn't time we talked about canapés. What do you think, Ruby? Maybe serve ice-related canapés, on account of the Buddha being found in an iceberg?"

Ruby, desperately wanting not to get stuck at the table talking to her mother about the mind-numbing subject of iced finger food, decided to make a swift exit.

"Mom, just gotta walk Bug."

"But I already walked him an hour ago," said Sabina.

"Oh, yeah, well, I promised him," called Ruby, already halfway down the stairs.

"Who promises a *dog*?" said Sabina.

On the way back from her walk, Ruby made a stop at the tree on Amster Green. She wanted to see if Clancy had left something for her. He had. A coded note, folded in two.

It translated as:

Are you in some kind of trouble? I saw that
butler guy of yours and his fancy car —
I don't trust him.

Ruby felt a pang of guilt as she carefully refolded the note and put it back in the tree as if she had never read it.

Back home she dejectedly climbed the stairs to her room. She closed the door firmly behind her and her thoughts returned to the watch. She knew it was safe inside her jacket pocket — only thing was, where was her jacket?

**Mrs. Digby had woken to
the unmistakable sound of
a knife ripping through a
white designer couch. . . .**

Luckily, Mrs. Digby had taken to sleeping in the bed at the far end of the warehouse in the Redforts' guest room. She had always wanted to try it out — the mattress was pocket sprung.

She pulled on her robe and tiptoed silently along the far side of the warehouse, where she was hidden from sight by huge cargo crates. From here she had a pretty good view of what was going on, and she did not like what she saw. There were several thuggish men tearing at the furniture, pulling open drawers and cupboards, opening jars, ripping into feather cushions. Mrs. Redfort's jewelery boxes were simply tipped upside down and emptied onto the floor. None of the thugs seemed at all interested in the contents once they had rummaged through them, yet these jewels were worth many thousands of dollars.

Mrs. Digby, who was finding it hard to restrain herself from marching right out there and giving them a piece of her mind, was relieved to hear a woman's voice shout out, "Just what do you numbskulls think you are doing?"

About time, thought Mrs. Digby.

The woman continued. "We are looking for something very small and highly valuable, how are we supposed to find it if you have turned the whole place on its head!"

Silence from the numbskulls.

Couldn't have put it better myself, thought Mrs. Digby. She couldn't see the woman from where she hid but she guessed she must be quite a force to reckon with, since for the next eleven hours the men went painstakingly through every item of the Redforts' home, picking it up, opening it, inspecting it, and then replacing it.

What in tarnation are those creeps looking for? wondered Mrs. Digby.

Whatever it was, it seemed they didn't find it.

CHAPTER 15
Strictly Confidential

RUBY GOT HERSELF UP AND READY nice and early. She was looking forward to going back to Spectrum and finding out more of its secrets. But first she had to find the Escape Watch, which meant locating her jacket. She was pretty sure that she must have left it in Hitch's car, in which case it was safe — but what if he had found the jacket and looked through her pockets? She wouldn't put it past him. In which case she was in big trouble.

But when she got downstairs Hitch was in the kitchen quietly studying a piece of toast.

"Is that piece of toast private or can anyone eat it?" she said.

He looked up. "Strictly confidential," he replied, hurriedly biting into it. "So, you excited about your first day as a code breaker?"

Ruby gave him a withering look.

He winked at her. "Just pulling your leg, kid, I know you're far too cool to get *excited* about things."

She gave him another withering look and started for the back door.

"Where you going?"

"To get my bike. I might as well leave now. I can pick up breakfast at the diner."

"No, that's not how it's going to be, kid. Strict instructions from the top: I'm going to drive you in to the Spectrum office each day and I'm going to collect you when you're done."

"Oh, man!" Ruby rolled her eyes. "I don't need you driving me around. I'll take my bike, OK?"

"Not OK, said Hitch firmly. "I gotta make sure no one tails you and I need to make sure you are all present and correct in one piece. If I'm not available then someone else will drive you home."

Ruby opened her mouth to argue but Hitch simply held up his hand. "This is non-negotiable."

Ruby said nothing.

"Get yourself in the vehicle pronto. We need to get going."

"But I haven't had breakfast!" protested Ruby. "Most important meal of the day and all that."

"We'll pick something up on the way, OK? Now scram. I'll be with you in a split second."

Ruby got into the car and was relieved to see her jacket crumpled on the floor behind the passenger seat. She felt around in the pocket until her fingers closed around the cold metal of the watch — *got you, you weasel.*

She looked at it. Of all the things she'd ever owned this was certainly the best — only thing was, she *didn't* own it, and sooner or later someone was bound to discover it was missing, along with the whistle *and* the key ring. It wouldn't take a master sleuth to figure out who the culprit was. What was happening to her? This was the kind of thing that happened to Red Monroe — not to Ruby Redfort.

She slipped the watch back into her jacket. The key ring was already clipped securely to her jeans and was tucked safely hidden in her back pocket. The whistle was around her neck, concealed under her T-shirt. She just had to find a way to put them back before anyone noticed they were gone.

On the way to Spectrum, while Ruby and Hitch were stopped at a light, who should cross the street but Clancy Crew, Del Lasco, and Elliot Finch, stuffing donuts into their mouths. Ruby slid down in her seat.

"Don't worry, kid. They can't see you, only me."

"How's that?" asked Ruby.

"Special glass," said Hitch, knocking on the windshield. "If this switch is flicked down," he said, pointing to a little silver lever, "then on the passenger side it just shows a blank space, as if you aren't there." To prove his point he wound down his window, stuck his head out, and called, "Hey, kids, don't suppose I could persuade you to let me have one of those donuts?"

"No way, man," said Del through a mouthful of donut. "I only have two left."

Clancy said nothing, but he certainly wasn't going to let that butler guy have anything of his, not for free anyway. He didn't like him, and he didn't trust him either.

Elliot looked thoughtfully at the remaining donut in its paper bag. "How much you offering?" he asked.

"How about I guess what flavor donut you got. I'm right, I get it for free; I'm wrong, I give you ten bucks for it."

Elliot couldn't believe his luck. This guy was never going to guess what flavor donut he had; this meant a big profit. "Sure," said Elliot, "I don't mind taking ten bucks off ya."

"So?" whispered Hitch out of the corner of his mouth.

"Well, the one he was just eating was banana, which means the one in the bag is chocolate raspberry with strawberry frosting and rainbow sprinkles," hissed Ruby.

"OK," said Hitch, holding his finger to his temple as if he were channeling the information. "I'm guessing . . . chocolate raspberry, strawberry frosting, rainbow sprinkles — am I right?"

Elliot, speechless, handed over the donut.

"Pleasure doing business with you," said Hitch as he pulled away from the lights.

"Who is that guy?" whispered Del.

"Some bozo who works for the Redforts," muttered Clancy.

"They got a magician working for them?" said Elliot.

"Pretty cool," said Ruby as they sped along toward Twinford Bridge.

"I aim to please," said Hitch, handing Ruby the donut.

When they arrived at Spectrum, Ruby was told to sit in the waiting area. She was kind of fidgety. She wasn't particularly looking forward to meeting Agent Blacker. So far everyone she had encountered at HQ had not exactly been Mickey Mouse friendly.

But when Agent Blacker turned up he actually smiled.

"If you don't mind my saying, you look kinda youthful," he said.

"I drink a lot of banana milk—keeps you young looking," said Ruby.

"Is that so? How many pints do you drink exactly?"

He was a disheveled-looking man and his badge was upside down and his hair didn't look like it had been combed since

Christmas. He had a nice voice though. It had warmth — she could tell from just a few words.

"So," he said. "You gonna solve this Lopez code for us?" He ruffled her hair and added, "You know what? I think you just might."

Messing with Ruby Redfort's hair would not ordinarily have been a good idea, but for some reason, today, Ruby didn't mind. Perhaps she was just relieved that someone was finally on her side.

"Thanks, but I'm not sure anyone else around here would agree with you. I feel about as popular as a person infected with the Black Death."

"Nah, they wouldn't talk to you at all if you had the Black Death," said Blacker.

Ruby was surprised when she was ushered through a door and found herself outside in an alley, facing a Dumpster and an old van that *looked* like a Dumpster. "There's our ride," said Blacker, walking toward the van.

"You're kidding, right?" said Ruby.

But he wasn't.

"Where we goin' — the junkyard?"

"Yeah, I hear what you're saying, Ruby. She is a bit of an old lady, but she runs OK. Inconspicuous too."

"Only if we are going to a real dump of a neighborhood," said Ruby.

Blacker laughed awkwardly. "Yeah."

Twenty minutes later Ruby understood why. They had pulled up in front of an old office building on Maverick Street on the east side of town in the area known as Trashford. It was a dump.

"Here we are — the file office," said Agent Blacker. "Lopez worked from here because it made for a good cover, and it was safe."

Ruby looked up at the derelict building that was sandwiched between an ancient-looking Laundromat and a boarded-up convenience store. "If you don't mind my saying so, it doesn't look very safe."

Blacker pointed at the door. "Try drilling through this baby in a hurry — it will take you upward of eighteen hours."

If that was true then it was disguised well.

He unlocked the door. It was brown — at least the top layer was — large flakes of ancient paint were peeling off to reveal many past color choices, all the colors of the rainbow. Ruby stepped inside. The small room was lined floor to ceiling with files, brown ones.

"If anyone did ever happen to tail Lopez, we wanted them to find some dusty old office. Lopez told everyone she was a bookkeeper. No one outside Spectrum knew what she really did."

"So, what, she never got to go out on any missions or adventures?" asked Ruby.

Blacker shook his head. "She never did anything for Spectrum that involved any danger. LB doesn't like losing her code breakers, not after . . . well, she just doesn't. She likes to keep her great minds safe and sound."

Ruby looked around at the dismal office. She couldn't help feeling it was capable of *depressing* a person to death.

"So every day she sat looking at these drab old walls? What did she do for kicks?" asked Ruby.

"Rock climbing," replied Blacker.

"She probably enjoyed the scenery," said Ruby, glancing at the window, almost black with dirt.

"So, I guess LB filled you in on the case," said Blacker, pointing at the far wall. "All these files on this shelf here cover every little thing we found out about the planned bank heist."

Ruby counted them. There were more than a few.

"We want you to read through every single file, and try to

spot what we missed the first time around. We know we musta missed something because old Lopez worked it out while she was on her vacation. Her mind musta been ticking over and suddenly — vavoom! — she figured something out. But that leaves us with a problem; we don't know what it was."

"So what tipped you off about the robbery in the first place?" asked Ruby.

"We had a call from the Gotz Bank in Switzerland. That's where the gold's coming in from. They reported that they were sure someone had infiltrated their security and possibly got their hands on information relating to the gold bullion which is due to be transferred from Gotz Bank to the Twinford City Bank on April twenty-second."

Ruby took some bubble gum out of her pocket. "Mind if I chew?"

Blacker shook his head. "Why should I mind?"

Ruby shrugged. "You'd be surprised." She popped the pink cube into her mouth. "So, anyway, what made them suspicious?"

"The person in charge was very, you know, fastidious. She liked everything all lined up 'just so,' and was the only person to have access to the documents and papers, and although nothing was missing, she was certain that her papers had been disturbed."

Ruby nodded.

"Not long after this we intercepted a call from a new customer who claimed she wanted to make a deposit of highly valuable jewelry in the Twinford City Bank. She also wanted to visit the vault it would be kept in."

"That's not unusual. I know my mom would do the same."

"But your mom probably wouldn't ask quite as many questions as this woman did."

"Questions like what?" said Ruby.

"Like, was it true that the basement was designed by Jeremiah Stiles? Was there really a trick to working one's way through the maze of passages?"

"Maybe just interested in architecture," suggested Ruby.

"Maybe," said Blacker. "According to the bank employee who showed her around, she certainly *seemed* interested. She actually seemed to be *memorizing* the corridors. And there was something a little *off* about her, apparently. She had a strange accent — strange meaning it sounded a little fake. Kinda staged, like she was trying to sound like she was from around here when she wasn't. She was wearing a hat with a veil — looked like something from out of an old movie — very stylish and all but a little over the top for a visit to the bank."

"So she was an eccentric — there are lots of strange people in Twinford," said Ruby.

"I can't disagree with you there, but when the bank checked out her ID later it was discovered that she had been dead for twenty years."

"Ah, now that is a little strange," agreed Ruby. "Even for someone from Twinford. So what about the security cameras — didn't they get a good look at her?"

"Something went wrong there," said Blacker. "Maybe it was her veil, but in every picture her face came out a blur, as if the camera couldn't see through it — couldn't even make out one feature."

"So then what?" said Ruby.

Blacker shook his head. "Nothing. No more inquiries about safes and security, no more eccentric ladies turning up at the city bank."

"But you didn't think whoever it was had given up?"

"Well, that's where we got lucky, I guess. We stumbled on something."

Agent Blacker walked over to the files, picked up a folder labeled FOOL'S GOLD — FILE ONE, and placed it on the desk where Lopez must have sat for all those years. It was a dated-looking piece of furniture, perhaps designed in the 1950s, and it had little colored drawer pulls, a built-in pencil holder, and a cool-looking pale-blue lamp. He switched the lamp on and motioned for Ruby to sit down.

"Take a look for yourself—you'll get the idea. Might as well make yourself comfortable, you're gonna be sitting here for a while. Don't rush it. Remember, there has to be something that Lopez missed, and she was careful, so you need to be extra careful." He handed her a crumpled brown paper bag, inside was a donut.

"You must be a mind reader," she said.

"Who *doesn't* like a jelly donut?" shrugged Blacker.

The file was full of newspaper clippings, lots and lots of newspaper clippings.

They were all from the personals. They seemed innocent enough:

LADY OF ADVANCING YEARS seeks companion with an interest in cats, crochet, and ancient history.

FITNESS INSTRUCTOR wanted for fitness phobic Finn.

LEARN TO COOK GREEK STYLE! When you're done—no need for tiresome dish washing, just throw them over your shoulder!

Silently, Ruby read page after page. There were hundreds of these absurd clippings, every one from the *Twinford Mirror*. There was nothing remotely suspicious or sinister about any of them.

What was it that Lopez saw?

After about an hour of reading Ruby shouted out to Blacker. "So what made you look out for personals in the *Twinford Mirror*?"

"Well, that's an interesting story," said Blacker, walking out of his room and sitting down on a box next to Ruby. "The police picked up a known felon by the name of Fingers Macgraw. He was driving an expensive car that didn't belong to him and he couldn't really explain how he had come by it. Anyway, when the car was searched it had a whole batch of these personal ads stuffed in the glove compartment."

"So? Fingers read the personals — there's no law against it."

"Right, but there was no way they belonged to Fingers; there wasn't a single fingerprint of his on them. It was obvious he didn't even know they were there. In any case what would he be doing with newspaper cuttings? Fingers can barely read — he is strictly a feel it and steal it kinda fellow — nothing complicated about him."

"And this looked complicated?" said Ruby.

"It looked like it was *something*," said Blacker. "A whole lot of carefully collected newspaper ads and tips from the *Twinford Mirror* — I mean why? What do they mean?"

"They look pretty random," said Ruby.

"Yeah," he said. "That's just it — they are *so* random, it made us wonder if they *were* random, if you get my drift. And why didn't the person they belonged to ever contact the police to report the car *missing*? It was a good car — almost new."

"But the police must have run a check on the license plates, found the owner?" said Ruby.

"Sure they did. We know who the car was registered to but it turned out to be the same dead woman who supposedly visited the bank."

"Well, I agree that *is* pretty suspicious," said Ruby.

Blacker nodded. "So we ran the ads past Lopez to see what she thought."

"And how long before you knew you were on to something?" asked Ruby.

Blacker pointed at another whole row of files. "Lopez started reading the *Twinford Mirror* very closely — wasn't until she had filled all of these before we began to see exactly what was going on with the personal ads."

"Boy, you people must really have patience" said Ruby, pulling the next file from the shelf. "What was it she worked out?"

Agent Blacker smiled. "Sorry, but LB wants to see if you can find that out for yourself."

For the next couple of hours Ruby barely moved from her chair. She just sat there, reading clipping after clipping.

Most of the clippings were personal ads. Some were titled TOP TIPS; people would write in from all over to suggest ways of, for instance, getting a cat down from a tree, or how to get shoe polish off a pair of corduroy pants. The pieces were at worst boring and at best faintly amusing but there was nothing suspicious about them — nothing, that is, until Ruby spotted the pattern. They were using a number of different variations on the same code, taking the first letter of the ad and then letters at fixed intervals, discarding the rest. The first code Ruby deciphered used every fifth letter or number to convey the secret message. After some tinkering, Ruby also discovered something else: three dots in a personal ad seemed to indicate a question mark in the coded message. After that you started with the first letter again.

As Ruby deciphered each short piece, it became clear to her what was going on: five or more people were communicating with one another about something, and it wasn't about how to get shoe polish off a pair of corduroy pants.

At around lunchtime Blacker ordered pizza.

"So, is it beginning to make sense, Ruby?" he asked.

"I can see where it's headed." She showed him what she had deciphered.

SCOTCH AMERICAN up for amiable dominos.
Anticipating players of minimal ages 20 to 22.
Shipment April 22

OVENS, PAINT, ELECTRIC TRAIN SETS, various
models, newer 100 to 200 mph outboards.
Uncle Ralph's jumble bonanza starts Easter.
Operation 12 hours later

WANT THAT STAIN OUT? Here is one super
trick: heat pear with soda, cool, rub in
gentle rotations . . . Slows or eliminates
most tough or dried-on nasty gloop. Powder the
pear, it cuts time. Store it under sink . . .
What is the target? Something precious?

WITCH HAS A CAT AND TOAD, lizards, charm,
all to order at special price. Reply early,
cuz this ace offer undersells the others.
Hats, wand, frogs also. Excellent deals . . .
What is more precious than gold?

VALUE A REST? U need latest calming comfrey + pea treatment. Sleep w/out any drugs, say bye bye to lost repose with simple tea. To hear more, you *must* try to phone Legera Botanicals.
Vault impenetrable without plans.

POOLS, LAWNS, AND SAND PITS: good, mature yard man looks for jobs. I've dozens refs and past works if you like. Classy home maintenance, DIY too. Own a van. Special rates.
Plans memorized—will hand over.

MADAM UNICE SEEKS Twinford's absolutely fab social denizens for deeply cool music, prayer, impact. Every Tuesday evening. Vanquish vices! Amen.
Must obtain security device.

DANCE EVENT. Very mixed acts. See the only pros waltz in 5 years, enjoy tango live. Hot dancing magic starts early December. You have to see what Ted Sarkey can do in only two hrs with those toes of his. Amazing skill in *our* town.
Device not yet located but we know who has it.

"Not bad," said Blacker. "I think you're gonna prove me right."

"So where is the security device?" asked Ruby.

"That's the thing, the gold vault at the bank doesn't have a security device — not as such. It has a two-part code: Freddie Humbert, the bank manager, has one half, and his security chief · has the other. There's no way anyone can get their hands on the code without kidnapping *both* of them, and since LB's brought in around-the-clock high security protection — kidnapping is near impossible."

Ruby frowned. If the Fool's Gold Gang were worthy of Spectrum's concern, then why hadn't the Gang noticed that Twinford City Bank security had been tightened? Why didn't they know that they had to get their hands on a code, not a device? They didn't stand a chance with a plan like this. These bozos might well know how to get shoe polish off a pair of corduroy pants but they had no idea how to go about robbing the safest safe in the U.S.A.

Ruby pondered all this for a while. Something didn't make sense . . . unless, of course, the gang had something much bigger in mind.

Was this plan only the beginning of things?

Was the real plan way more cunning? Is that what Lopez had discovered? Did the Fool's Gold Gang know more about the Twinford City Bank than anyone gave them credit for?

At three o'clock Hitch called to see how she was doing. "Look, kid, I'm sorry but I'm going to be a little late picking you up. Something has come up at HQ. Just hang on till seven and I'll be there."

Ruby was exhausted and the idea of staying into the early evening was not very appealing. To make things worse, Blacker poked his head around the door and said, "I'm sorry Ruby, I've been called in to HQ. Got to deal with a crisis. A replacement agent is coming over to watch over you. I'll stick around till they get here."

"Oh," said Ruby. "OK."

She started reading, and ten minutes later a voice broke her concentration. She looked up to see the smug face of the Silent G.

"Well, well, well, if it isn't Little Ruby Redfort."

"Oh, brother!" sighed Ruby.

"Believe me, little girl," Froghorn said, "I'm not exactly turning somersaults to be here."

Blacker frowned. "You play nice, Froghorn, you hear? Ruby, I guess I'll see you tomorrow." He grabbed his jacket and made for the door, calling out, "Be nice, Froghorn! You remember how to be nice, don't you?"

Froghorn pinched his lips together like he had just sucked a lemon.

"Never fear," he said. "Your little babysitter friend will be back to keep you company tomorrow. And I'm sure Hitch will make you an ice-cream sundae when you get home."

Geez, this potato head was really winding her up, but she decided to keep her cool.

Keep a lid on it, Ruby.

That day Ruby did about as much reading as she had ever done, and Ruby was a big reader. She had once read one hundred and two *Spy-Scoundrel* comic books in one day, but this was a whole different type of reading.

By six o'clock she was exhausted — she had barely looked up all afternoon. She stretched back in the chair and absentmindedly pulled the key-ring puzzle out of her jeans pocket. She stared at it without thought — she was too tired to think. She sat there motionless for a few moments before being brought back into focus by a buzzing sound — a housefly had roused itself and was hovering over in the corner of the office. She watched as it settled on the seat of a bike that was propped against the wall. It was a woman's bike; she guessed it must have belonged to Lopez. Ruby looked at the door and looked over at Froghorn — he was chatting on the phone. She paused for one whole split second just weighing something up.

"Excuse me," she said, "but I gotta be going. Hitch phoned to say I could ride home if I liked. He's not gonna be finished for a while."

Froghorn put his hand over the receiver. "Sure, sure, run along home, little girl, what do I care?" He motioned for her to go. "Maybe you'll be allowed to watch some TV before bedtime."

Ruby thought she might just do that — she had done enough reading to last her a week.

**Mrs. Digby, on the other hand,
was missing her reading. . . .**

She was without her beloved paperbacks, which had apparently been rejected by the burglars and left in her basement apartment. Mrs. Digby was a voracious reader and loved her crime fiction even more than she loved her TV thrillers.

If they had to go and steal everything, including me, then why in tarnation couldn't they have the decency to steal my valuables too?

Then she stopped to think.

Aha! But they will have stolen Ruby's valuables, and I can count on that kid to have a little old thriller I can settle down with.

Then she noticed the clock — nearly seven.

Quick, not much time.

Although unable to escape her luxury prison, Mrs. Digby could at least make herself a cup of tea — although the milk had gone bad. "Rats!" she muttered, before settling down in an armchair to watch her favorite game show, *What's Your Poison?*

She was just getting comfortable when she was startled by an alarming, high-pitched scream.

Before Mrs. Digby could turn around, she heard the voice of a woman. "Stay right where you are, lady. Don't move a muscle. Don't even twitch an eyelash."

Mrs. Digby was a tough old bird, but even she knew when it was wise to twitch an eyelash and when it was not.

CHAPTER 16
Don't Look Now

IT WAS NICE TO BE BACK ON A BIKE AGAIN, and Lopez's bike, although a good deal too big, was a pretty deluxe one. It was fast and light and Ruby seemed to be gliding along speedily with little effort, which was lucky since it was beginning to get dark and the bike had no lights. She was just making her way up the steep hill—a deserted stretch of road—which connected East Twinford to West Twinford, when she started to feel the unpleasant sensation of a deflating back tire.

Oh geez, that's all I need! She hopped off the bike and surveyed the flat. There was no way of fixing it; she was going to have to walk home, and it was a long way. To make matters just that much more miserable, it began to gently drizzle.

Fabulous, just fabulous.

A few cars passed her as she trudged up the hill—some of them slowed down but none of them stopped. She didn't want them to either, not unless it was someone she knew, someone she could count on. By now it was pitch black. There were a few streetlights but this was the industrial part of town and the mostly abandoned warehouses were unlit. The drizzle had become rain, real drenching rain.

Ruby thought about her own bike with its sturdy, heavy-duty, all-terrain tires — speed was all very well but given the choice she would take reliability any day.

Darn it!

She was so busy cursing and complaining to herself that she didn't at first sense the car behind her. She had vaguely heard it in the far distance as it approached the hill, its gears shifting down as it began to climb. But what she hadn't noticed was the sound of the engine slowing to almost walking pace; not overtaking, just following. Puddles were beginning to form on the road, and her feet were soaking wet. The lace of her left sneaker had come undone, and she bent to tie it. It was sodden and her fingers were cold, unable to get a proper grip. She made an ugly knot and stuffed the ends into her shoe.

And that's when she really became aware of the car.

Still crouching, she turned her head; the headlights were on full beam and she held her hand in front of her eyes to protect them from the glare. The car was moving very slowly toward her but she was unable to make out the driver's face. Ruby's mind began to weigh the options — friend or foe? What kindly stranger would be so stupid as to shine their lights in a person's face and edge nearer to them in this creepy way?

Foe, it had to be.

Panic took hold and Ruby, stumbling to her feet, began to run. She felt the rough stones beneath her soles and heard the sloshing of her shoes in puddles, but mostly she was aware of the thumping of her heart and the single thought that was echoing in her brain: *how could you be so dumb?*

She quickly turned to check on the car, stumbled, and went sprawling onto the road. The car stopped. Through the dazzle of the headlights she saw the door open and the black shape of a figure step out. A man. He paused, faceless behind the light, and then he moved, stepping steadily toward her. *Tap, tap* went his shoes on the shiny wet asphalt. *Thump, thump* went Ruby's uncertain heart. She held her breath, her hands unable to make a fist . . . she felt around for some stone or stick, some inadequate weapon to fend off who knew what. The man leaned down toward her, she could smell his cologne.

"When are you going to start paying attention, kid?"

"Hitch?" croaked Ruby. "That you?"

"You better believe it, buster," came the reply.

CHAPTER 17
Strange and Uneasy

THE JOURNEY BACK WAS NOT A PLEASANT ONE. Hitch wasn't mad. He didn't need to be — Ruby was far too mad at herself already. She was, however, relieved — relieved to be sitting in a nice warm car and not to be in the hands of some mad murderous crazy type. Not that there were *a lot* of those around, but you never could be quite sure and with Ruby's luck lately, she felt the odds of meeting a mad murderous crazy type were high.

Hitch drove in near silence while Ruby mumbled on. Every now and then he would raise an eyebrow or nod in agreement but he never bothered to say, "I told you so."

He didn't have to.

When they got back to Cedarwood Drive, Ruby slumped down at the breakfast bar while Hitch unloaded Lopez's bike from the trunk. When he came in he said, "Look, kid, maybe part of this is my fault, I accept that. I've been kinda ribbing you and talking down to you — so maybe you and I need to start over?"

Ruby was astonished — it was the very last thing she was expecting.

"Yeah well," she said. "I guess I should have listened but I just like to be independent, you know what I mean?"

Hitch nodded. "OK, so how about you get yourself to and from Maverick Street but on *your own bike* and on the condition that you attach this tracker device to the handlebars." He took out a small, round, orange metal thing that looked exactly like a bicycle bell. "The first sign of anything suspicious, you press the green button in the middle and I'll find you."

It seemed like a pretty fair deal. "Sure, I can do that."

"One other condition," continued Hitch. "If someone ever does tail you, someone meaning someone relating to the work you are doing, someone who's figured out what you are up to, then we have to pull the plug — no more code cracking."

"OK." Ruby nodded reluctantly. "I guess I can live with that." She had no choice other than to agree. But in any case she was determined that no one was ever going to tail her.

On Saturday morning Ruby pulled on her jeans and a T-shirt that simply said, **help is at hand.** She looked out the window. Mrs. Gruber was walking her cat, as she always did in the morning. Apart from that, there wasn't a whole lot of action. She went downstairs, scratched Bug behind the ears, grabbed her bike, and rode to Maverick Street. Halfway there she got, well, not so much a strange feeling, as an *uneasy* one. She had no idea why but she sort of felt as if a pair of eyes was watching her every move.

Getting edgy, Rube, that's not good. **RULE 76: STAY ALERT BUT DON'T EVER GET EDGY.**

But she couldn't shake the feeling that something bad was going to happen. This feeling was justified when she arrived and the door was opened by none other than Froghorn — the Silent G.

"Oh, look, it's the wonder kid." He tapped his watch. "You're late."

Ruby's smile faded. "I've been missing you too. Where's Agent Blacker?"

"He might be in later but right now I'm the lucky babysitter."

Ruby gave him her best Ruby Redfort bozo-look. "So where's the baby? Don't tell me you lost it already?"

Froghorn extended his index finger and jabbed it in her direction. "You think you're the cat's pajamas, right?" he hissed. "Well, let me tell you, I'm in charge, so you better toe the line, little girl. You already got me in trouble once by riding home on your own. But I've got my eye on you now, and not much gets by me."

"Oh, brother!" muttered Ruby.

There was no jelly donut on her desk today, and there would

be no helpful conversation, let alone convivial chitchat, to speed up the work.

Ruby picked up where she had left off and started to read Lopez's notes.

She saw the way Lopez had put everything together, piece by piece. She had put the decoded messages in some sort of order so that they made a kind of conversation. It was easy to see what it all meant when you were looking at the whole picture. Just knowing any one piece wasn't enough — it meant nothing. It occurred to her that this whole thing was cleverer than it looked; Lopez had seen that only the person masterminding the bank heist had actually known what the whole plan was. Each gang member had their piece of the plan, but that was all.

Smart, thought Ruby, *very smart. Now that's what I call keeping a secret.*

Froghorn walked into the room. "There's a sandwich if you're hungry — hope you like liverwurst. I don't, so I took the egg."

Jeepers, thought Ruby, *remind me never to recommend your charm school.*

Ruby sniffed at her lunch and cautiously took a bite. It wasn't great but she had eaten worse.

She had almost worked her way to the very end of the very last file. There was another clipping which she translated as:

Handover to take place at fountain—
plan to be there at 18:00 hours.

That was it, nothing else.

Ruby had reached the end — but what did she know? Not as much as Lopez, that was for sure. She wished she could talk it all over — get a different perspective — but there was no use trying to talk to old Froghorn.

She looked around the dingy office. She could hear him talking on the phone. He barely took a breath, and Ruby began to wonder how Lopez could have stood this. Day in, day out, sitting in an office chair trying to figure out things that might in the end lead nowhere — what kind of life was that? A lonely one.

She caught her reflection in the glass of the adjoining door. She looked at the words of her T-shirt, **help is at hand.** She tore off a piece of packaging tape and stuck it over **is at hand** so the shirt now simply read, **help.**

And then, like a miracle, Blacker walked in.

He looked at her. "Did you get into a fight with the tape or are you sending some sort of SOS?"

Ruby kind of smiled. "Well, let's put it this way, your timely arrival may have prevented a major felony."

He motioned toward the little office where Froghorn was working. "You two not hitting it off?"

"Oh, me and Froghorn, we are getting along like cats and dogs — couldn't be better."

"Yeah, well, he's an acquired taste, that's for sure." Blacker handed her a donut. "So I'm guessing you've cracked the case."

"Yeah, yeah, very funny. I got as far as the fountain. Did you ever work out where it was?"

"'Fraid not, there must be more than a hundred fountains in the area. We knew it was likely to be in a town, 'cause most fountains are, but which town is what we couldn't figure out."

"So you didn't follow it up?"

"No way we could. Anyway, Lopez was feeling kinda itchy, couldn't sit still. It was bugging her that we couldn't work out who these people were — we'd sorta reached a dead end. We went and got a drink at Blinky's bar and then at around four I dropped her off at that fancy salon off of Twinford Square — she was always in there getting her hair manicured or whatever — never a nail out of place!"

"That's not how I pictured her," said Ruby. "I guess I thought she might be kinda dowdy."

"Dowdy, oh no, not Lopez. Always looked like two-and-a

quarter million dollars, always perfect — well, apart from the week before she went away of course."

"How do ya mean?" asked Ruby.

"The day after I dropped her off at the salon, she came into work with only half a manicure."

"Did you ask her why?"

"Who am I to comment?" said Blacker, pointing at his dirty fingernails. "A person wants to go about with nail polish on one hand but not the other, that's up to them. But something wasn't right — she was distracted."

Ruby thought about this. "I bet you miss her, huh?"

"Yeah, I miss her all right. She was one nice person." He paused before saying, "I've just packed up the things she had with her when she died — got to mail them back to her family." He pointed to a small box, high up on the shelf by the door. "Doesn't look like much, does it?"

Ruby could only agree.

Blacker said good-bye and wished her luck. "Maybe I'll see you on Monday, Ruby. Just keep thinking. I know you'll get there."

But Ruby wasn't so sure. She had been looking forward to the challenge of finding the missing link, the final piece, but three-and-a-quarter hours later she had found exactly zip.

Back at Cedarwood Drive, Ruby went downstairs to find Hitch, who was sitting in his small but comfortable apartment, listening to music and reading some papers.

He looked up. "Hey, kid, long time no see. How's the world of crime?"

"Oh, you know, full of criminals."

"But no one's been tailing you? No strange or uneasy feelings, I trust?"

"No," said Ruby. "No strange feelings." She decided to keep the uneasy ones to herself.

"Know anything we don't know?"

She paused for a second, but, realizing she had nothing to say, she shook her head. "Afraid not."

"That's a shame," sighed Hitch. "We were all kind of counting on you."

"There's still time though," said Ruby. "I mean, LB didn't give me a deadline."

"She never does," said Hitch. "Likes to keep everyone on their toes. Yep, you could have hours before she fires you. Let's keep our fingers crossed."

CHAPTER 18
If in Doubt, Say Nothing

RUBY WENT UP TO HER ROOM, and ignoring the blinking light
of her answering machine, she opened her notebook and began
writing up the day's interesting events. She had barely started
when she heard the doorbell ring. She slipped off the window
ledge and went to look at the door monitor. It was Clancy Crew,
standing with his face right up close to the camera so that his eyes
looked huge and ridiculous.

Yikes, thought Ruby. It wasn't that she didn't want to see
Clancy, it was just she didn't know what to say to him. She decided
to keep quiet — RULE 4: IF IN DOUBT, SAY NOTHING. *Would
Hitch answer the door?* She waited a few moments. No, it seemed
he couldn't hear over his music. There was no way Clancy could
know that she was home unless he had staked out the house,
and that seemed unlikely.

Eventually she heard something drop through the mail slot

and his footsteps as he walked back down the drive and through the wooden gate.

Ruby went downstairs and picked up a carefully folded piece of paper. A snake.

On it Clancy had written in code:

```
What is going on Rube??? You aren't even
    answering my calls — is that butler guy
            holding you hostage?
```

She went back upstairs, heavy with guilt. Flicked the *Play* button on her machine and listened to her messages. The first voice was Clancy's. He was asking her if she was going to stop in at the Donut Diner on her way to basketball: *"We could grab some French toast — hey, I'll even pay."*

There was a message from Del, who wanted to discuss the game: *"We need to talk tactics, man. Bugwart's not gonna slam us again."* One from Red asking if she could borrow Ruby's violin because she had accidentally sat on hers and it was now *"in several pieces"* and *"beyond fixing"* and her mom was going to *"most likely kill her,"* and another from Clancy. This time it just said, *"Rube, it's Clance, please call."*

Ruby felt a little stab to her gut. She sat there for a while just thinking. She was in an impossible situation—lie to Clancy or break Spectrum rule number one. What kind of choice was that? She became aware that there was noise coming from the kitchen and she took a look through the periscope; Consuela had arrived and was chatting with Hitch as she prepared dinner. All at once Ruby knew what she had to do. She needed to talk to Hitch. He would just have to see her point of view.

She walked into the kitchen and found Hitch drying martini glasses while he chatted with Consuela, who was busy stuffing fourteen large tomatoes with what looked like more tomato. It occurred to Ruby that Consuela was rather overdressed for this task, the stiletto heels and painted fingernails seeming to be more of a hindrance than a help. She was also laughing rather too much, that sort of random giggling that certain girls at Ruby's school broke into whenever Richie Dare walked past.

"Oh, brother!" muttered Ruby. She took a breath. "Hitch, can I ask you something?"

"I am sure you can and I have no doubt that you will," he replied.

Consuela giggled, and Ruby glared at her.

"Well, if I could *drag* you away from the kitchen for five

trilliseconds." She made an eye signal, meaning "not in front of *her*" and Hitch put down his dishcloth and asked Consuela to excuse him. Consuela adopted a fake pout and giggled again.

"Jeepers!" muttered Ruby.

When they were out of earshot Ruby said, "What am I gonna do about Clancy?"

"What do you mean? What's Clancy got to do with anything?"

"He has everything to do with everything and now that I'm involved with Spectrum I can't talk to him about anything!"

"Goes with the territory, kid — you can't talk to him, you can't talk to anyone."

"But . . ."

"Kid, you blab and you're going to be in the deepest deep water you have ever been dunked in — that clear?"

Ruby nodded. This guy was never going to give in. She felt her spirits sinking as if there was an impossible weight pushing down on her. Lying to Clancy — an impossible task. She was dead meat.

She decided to get some air — take Bug for a walk. She headed off in the opposite direction from Amster Green.

When Ruby got back, her mother was there to greet her.

"Well, hey there, stranger, where have you been?"

Ruby was a little surprised by the question and wasn't sure what to say — she couldn't quite discern whether her mother's tone was serious or playful.

RULE 4: SAY NOTHING. When in a tight spot people often give themselves away by over-talking.

"Um, well, you know," said Ruby.

"Yes, I do, young lady. I came to pick you up after the game. I was going to take you to get your haircut — remember?"

Ruby *did* remember now her mother brought it up — how could she have forgotten something which could so easily have blown her cover? **RULE 7: NEVER FORGET THE LITTLE THINGS — IT'S THE LITTLE THINGS THAT WILL LEAD PEOPLE TO NOTICE THE BIG THINGS.** This was something Ruby had seen time and time again in *Crazy Cops*. It was one of her most important rules.

"Hey, you've ripped your new jacket," said her mom. "How did that happen?"

Yeah Rube, explain that, why don't ya.

"Uh, well, let me tell you." Ruby was thinking fast but, unusually, nothing was coming to mind.

"I guess it was at Mrs. Beesman's, right?"

"Uh . . . ?"

"I was about to go and call Coach Newhart," said her mother,

"I was worried, but luckily I ran in to Clancy and he tells me you went off to do some volunteer work helping out poor old Mrs. Beesman. Ruby, you never told me about that—so sweet of you, honey! But you ripped your jacket, huh? Well, I'm hardly surprised—state of her yard."

"Yeah, well, you know," mumbled Ruby. Her mother was asking her all kinds of questions about Mrs. Beesman but what Ruby was thinking was, *Clancy covered for me even though I have been ducking his calls and deliberately avoiding him—he still covered for me. Wow, he's some friend.*

This made her feel bad.

Her mother was still talking about Mrs. Beesman and how proud she was that a daughter of hers was kind enough to go and help a poor old lady out.

"Ruby, you really do make me feel ashamed! I have *never* done anything to help her."

This made Ruby feel worse.

She tried to make light of it. "Don't beat yourself up, Mom, we can't all be saints."

But her mother wouldn't let go. "Be modest if you want, Ruby, but as your mother I am proud of you, you can't change that." Then she started kissing her on the cheeks—Ruby decided that perhaps this was Clancy's idea of revenge after all.

At dinner, Sabina was still bragging about Ruby's charitable work, this time to her father.

"That's swell, honey," said her father.

And later, on the phone she bragged to Mrs. Irshman. "She cleaned up Mrs. Beesman's yard. . . .Yes, Mrs. Beesman with all the cats."

Ruby was feeling steadily more and more horrible. She would have to actually go over and clean Mrs. Beesman's yard now. She was sure to go to hell otherwise. She was really beginning to dislike Clancy. *Wow, some friend you are.*

As if preventing a bank heist wasn't enough — now she had to clean some cat lady's yard.

CHAPTER 19
One Little Lie

THE NEXT DAY WAS SUNDAY and Ruby wasn't expected at Spectrum. She decided that it was about time she saw some of her friends — Clancy in particular. She wasn't quite sure how she was going to explain her absence from school but she thought maybe she should tell them the truth — well, the truth that was the lie that Hitch had told, about her grandmother being sick. It was just that Ruby wasn't good at lying to her friends. Mrs. Drisco? No trouble at all. Her parents? Easy. But not her friends — it didn't feel right.

She just hoped none of them would remember that the grandmother in question had actually long since departed this earth.

It's just one little lie, thought Ruby.

She got out of bed and walked over to the heap of clothes lying on the floor. She had been so preoccupied the night before that she had completely forgotten about the watch. Now she finally had the chance to take a close look — see just what it could do. However, it seemed her jacket was no longer in the pile. Nor, indeed, was it anywhere in her room.

"Hey, Mom," called Ruby. "You seen my jacket?"

"I grabbed it while you were sleeping honey — got Hitch to take it to the tailor."

"I don't believe it."

"Ruby, you can't wear a ripped jacket!" said her mother. "Besides, you have plenty of others."

"That's not the point," muttered Ruby. "People shouldn't mess with other people's stuff." Boy, if she lost that watch she'd be toast.

She slipped a T-shirt that bore the words *you better believe it, buster* over her head and was just pulling on a pair of jeans when the phone in her bedroom rang. Without considering who it might be, she picked up the receiver.

"Twinford Retirement Center, just sit in a chair while we vacuum around you."

"Hey, Rube, where you been?" It was Clancy.

Ruby took a deep breath. "Haven't you heard, my grandmother's sick and I, you know . . . have been cheering the old lady up."

"Oh yeah? I'm sorry to hear that. Your mom must be real upset."

"What makes you think it's my mom's mom?"

"Only 'cause I spoke to your other grandmother this morning. She called to speak to my mom about some party she's planning, and I guess she wouldn't be planning a party if she was real sick. Planning a party would be the last thing she would be thinking about — don't you agree?" Clancy said this casually.

"Well, yeah, you're right, it's my mom's mom — poor thing. She's been pretty sick but I reckon she'll pull through, she's a tough old bird."

"Mm, she must be," agreed Clancy.

Ruby gabbled on about her grandmother until Clancy finally interrupted.

"Rube, this is me you're talking to. Clancy Crew, remember? Your best buddy? And I hate to break it to you this way but your grandmother on your mother's side, she isn't sick — she's dead!"

"Aw, now, come on Clance, that ain't nice. You don't wanna break bad news like that!"

"Ruby, what is going on? First you tell me all that stuff about the butler who plainly isn't a butler and then this stuff about phone calls and codes and now, zip, nothing — like you just made it all up."

"Yeah, well, maybe I did," said Ruby.

"Yeah? That sounds likely! I can't believe I was actually

worried about you, when all you are doing is lying your head off. And by the way, for your information, you might as well tell me what's going on 'cause if you don't — you know I'm gonna find out."

Ruby thought about this for just a minute and knew it to be true. But what she said was, "Look, I think I can hear my mom calling. I gotta go."

"You can lie to yourself, Ruby Redfort, but you can't lie to me,' said Clancy as he slammed the receiver down.

Yeah, you got that right.

Pulling on her sneakers, she grabbed her jacket and left the house. Bug followed.

"Hey Rube," said Elliot. "Where've you been?"

"Oh, my grandmother . . . she's sick," said Ruby.

"Sorry to hear that," said Elliot. "She gonna be OK?"

"I guess there's no way of knowing."

Elliot looked at the ground and kicked an old tennis ball that was lying by the curb, then he looked up and said, "Hey, who's that guy I keep seeing driving your mom around?"

"Oh, you mean Hitch. He's our new butler," replied Ruby.

"Your butler?" spluttered Elliot. "You have a butler?"

"Well, house manager — I call him a butler but he's a house

manager." Ruby was kicking herself — why did she have to go and say butler?

Elliot obviously thought this was the funniest thing he had ever heard. "Butler!" he repeated. "Butler!" He was laughing so hard that he no longer seemed to be able to hold himself up — his spine seemed like a concertina. Tears were rolling down his face.

Mouse Huxtable came around the corner. "Hey, what's so funny?"

"Nothing," scowled Ruby.

Mouse looked at Elliot. "Do ya think his head will fall off?"

"It's hard to say," replied Ruby. "It never has before."

This scene wasn't unusual. Elliot was prone to terrible giggling fits. At the most inappropriate moment he would break out into uncontrolled, often silent laughter, shoulders shaking, tears streaming down his cheeks. The worst thing about it was that Elliot had a very infectious laugh and it was hard not to get caught up in it once he got going.

But this time, Ruby did not want to see the funny side.

"Give me a break, bozo — funnier things *have* happened." But Elliot did not seem to think so.

Ruby felt the corners of her mouth twitch — she didn't want to give him the satisfaction, so instead she said, "Come on, Mouse, let's go and get a fruit shake."

The two girls and the dog left Elliot on the sidewalk and made their way across the road to the fruit bar, Cherry Cup. Ruby liked the fruit shakes here because they had an unlimited choice of both the interesting and the more pedestrian fruit. The owner, Cherry, was a man in his late fifties. Five years ago he had given up his job selling insurance and opened this place. Now he was just happy to be liquidizing fruit, any combination, however unlikely. If anyone ever asked him how he was, he would reply, "Not too shabby," meaning, pretty darn good.

"So where've you been, Rube?" asked Mouse.

"My grandmother has been sick," said Ruby.

"Really? How bad is she?"

"Tragically bad," replied Ruby in a hushed voice.

"I'm sorry to hear that," said Mouse. "What hospital's she in?"

Ruby looked down at the floor. "Uh, one in New York — I've sorta been flying back and forth."

Another lie, she thought.

Mouse took Ruby's unease as a signal that she no longer wanted to talk about it, and fell silent. The door opened, and in walked Clancy Crew. He barely even glanced at Ruby.

"Hey, Clance," said Mouse.

"Hey, Mouse," said Clancy. Ruby said nothing.

Clancy went over to one of the booths and sat down. He pulled out a comic, appropriately titled *Buzz Off*, and began to read it intently. Mouse looked first at Ruby then at Clancy and then back to Ruby. "Something you want to tell me?"

"Like what?" Ruby was staring hard at the Cherry Cup menu.

"Like did you guys have a fight or something?"

"Nah," said Ruby.

"Are you sure? I haven't seen old Clance like this since that time you stepped on his turtle."

"Look, Mouse, could you just drop it? I don't feel like talking about Clancy Crew right now, OK?"

"Whatever you say, Rube," Mouse said, sighing.

"Listen, Mouse, I got bigger things on my mind than some boy with a bad case of the grouches."

"Course you do, Rube," said Mouse, biting her lip.

Ruby felt guilty. She didn't like to lie to Mouse, and now she was making it worse by snapping at her. "Look, I didn't mean to bite your head off, it's just my brain is overloaded and all — what with my grandmother being so sick and my mom all racked with worry so she can't sleep anymore."

Another lie.

"That's OK, Rube — no offense taken. Let me order you a fruit shake."

"Thanks, Mouse, my old pal — make mine a pineapple quince, two straws. Here." She held out a five-dollar bill. "They're on me."

Mouse ordered the drinks and waited at the bar. She was fiddling with toothpicks, sticking them into the plastic cherries that decorated the bar top. She looked up at Ruby. "Hey, I bet it has to do with his teeth."

"Huh?" said Ruby.

"Clancy being all grouchy — it must be to do with his teeth. I overheard his mom talking about how one of his molars is infected — how it's gotta come out. You know what Clancy's like about the dentist. I'll bet that's what's making him act weird."

Ruby smiled. "You know what, Mouse, you're probably right. You usually are."

Mouse was pleased with that. "So you heard about the TV people coming to film the 'safest safe in the U.S. of A.'?"

Ruby looked blank.

"Twinford City Bank, you know — the gold?"

"Oh yeah, I read about that in the paper — the 'unstealable gold,'" said Ruby.

When they got up to leave Mouse called out, "See you, Clancy."

"Yeah, see you, Mouse," he replied.

It was as if Ruby didn't even exist.

It was late afternoon by the time Ruby got home, and as she climbed the stairs she could hear the singsong voice of Barbara Bartholomew. She stuck her head around the living-room door; Ruby's mother was reclining on a new and elegant sofa, Barbara sitting cross-legged on a pile of silk cushions — both were sipping on elaborate cocktails. They were deep in conversation.

"I can't tell you, Barb, how super great Hitch was this morning. I had quite the lucky escape."

"Really, no kidding?"

"Well, he drove me into town — I needed to stop off at Glenthorn's jewelers, they are altering that necklace of mine."

"The white jade one?" asked Barbara.

"The white jade one," confirmed Sabina. "I want to wear it at the launch and it needs a better setting — more modern."

"Oh, that will be nice," cooed Barbara

"So Hitch stays in the car because there are no free parking meters, as per usual."

"Oh, Sabina darling, there never are — it's terrible."

"Isn't it? Why the mayor doesn't do something, I don't know. Anyway, where was I?"

"Hitch stayed in the car," said Barbara.

"That's right—anyway, I am in there a little while, thirty minutes, maybe forty, and Hitch is driving around the block and I come out and I stand there waiting on the street for him to reappear and then you won't believe what happens."

"What?" whispered Barbara dramatically.

"I only get my purse snatched by some criminal is all!"

"You don't!"

"I'm telling you, and no one does anything, I mean the guy's fast but still . . . you'd think . . ."

"You would," agreed Barbara.

"Anyhow, suddenly Hitch drives around the corner, sees me screaming at the thief; I tell you Barb he was out of that car before you could blink and run. I've never seen a man move so fast."

"Hitch, your butler? You are kidding!"

"I am not kidding, Barbara. He is after that guy, catches up with him, karate kicks him in the back of the legs, and the guy drops my purse."

"No way!"

"I get my purse back, no harm done."

"What about the guy?"

"Hitch chases him up a fire escape and over the top of the Wilmot building but the guy leaps down about forty feet into a passing garbage truck and he's gone."

"Wow, Sabina. That's some butler you have there — hold on tight to that one."

"You can be sure of it, Barb!" And the two women dissolved into unexplained giggles.

Ruby walked into the kitchen, where Hitch was preparing snacks.

"So I hear you were quite the action hero today."

"Yeah, well, stopping purse snatchers isn't usually what I do but it makes a change from arranging cheese straws."

"But you do it so nicely," said Ruby, adopting her mother's voice.

"It's not as hard as it looks. Want to try?"

"Nah, I'd cramp your style. So I guess your shoulder's getting better if you can chase a thief up a fire escape?" said Ruby.

"Yeah, it must be, finally — which can only mean one thing. I'll be moving on soon. I'll have to get someone else to babysit you."

"Just like Mary Poppins, you'll be gone," said Ruby, pouring herself a glass of banana milk.

"Yeah, well, kid, I'm not saying it hasn't been supercalifragilistic to know you, but I'm kind of glad to be getting back to the day job, know what I mean?"

"I know what you mean."

Ruby walked upstairs to her room and met Consuela coming the other way with a tray piled high with dirty cups and cereal bowls.

"I was just about to bring those down," said Ruby, correctly predicting trouble.

"I shouldn't have to be going up and down cleaning up after you. I'm a dietician, not a housemaid," said Consuela. "But we are running out of dishes — they are all in your room!"

"Look, I'm sorry, I really am." Ruby gave Consuela her best "I'm sorry" face, and Consuela's scowl instantly softened.

"Oh, your friend Clancy called," she said. "He wanted me to ask you how your grandmother is doing? He seems to think she is sick or something."

"Yeah, poor Clance, he can get very confused about things — gets facts very mixed up. He's got some sorta disorder."

"Oh, that's a shame," said Consuela, unusually concerned.

"Yeah, it's too bad," said Ruby, and as she closed the door to her room, she remembered how every little untruth always led to a hundred others. This was **RULE 32: TELL ONE LIE AND GET READY TO TELL A WHOLE LOT MORE.**

＊ ＊ ＊

The next day, riding her bike through Twinford, she had the same "watched" feeling she'd had before, but there was no sign of anything that might suggest she was being tailed.

After sitting at the desk in the dusty brown office for six hours, it dawned on Ruby that she was bored. It wasn't the work exactly, although today it *was* painstaking, reading files over and over, trying to find a loose thread or something that would lead her to the next thing. No, it was the environment that was the problem, cut off from the world with only a supreme potato head for company. She wondered if this was how Lopez had felt.

Only it was doubly bad for Ruby because it looked like she was going to fail, and the fear of failure was indeed a strange new feeling.

She started absentmindedly rolling her pencil up and down the desk — she wasn't even aware that she was doing it. She was lost in thought when she heard Froghorn shout, "Hey! Little girl, could you stop doing that!"

Ruby jumped, and the pencil rolled across the desk and disappeared off the edge.

Darn it.

She slipped off her chair and took a look underneath the desk — she could see the pencil there on the floor but she couldn't reach it. As quietly as she could, Ruby began pulling at the heavy piece of furniture until it moved a couple of inches. She slid her hand along and felt around until it found what she was looking for. But the pencil she retrieved was not her pencil; it was green with white writing. The writing said:

The Fountain.

Ruby sat still for so long that Froghorn came in to see if something had happened.

When he saw her sitting there, just staring at a pencil, he made some pathetic attempt at a smart remark. Ruby noticed that he had a mayonnaise stain on his tie but she really couldn't be bothered to point it out — she was far too busy thinking about Lopez.

**Mrs. Digby was busy
trying to get a tea stain
out of Mrs. Redfort's
evening gown . . .**

... when she heard a voice, or rather voices.

"We better go and talk to the old lady, get her to *cooperate* if you know what I mean."

Oh I know what you mean, said Mrs. Digby to herself. She sat back in her chair and waited for the inevitable. The door was opened and in walked two men: the one with the nice face who she had met before and another much bigger man, almost a giant, who she hadn't had the pleasure of meeting yet. There was no sign of the woman with the high-pitched scream.

The nice-looking man seemed to be in charge — at least he did most of the talking.

Mrs. Digby stood there with her hands on her hips. "What is this? Kidnap-an-old-person week?" She wasn't taking captivity lying down. The Digbys had always fought tooth and nail, no matter what the odds.

"All we want you to do," said the man, "is call your employers and tell them that you are safe and sound in Miami."

She folded her arms.

"And why would I tell them that, when it is perfectly obvious to me that I am not?"

"Well," suggested the man softly, "why don't you just *say* that you are?"

"Because that would make me a liar and I'm no liar." Mrs. Digby pursed her lips.

"Well," said the man, "cross your fingers behind your back and *pretend* that you are."

Mrs. Digby sighed heavily. "And just what am I *doing* in Miami?"

"Perhaps you are playing a game of blackjack. Perhaps you have friends there."

"And what if I'm not in Miami? What if I'm being held at gunpoint in a warehouse, what are you going to do then?"

"Then," said the other man, the one with the big hands and the silver rings that looked a little bit like brass knuckles, "then perhaps you are gonna wish you was in Miami playing blackjack."

"OK, OK, I get the picture, tough guy." Mrs. Digby picked up the phone, praying Ruby might have skipped school. If Ruby heard her voice she would know in a moment that something was up. Ruby was one smart cookie. Mrs. Digby dialed the number — but no one answered.

"So leave a message," hissed the tough guy.

Mrs. Digby glanced at his silver rings and decided she would do as she was told.

"They won't believe it, you know," she said. "You can force me to say a whole lotta mumbo jumbo on an answering machine but the Redforts know me inside out — they'll know I was made to do it. It just won't ring true, they know I have no cousin Ernie — believe you me, you all are gonna be stitched up like a pack of kippers." Mrs. Digby was defiant as ever, but her captors merely laughed.

"Don't wait too long to be rescued, old lady — you might pass your sell by date."

CHAPTER 20
Unlikely But Not Impossible

WHEN RUBY RODE ONTO CEDARWOOD DRIVE she noticed a Sushi-land van parked across the street. She was greeted at the front door by Bug, and as she walked upstairs the sound of her parents' chatter drifted down from the kitchen.

"That was so nice to get a message from Mrs. Digby, wasn't it honey?"

"Yes," agreed Brant. "I had no idea that she had a cousin Ernie."

"No, nor me — just shows, you can know someone your whole entire life and never know a thing like that. Still, I am glad she is having a high old time — it's probably done her the world of good to have a break." Sabina picked up her magazine. "It'll be nice to get her back though."

"Yep, I can't wait to tell Ruby. She's going to be pleased as a pie," said Brant.

"Can't wait to tell Ruby what?" said Ruby, dumping her backpack on the floor and walking over to the fridge.

"That Mrs. Digby called!" said her father.

Ruby nearly dropped the carton of banana milk. "She did? You spoke to her? Where is she?"

"She left a message — she's in Miami, just as your father said she would be," said Sabina proudly.

"Oh, I'll go listen," said Ruby, turning to leave.

Her mother bit her lip. "Sorry honey, your father erased it."

"Sorry, Rube," said her father, grinning awkwardly. "You know what a dunce I am with those answer phone gadget things. Never can work out which is the right button."

Ruby tried not to say anything unkind. "Can you at least tell me what she said?"

"She's living it up in Miami with a long-lost cousin!" said Sabina brightly.

"Which long-lost cousin?" said Ruby, but before anyone could answer, the doorbell rang and her father went off to see who it was.

"Oh, heavens!" said Sabina, jumping up. "That'll be the sushi people!"

"The what?" said Ruby.

"We have the museum committee coming over tonight — the museum curator, Enrico Gonzales, the Humberts, and of course most excitingly what's-his-name-Gustav should be flying in."

"No, honey," said Brant, walking back into the kitchen. "He called to say he couldn't make it."

"Oh drat!" said Sabina.

"Nor can Freddie Humbert, he's tied up at the bank."

"Double drat!" said Sabina. "Anyway it will be such fun."

Ruby rolled her eyes. "Do you mind if I watch TV?"

"Well, the thing is, honey, I thought we might go sort of Japanese and eat low — at little tables on the floor in the living room, on account of us having no dining-room set. Seemed like the perfect solution — it will be completely darling!"

"What, you can't go Japanese in the dining room?"

"It's being redecorated."

"You are welcome to join us, Ruby sweetie — do you want to invite Clancy over?"

Clancy — Ruby felt that pang of guilt again. "You know what, I think I might just go Japanese on my own — in my room, do ya mind? I gotta lot of homework to do."

"Oh, but honey, won't you just say hi to everyone? They so want to meet you."

After Ruby had spent two hours saying "hi" to everyone, she finally managed to slink off to her room where she made a list of all the things she knew about Lopez.

LOPEZ WAS LIKED BY BLACKER

and it seemed most of the Spectrum team so
it was safe to assume she liked them back.

. . . .

DID FROGHORN BUG THE LIFE OUT OF HER?
It seemed more than likely.

. . . .

SHE SOUGHT ADVENTURE,
so she was no shrinking violet.

. . . .

SHE WAS ALWAYS WELL-GROOMED AT WORK,
except for that one day when she had come
in with just one hand manicured.

. . . .

SHE SEEMED LIKE A PERSON WHO HAD SECRETS—
did anyone know what they were?

Ruby took the Fountain pencil from her bag.

Where did this pencil come from?

. . . .

How had it ended up under Lopez's desk?

. . . .

MIGHT LOPEZ HERSELF HAVE OBTAINED IT SOMEHOW?

Now that was an interesting thought. What if Lopez had gotten tired of sitting on her little old behind and decided it was time to get a piece of the action? What if she had worked out where the Fountain was and had followed whoever it was to the meet?

It wasn't at all likely but it was possible.

CHAPTER 21
The Blink of an Eye

TODAY RUBY WAS DEFINITELY ON EDGE. She got up a half hour early and, using one of her mother's powder compacts for a mirror, taped it to her bike's handlebars — this way she could see behind her without turning around.

So, maybe she *was* being paranoid but better that than . . . well, never mind.

Amster was busy as ever, people jogging, people walking their dogs, walking to work, people sitting on benches reading the paper, nothing sinister — but just to be sure, she would take a new route. This time, when she got to the left turn she sailed on past it. She was taking the long way around, the route which took you over the wooden bike bridge.

Every couple of minutes she glanced in the mirror. There was quite a bit of traffic and Ruby was managing to keep ahead of most of it by riding on the sidewalk. Each time she thought a car was on her tail, it would peel off in another direction and she would feel a wave of relief. However, there was one vehicle, a taxi, which seemed to have been behind her for a long time. There were a whole lot of yellow cabs on the road, each displaying its own individual number:

6582,

8874,

902,

5677,

etc.

Ruby had a particular gift for remembering numbers even when they were displayed backward in a tiny mirror, and this one was sticking to her like gum:

ㄥㄥ85

Ruby cut across one of the parks to see if she could lose it but when she rejoined the road a few blocks up, there it was — just as if it could read her mind. She rode three blocks down a tiny pedestrian alleyway but sure enough, when she reached the end, there was the cab. This was someone who could second-guess her every move.

Ruby was beginning to sweat.

She was tired and her mouth was dry. The cab neither slowed down nor sped up, it just kept following. Her finger hovered over the little orange bicycle bell but she couldn't press it — if she did, Hitch would swoop in and all this would be over. At last she reached the bike bridge, not wide enough for cars — the nearest vehicle bridge was a quarter mile away so it was the end of the road as far as this guy was concerned. So she was surprised when she heard the car's engine cut out and alarmed when she heard the clunk of the door opening and closing. But no one appeared on the bridge.

What are they up to? She heard the sound of movement in the marsh reeds below. Ruby froze; for seven minutes she stood completely still, not even blinking. **YOU CAN MISS A LOT IN THE BLINK OF AN EYE {RULE 52}.**

Then, suddenly, she saw it. Something definitely glinted in the long grass, just for a split second. *What was it?* Something glass — a camera, binoculars . . . glasses?

Suddenly, something or someone was moving through the marsh reeds at great speed. Curiosity overtook fear and Ruby found herself climbing over the railings, straining to see where whatever it was had gone — holding on with one hand, she leaned her body out as far as she could. She wanted to see under the walkway, then just like that, she heard the clunk of the cab door closing and the rumble of the engine as it drove away.

"Who are you?" shouted Ruby, and that's when she lost her footing. Slipping on the iron support, her hand let go of the rail and she felt herself falling to the soggy ground below. She landed heavily but not awkwardly and nothing seemed to be broken. Whoever had been there was gone but they had left behind footprints, two smallish footprints; she crouched down to get a better look. The soles had a crisscross pattern like a lot of sneakers but what was interesting was that in the left shoe there were two round indents — the size of thumbtacks.

Now who can I think of who might have stepped on a couple of thumbtacks recently?

She turned her bike in the direction of Ambassador Row.

Ruby was buzzed through the high black curly-metal gates, and there sitting on the steps was Clancy. His top lip was all puffy and he had his dog with him — they seemed to be sharing a soda.

"I'm not sure soda's good for dogs, Clance," said Ruby.

"Oh, I just wondered if Dolly could drink through a straw."

"And?" said Ruby.

"No, she just starts eating it," replied Clancy.

"Oh, too bad, you won't be able to get her on *My Pet Genius* after all."

My Pet Genius was a program that Ruby and Clancy were crazy about. It featured birds that could operate remote controls, dogs that seemed to be able to read, and cats that could make their own supper—it was highly entertaining.

Clancy smiled. "No, I guess not. Dolly is not exactly top of the class."

"By the look of you, I'd say you had to take a seat in the dentist's chair—either that or your dentist punched you in the kisser."

"Does it show?" said Clancy, pointing to his puffy lip.

"Uhhh—did you look like a duck before? I can't remember," said Ruby, ruffling his hair.

"Thanks, Rube, that's really reassuring—how would you like to go to the dentist at seven a.m.?"

"That stinks," agreed Ruby. She looked down at Clancy's feet; his shoes were not quite clean, there was still the residue of dry mud around the sides, and in the sole of the left shoe were two brass thumbtacks.

"So, you been following me, Clance?"

"How'd ya know?" he asked.

Ruby nodded at his shoes. "You left tracks," she said. "Or should I say tacks?"

"Oh."

Neither of them said anything for a couple of minutes until Clancy took a deep breath. "So, you going to tell me what you've been up to, Rube?"

"It's kinda a long story," said Ruby. "Very involved."

"I got time, got the whole day off as a matter of fact—on account of my puffy lip."

Ruby looked up. "So you know where I've been going?"

"Not exactly—you ride fast, I've only tailed you up as far as the west side of East Twinford."

"Well, that's a relief, I guess."

"So, how about it, Rube, you might as well tell me. Remember that time a couple of years ago when you knew what my mom and dad had gotten me for Christmas and you didn't wanna tell me but I just wore you down until you did?"

Ruby sighed. She remembered it well. "OK, Clance, I'll tell you, but you to have to swear you won't under any circumstances breathe a word—not even in your sleep."

"I know, Girl Scouts' honor and all that."

"Not even under torture," Ruby insisted. "Not even under torture in your sleep."

"I'll gag myself, how about that?" Clancy smiled.

Ruby wasn't smiling. "This isn't some little secret, Clancy — this is big."

"You know me, Ruby. I never blab — never," said Clancy earnestly.

It was true, Clancy never blabbed — you could dangle him over a crocodile pit and he wouldn't say a thing.

Ruby looked at her friend. It was her sideways look, a look she gave when she was measuring up a situation. Clancy Crew knew that look well and held her gaze.

"OK," she said. "This is the story."

It took a lot of explaining, and Clancy spent a lot of time saying, "You have to be kidding" and "This is unbelievable — a real spy agency underneath Twinford City?"

"It's all true," she said. "Every word."

"So what are we going to do now?"

"What I am going to do is to get myself over to Maverick Street before the Silent G gets on my tail." She picked up her bike. "I need to keep thinking but I'll be in touch, Clance, I promise — just keep it zipped, OK?"

CHAPTER 22
Don't Breathe a Word

CLANCY WAS SURPRISED TO SEE RUBY standing on the curb by the side of his house; it was Wednesday morning, pretty early, and she didn't usually bike to school with him.

"Hey, what are you doing here?"

"Thought you might be interested in taking a little trip with me," said Ruby.

"Sure I would but I've got school — remember school? It's that big building where all the kids hang out."

"Don't stress it — I made a call. You're off sick — that tooth of yours is a real pain in the cheek — which, by the way, still looks puffy."

"You called the school and told them I was sick?" Clancy was flapping his arms.

"Well, your mom sorta called. I do a pretty good impersonation of her — Mrs. Bexenheath certainly thought it was good."

It took about seven minutes but Ruby managed to convince Clancy that no one would suspect a thing if he skipped school — just this once.

"So where are we going?" he asked nervously.

"Just taking a little trip to Tony's Hair Salon, see if we can't get some more information."

"But aren't you gonna be missed — at Spectrum, I mean?"

"I took care of that," said Ruby. "I phoned Blacker and told him I needed to figure some things out. I explained I do it better in my own space."

They pulled up at Tony's — the fancy hair salon just off Twinford Square.

"So what are we doing here?" asked Clancy.

"Getting information. Just follow me, don't speak — just you know, keep it zipped."

"Sir, yes sir," muttered Clancy.

"Hey, Ruby!" said Marcia. "What are you doing in here? You retired from school or what?" Marcia did Sabina's hair, and Ruby had been coming here since she could remember.

"They've run out of things to teach me so they let me off for the day."

Marcia winked. "Oh, I get it — don't worry, honey, I'm no

snitch." She looked at Clancy. "What happened to you, kid? Get in a fight with a dentist?"

Clancy rolled his eyes.

"So," said Marcia. "What can I do for you?"

"I was wondering if you knew a person named Carla Lopez?"

"I know her, 'course I do — she's a regular. Why you asking?"

"The last time she was in, did you notice anything odd about her?"

"Odd? Like how?"

"Was she out of sorts, distracted?" suggested Ruby.

"Well, she did walk out of the salon with a couple of heated rollers in her hair, so I guess you might say she was distracted, but it's Sandy you might wanna talk to — she did Carla's manicure." She pointed over to a tall young woman who was busy filing the nails of a dumpy lady with slightly blue hair. "Hey, Sandy, the kid wants to talk to you!"

Ruby walked over to the nail bar and sat down on the stool next to Sandy. Sandy kept on filing.

"I was wondering, do you happen to remember doing the nails of a friend of mine a few weeks ago — Carla Lopez, long black hair, pretty, mid thirties?"

"Yeah, I do!" replied Sandy, filing more furiously. "She owes me a tip."

The lady with blue hair coughed—it wasn't a real cough, more of a "do you mind?" sort of cough.

Ruby ignored her.

"What, she left without paying?"

"I do her nails, get them all filed and regular and then I start applying the red polish and there I am telling her about my cousin's fancy wedding at some fancy hotel and she suddenly jumps out of her seat and asks to see a phone directory. I say, 'But, lady, I haven't finished painting your nails.' I wasn't even done with the left hand but she doesn't seem to care—she goes over to the phone booth, flicks through the phone book, and then runs out the door. I thought, that's one serious nut we got there."

"Thanks, you have been super helpful, Sandy," said Ruby, who was already moving toward the phone booth.

"When you see her, tell her she still owes me that tip," called Sandy.

Ruby flipped open the directory that was attached to the wall by a string, and hurriedly turned the pages.

"What are you looking for?" said Clancy.

"Something beginning with *F*," she replied.

Ruby scanned down: *Fountain Farm, Fountain Fresh Eggs, Fountain Garages, Fountain Gardens, Fountain Hotel.*

Bingo!

And as if to confirm that she was exactly on the right track, there was a little smudge of red nail polish next to the name.

Ruby took her yellow notebook from her bag and scrawled the address and phone number on the inside cover.

"Could you let me in on whatever it is you are doing?" said Clancy.

"We gotta go somewhere — it's out of town."

"Where out of town?" said Clancy.

"Everly," replied Ruby.

"Everly? But that's miles away — how are we gonna get there?"

"Don't suppose that chauffeur of yours is free?"

"Oh no, Rube you better not be thinking what I think you're thinking."

Two minutes later Clancy found himself listening to Ruby doing a pretty good impersonation of his dad's secretary.

"Hello, Bill? Yes, I need you to drive Mr. Crew's son Clancy out to Everly . . . yes, Everly . . . it doesn't matter why, he has to pick something up for his father . . . it's a surprise, so don't mention anything about this. That clear? Good. All right, pick him up from Twinford Square right away. Thanks so much. Oh, and Bill, I mean it, no blabbing."

Ruby replaced the receiver and smiled at Clancy.

"If my dad finds out, I am going to be dead meat, Rube. I mean it, dead as a dingo."

"Dodo," replied Ruby.

"Now you're calling me a dodo?"

"No, it's dead as a dodo, not dead as a dingo."

Clancy sighed. "Well whatever I am as dead as, it doesn't change the fact that I will be *dead,* so who cares if it's a dog or a bird!"

Seven minutes later a large black limousine cruised by and they got in.

"This beats the bus," said Ruby, nudging Clancy with her elbow. Clancy rolled his eyes. "I just might throw up."

"I don't think your dad would like that," said Ruby.

"Could you at least quit clicking—it's getting on my nerves, and my nerves are a little frayed right now," said Clancy in an exaggerated whisper.

Ruby hadn't really been aware that she *was* clicking, she had been too busy thinking.

"What is it, anyway? That thing you are clicking?"

She pulled LB's key ring out of her pocket. "Just some old key ring I found."

"Looks kinda dumb," said Clancy. "Cool in a way but sorta dorky — where'd ya get it?"

"Just sorta picked it up," said Ruby, stuffing it back into her pocket.

CHAPTER 23
Funny Peculiar

FORTY MINUTES LATER THE CAR PULLED UP in front of the Fountain Hotel, an attractive old building with a courtyard and a fountain that was struggling to bubble water out of a trumpet held by a statue of a fat baby.

"Now what?" said Clancy.

"Follow me and remember no talking, no—"

"Yeah, yeah—keep it zipped," grumbled Clancy.

Bill took out his newspaper and started to read the sports pages.

Clancy and Ruby walked across the courtyard and in through the main door. A young couple was at the desk, checking in. They were taking a long time about it, and Ruby was beginning to lose her nerve.

"Yes? Can I help you?" The concierge was looking at them sternly.

"Uh, yes, I was wanting to know about a person who may

or may not have visited your establishment a few weeks ago —
a lady, medium height, long black hair, pretty?"

The man behind the desk adopted a very tired look. "If this is
some kind of childish time-wasting prank then I am not amused."

"No, it isn't," said Ruby, giving the man her Ruby Redfort look
of sincerity. "I just really need to know if you saw this lady. She's
my aunt you see, and she mentioned that she was lucky enough
to visit a beautiful hotel in Everly and we want to surprise her
by booking her a room . . . as a, a *surprise*! And we think it must
be this one because it is of course, you know, completely divine."

The concierge was perking up. "Oh I see, well I'm sure it must
have been the Fountain — when did you say she was in town?"

"March 25th around six p.m.," replied Ruby.

"I was away that week — let me call Felix."

A skinny young man came out from the back room and the
concierge explained what Ruby needed to know.

"I'm not sure," pondered Felix. "She sounds like a lot of our
customers. We did have one lady I do remember — I thought it
was odd 'cause she had this fancy salon type hairdo but she still
had a couple of rollers in. Oh, yeah! And she only had nail polish
on her left hand."

"That's her!" said Ruby.

"Yeah, she was behaving really weird, kinda ducking behind

the furniture and holding her menu in front of her face — weird! Extremely weird!" he said again just for emphasis.

"What — like she was spying on someone?" asked Ruby.

"Yeah, like she thought she was in some kinda secret-agent movie or something. She wasn't the only fruitcake in that day either — there was an old-fashioned lady sitting in the dining room with a big hat and a veil. She was the one the other fruit loop . . . I mean, your aunt . . . was spying on. All this old gal did was write something down on a pad, tear it off, and leave. Didn't even drink her iced tea, and when she was gone, your aunt went over and took the pad — and there was nothing written on it! I tell you we get them all in here."

The concierge coughed but Felix had more to say on the subject of fruit loops. "Well, I guess your aunt wasn't too good at the whole spying game because this other fellow comes by as if to sit down at the table; he looks pretty mad about her taking the notepad."

"Now why would she pick up a blank piece of paper?" said Ruby.

"Who only knows what that loony tune was up to."

The concierge gave Felix a swift dig in the ribs and said, "That will be all, thank you, Felix."

Ruby and Clancy thanked the concierge, promised to be in touch, and returned to the car.

"*Now* are you going to tell me what this is all about?" Clancy said.

"Not now," said Ruby through gritted teeth. "Not when people might overhear." She motioned to the chauffeur with her eyes—though it was clear he wasn't a bit interested.

"Just tell me in code," hissed Clancy.

"Look, why don't you come over tomorrow night—you can watch my dad's slide show, since I figure you owe me one."

"How do I owe you? You're the one who got my dad's chauffeur driving us all over town," whispered Clancy.

"Yeah, and if you hadn't been such a sneak I never woulda asked you in the first place so it really is your own fault."

The two of them continued to whisper insults to each other all the way back to Twinford. When they reached Cedarwood Drive, Ruby thanked Bill and got out of the car. "So Clance, see you tomorrow night, six p.m.—I have to warn you it's gonna be a total yawn."

When Ruby got in, she could hear her mother's voice. She was talking on the phone. Out of habit Ruby tried to tune in to what her mother was saying. Her mother's conversations were rarely interesting but Ruby was a slave to curiosity. Her mom's side of the conversation went something like this:

"The funniest thing happened to me today, Barbara . . . uh, funny strange . . . not so funny ha-ha . . . So I was walking through Clavel Square . . . no, Clavel Square is the one with the statue, you are thinking of Clara Square, that's the one with the roses . . . yes, that's right, the one where you slipped on a hamburger . . . I know, it is terrible the way people just drop their garbage anywhere they feel like it. You are so right, it could have been worse, luckily it was just a trip to the emergency room."

Ruby listened as her mother broke into peals of laughter.

"You're not kidding . . . you're not kidding! Oh, I know, that doctor was very cute . . . I can't say I would have blamed you . . . who wouldn't!"

More laughter. Barbara always made Ruby's mom laugh like this, and it was hard to know if she would ever get to the end of this story because she and Barbara had a habit of going off the subject.

"Oh yes, what was I saying? The funniest thing happened to me . . . yes, I was just walking across Clavel Square when this man sort of grabbed me by the arm . . . yes, it was a grab, no doubt about it . . . it did sort of hurt, yes . . . there might be a bruise, I'm not sure, Barbara."

Now Ruby's ears had truly pricked up; she stopped chewing her bubble gum.

"So then he starts to pull me across the square . . . yes, by the arm . . . no, there was no one around . . . you're so right, I know it can get that way after lunch . . . I do too."

Get on with it! thought Ruby.

"So then he is pulling me across the square to who-knows-where when suddenly all these Italian tourists walk by, he lets go of my arm and says, 'I'm so sorry I thought you were my wife.' And I say, 'Well, to be honest I'm surprised you've got a wife if that's how you treat her!' . . . I know, some people . . . uh-huh . . . uh-huh, lucky for him his wife came along because I can just about promise you I would have made quite a fuss . . . well, as a matter of fact he did have a

wife . . . sure, we looked something alike and yes, I was
wearing a head scarf but even so . . . no, she definitely had
red hair and mine is unmistakably auburn . . . thank you,
Barbara, that's very sweet of you, yes, I will absolutely give
you my stylist's number . . . Well, you could be right, maybe
he was without his glasses but you would think he ought to
know what his own wife looked like . . . you're right, I am
having a run of bad luck, you are so right — first we lose our
luggage, then all our furniture is stolen, then our housekeeper
goes off, then my purse gets snatched, and now Brant almost
loses his wife to a thug!"

Ruby's mother was laughing so hard she nearly fell off her
chair.

"Some men really lack charm — don't they, Barbara? Do you
remember Walt Waverly, wasn't he the worst! So rude . . ."

Ruby gave up listening. This type of conversation could go on
for hours between her mother and Barbara, and it was unlikely
that they would return to the point. Ruby wandered upstairs to the
kitchen, deep in thought. Grabbing a cookie, she made her way

to her room, pulled out her notebook and jotted down everything she'd overheard. Her mother might be convinced it was just a case of mistaken identity but Ruby wasn't so sure.

One thing her mother was right about, however, was that she *had* been having a lot of bad luck lately.

CHAPTER 24
A Total Yawn

THURSDAY CAME AND IT STARTED WELL — that is to say, the sun came up. But things went downhill from there.

First of all, Ruby was woken early by Consuela.

"Hey, Ruby, get up. Your new bed has arrived."

"I have a bed, I'm in it," muttered Ruby. She had the covers pulled up to her nose and an eye mask printed with the words, *wake only in case of emergency.*

Consuela lifted the mask. "Well, your mother has bought you a whole bedroom set so you better snap to it, *señorita.*"

Ruby pulled the covers over her face. "Tell her I like it the way it is. I like the space, it's very Zen, you know what I'm saying?"

"Well, you can discuss it with her yourself. I'm not interested — but furniture or no furniture she wants you out of here," said Consuela.

"As far as I am aware," said Ruby confidently, "today is Twinford Blossom Day, and *that means* a local holiday, which means I get to stay in bed."

"Not today, missy," said Consuela, tapping her foot. "*Today* you have lunch with the Humberts."

Slowly Ruby peeled the sheet from her face. "You are not serious?"

Consuela, who was standing with her hands firmly on her hips, nodded. "Sorry to ruin your Thursday but you better get dressed, missy — *rápido.*"

Ruby was missing Mrs. Digby; *she* would at least have looked sympathetic.

The thing was, Brant Redfort was a stickler for manners, and the very thought that anyone might feel in any way snubbed by a member of the Redfort family made him shudder. There were no two ways about it — she would have to go.

"Hey, is my jacket mended yet?" asked Ruby.

"No, Hitch sent it away," said Consuela.

"Sent it away where?" asked Ruby.

"To the place that's cleaning your mother's jacket — Clean and Crisp or something — he says it's the best for repairs."

Darn it, thought Ruby, *that watch sure would come in handy on a boring day like today — hey, I might even have been able to rappel out of there.*

Ruby picked up a T-shirt from the floor — it bore the slogan **what a total yawn.**

Consuela clicked her tongue. "You wear that, young lady, and your mom's gonna freak."

"Yeah, you got that right," said Ruby, throwing it back into the closet.

When the Redforts arrived at the Humberts' impressive home, they were greeted enthusiastically. "How wonderful that you all could come," and "Oh, Ruby, you look just darling in that dress!" and "Quent's just dying to show you his new magic trick."

The Humberts were really very nice people — it was just, well, they were also kinda boring.

Quent had invited a few of his friends over and Ruby found herself sitting at what was quaintly referred to as the "kiddie table." If that wasn't insulting enough then the level of conversation she had to endure during lunch was the final slap in the face.

"Hey, Ruby, can you do this?" Quent was holding his thumb in front of Ruby's face and was bending it back and forth to show her how it could go in either direction. "It's double-jointed! Isn't that neat?"

"Neat!" said Ruby in an overly bright tone that anyone but Quent might regard as sarcasm.

Ruby strained to hear what was being discussed next door

in the dining room. "Freddie has had quite the week, haven't you, dear?" said Marjorie Humbert.

"I'll bet he has," said Brant. "This gold delivery must be big news for your team at the bank?"

"Oh, it's big news all right but what I haven't told you — and I say this confidentially just between us," said Freddie Humbert, reducing the volume of his voice to a loud dramatic whisper. "Is that we have a threat to the bank's security!"

"Oh, my good gracious — can this be true?" cried Sabina. "I heard that Twinford Bank has the safest safe in the whole of the entire country?"

"And so it has!" boomed Freddie. "But even so it has recently come to light that there is a sophisticated plot to steal the Twinford City gold the very night after it arrives from Switzerland."

Brant was astonished. "No wonder you have been so on edge — I haven't seen you on the golf course in days!"

"He's been so busy," exclaimed Marjorie.

"But how could anyone possibly find their way into the bank vaults? I thought they were designed like an actual maze," said Sabina.

"That's true," assured Freddie. "Navigating your way through the basement is the first problem any would-be bank robber will encounter, and that's before they even get to the safe."

"I know all about that, Freddie," said Dr. Gonzales, the museum curator. "The museum basement was designed by the very same architect, Jeremiah Stiles, and is almost identical to yours. Great idea to have a maze leading to your bank vaults but not so good if you are trying to locate antiquities in a museum!"

"Makes the buildings pretty impenetrable, though," said Freddie Humbert. "You have to know the passageways like the back of your hand."

"They don't stand a chance," said Marjorie earnestly. "Not with the security team Freddie has lined up."

"Sounds like you could use some of the experts we have had working on the museum security," said Dr. Gonzales, competitively. "We have gone *very* high technology."

"Yes, that whole Buddha rising through the floor thing — that is impressive," agreed Freddie.

"Not to forget the amazing display cylinder," said Dr. Gonzales, proudly.

"Well, that's not so impressive — it's just glass," scoffed Freddie. "One knock and it's in pieces."

"Not *just* glass, *unbreakable* glass," corrected the curator. "And it comes with a unique locking device that will be delivered to me and me alone on the night."

"How exciting," said Sabina, who sounded like she was just about on the edge of her seat.

To Sabina, the Jade Buddha seemed a whole lot more thrilling than all that dreary old gold.

"Well," grunted Freddie Humbert, "I can assure you, it is nothing compared to the Twinford City Bank's security — *no one* will be breaking in, not if I have anything to do with it. Safest safe in the U.S.A., I promise you that."

It ought to be, thought Ruby, *with the whole of Spectrum working to keep it that way.*

"So how about it Ruby? Ruby?" Ruby felt a tug on her arm,

"Huh?" said Ruby. Quent was pulling at her sleeve, trying to get her attention.

"You up for a game of sardines?"

Oh boy, thought Ruby. Five eager faces were looking at her. "Yeah. Sure I am — nothing I'd like more."

"All right!" shouted Quent triumphantly. "You wanna hide first?"

"Nah, it's OK. You hide, Quent. We can all split up and find you."

"You don't want to team up?" asked one of the other kids.

"Nah, I'm better on my own — focuses the mind, if you

know what I mean. Why don't you guys team up and I'll go solo."
She had her notebook with her and a list of things she needed to
figure out.

One was:

```
What did Lopez see in the Mirror?
```

It seemed to Ruby that it was no accident that so little was
known about Lopez; she had wanted it that way. But when you leave
no clues, that in itself becomes a clue. As soon as she'd found a good
hiding place, she took out her notebook and studied her questions.

```
QUESTION
Why did Lopez stake out the Fool's Gold Gang?
ANSWER
Because her life lacked adventure
. . . . . . . . . . . . . . . . . . . . . . . . . . . . .


QUESTION
Why hadn't she told anyone?
ANSWER
Because she was breaking the rules
. . . . . . . . . . . . . . . . . . . . . . . . . . . . .
```

```
QUESTION
Was she spotted by the gang?
ANSWER
Certainly
```

• •

```
QUESTION
Did they think she was up to something?
ANSWER
There was no way of knowing.
```

Ruby had the foresight to bring the Spectrum dog whistle with her — she had a feeling it might come in handy. And she was right. Every once in a while, Ruby put the whistle in her mouth, inhaled, and shouted, "Where are you guys?" This gave the impression that she was moving around looking for them, rather than sitting on her behind in a cozy linen closet down in the Humberts' laundry room.

At four o'clock Ruby went and found Quent and his friends, who by now had given up on the game and were desperately trying to find her.

"My gosh," she said. "You are all so good at this, I couldn't find you anywhere."

That evening, at five minutes to six, Clancy Crew was leaning on the Redforts' doorbell as if his life depended on someone letting him in.

"Hey! Where's the fire?" said an irritated Consuela.

But Clancy just shouted "Sorry" as he ran up the stairs two at a time.

He burst into Ruby's room and plopped himself into the huge beanbag and said, "So?"

"Jeepers, Clancy, take a breath."

"So what were we doing yesterday in Everly?" he asked.

"Well, I sorta had this hunch that the code breaker I have replaced — well, am standing in for — had a secret."

"A secret? How do you mean?"

"I think old Agent Lopez got bored of sitting at her desk cracking codes and started to wonder what it would be like to be an action agent. So one day there she is getting her nails done when bingo, she figures something out and rather than call one of the trained action agents she decides that she will go and stake it out herself."

Clancy was impressed. "How'd ya figure that?"

"I got a little clue in the form of a pencil." Ruby dropped the Fountain pencil in Clancy's lap. "I found it behind Lopez's desk, and then I figured she must have worked out that the fountain in the code was the Fountain Hotel."

"Nice work, Rube."

"So now I see why I can't find the missing code in the files."

"Why?" asked Clancy.

"Because it isn't in the files, it's on that little piece of paper that Lopez picked up."

"But Felix said there was nothing on that piece of paper," said Clancy.

"Maybe nothing you could *see*," corrected Ruby. "But what if that was the point?"

"How do ya mean?" said Clancy.

"OK, so the lady writes something on the pad like so." Ruby took out her ballpoint pen and wrote something on her notepad. "Then she tears off the top sheet and walks away, leaving the blank pad on the table for her accomplice to pick up."

Ruby tore out the page and handed the pad to Clancy. "And I'll bet if you rubbed a soft pencil over that blank sheet you would see the message."

Clancy did as Ruby suggested and the impressions made by Ruby's pen were revealed on the paper.

"Pretty smart," said Clancy. "But how come Lopez didn't tell anyone?"

"Because she didn't want to get into trouble with Spectrum," said Ruby. She paused. "And you see now I find myself in exactly the same position. What do I do? Should I tell LB how Lopez is not the goody-goody they think she was, or what?"

Clancy was torn. He understood the problem: never rat on a friend or ally — that was his rule. He would rather die a thousand horrible deaths than betray a comrade.

"I can see another problem," said Clancy.

"Yeah, and what's that?" said Ruby.

"You are going to be in same trouble yourself if you tell Spectrum how you know what you know."

"You're not wrong there my friend, I just gotta get some proof and then they'll listen."

"And if you can't?" said Clancy.

"Then I just have to convince them with the old Redfort gift of the gab."

"Good luck with *that*," said Clancy.

When Clancy and Ruby walked into the living room they were greeted by a smiling Mr. and Mrs. Redfort, who were sitting on lawn furniture while Hitch set up a brand-new slide projector. Hitch gave her a look which Ruby took to mean, "Better you than me."

"I'll make some popcorn," she said, and she and Clancy disappeared into the kitchen. Clancy chatted excitedly while Ruby set up the popcorn popper.

"Hey, you two," called her mother. "Almost ready!"

"Just coming," said Ruby, adopting the face of a condemned prisoner.

"Hey, Clancy," came Brant's voice. "Come and tell us what you have been up to — we haven't seen you for a while."

Clancy reluctantly slipped off his stool and went into the living room.

While Ruby waited for the corn to pop she felt around in her pocket, pulled out the key ring, and started sliding the rainbow colored letter tiles up, down, and across. *Maybe it transforms into something cool,* she thought. But no, it really did seem to be just some dumb old puzzle. She had made a word: **FLY.**

Big deal, she said to herself.

From the kitchen she could hear Clancy doing his best to fake enthusiasm. "Wow, Mrs. Redfort, that looks like a great portrait of your shoes." And, "Nice close-up of your thumb," and, "Gee, Mr. Redfort, that's a very snowy picture of snow."

"Isn't it?" Brant Redfort beamed proudly.

"And what's that one, Mr. Redfort?"

"Oh, that's the tile floor of the airport."

Ruby started making the drinks; she took a long time about it. As she turned the blender off, she could hear her mother saying, "And this is us at the airport, just before that funny little man with the mustache spilled his drink over me."

"Oh, there he is, honey," said Brant Redfort. "Boy, was he in a hurry."

Ruby turned the blender on again. *How am I gonna explain Clancy to Hitch?* she wondered. *But maybe I don't have to. Clance won't blab. Hitch never needs to know.* Ruby poured the liquid into highball glasses and put them on a tray. The conversation hadn't gotten any more interesting.

"And who are *these* people?" asked Clancy, in a desperate attempt to sound interested.

Bad move, Clance my old pal, said Ruby to herself. *Cause now they're gonna tell ya.*

"Well," started Sabina, "that couple there, they're the Zimmermans, and that's Mr. Rodrigez, and let me think, oh yes, the blond couple must be the Summers, and the redhead in the background there, did we meet her, honey?"

"No, darling," replied Brant.

Oh, boy! Poor Clance. Better get him outta there before he loses his mind.

Ruby entered the room, all smiles. "Fruit drink anyone? Hey, where's Hitch?" she said, looking around. "I thought he wasn't leaving until eight?"

"He looked at his watch and suddenly *decided* that he had to go out and fix something in the yard," said Clancy pointedly. "It seemed kinda urgent."

"I'll bet it did," said Ruby, glancing up at a slide that showed her mother and father looking into each other's eyes while biting into the same strudel.

CHAPTER 25
Some Likely Suspects

RUBY GOT UP VERY EARLY THE NEXT MORNING, walked into the bathroom, looked in the mirror, made a face at herself, and said, "Ruby, my old pal, you look terrible."

Her mind was buzzing with thoughts — she had not been sleeping well.

She went downstairs. Hitch was in the kitchen drinking a cup of coffee. "Hey," she said, "that was a neat trick you pulled last night, disappearing at the last minute."

"Well, it wasn't planned. I got a strange signal on my watch — flashed up for just a second. Didn't make any sense — like a call from beyond the grave."

"Huh?" said Ruby.

"It was a signal from a non-existent agent," explained Hitch.

Ruby paused before dropping some bread into the toaster. "Meaning, an *extinct* agent?"

"Yeah, he's dead all right — though there's not a soul in

Spectrum who doesn't wish he wasn't. I had to check it out, though of course it was nothing."

"This dead agent, he wouldn't be this guy Bradley Baker would he?"

Hitch flinched, almost imperceptibly, but Ruby caught it. "It's confidential," was all he said.

Ruby let the subject drop. She was thinking about another extinct agent—just what *had* happened to poor old Lopez?

But all she said was, "Well, call it what you like but I figure you were saved from a fate worse than drip torture."

"I'm glad you survived it, kid. So you know I've got to ask you—you going to have anything to report tomorrow?"

"Maybe," said Ruby. "1 just need to check out a couple more things before I know for sure—but I'm close."

"That's not what Froghorn said—he seemed to think you'd struck out."

"Yeah well, you know Froghorn—always likes to rain on someone else's parade."

Ruby's toast popped up and Hitch slid it on to a plate.

"Looks like you're out of time, kid—LB wants to see you *today.*"

Ruby looked down at the plate and instantly lost her appetite.

When they arrived, Buzz informed them that LB was giving a briefing to some of the Spectrum staff.

"She's in the screening room — looking at key suspects for the City Bank robbery."

Hitch led the way down a black-and-white tunnel until they reached the circular doorway of the screening room.

"You better wait here, kid, this is highly confidential — I'll call you in when we're done." Hitch entered, and the door locked shut behind him.

Ruby stood around gently kicking at the wall until she heard footsteps running down the passageway. Agent Blacker appeared, out of breath and even more crumpled than usual.

"You meant to be at this thing too?" he wheezed.

"Yeah," replied Ruby. "I forgot the password — talk about dumb!"

"No worries," said Blacker. "We can probably slip in unnoticed if we sit in the back — I know all this stuff anyway so I'm not missing anything."

He tapped in the password and they crept in silently; a projector was whirring, and grainy pictures were being thrown up on to the screen. Twenty or so people sat listening as LB talked. Ruby caught sight of the back of Hitch's head and sank as low as she could into her seat; Agent Blacker made himself comfortable, propping his feet up in front of him. The image being projected was of a big, thuggish man in a raincoat.

"I wouldn't like to meet him on a dark night," whispered Ruby.

"I wouldn't want to meet him on any night," replied Agent Blacker.

The next picture came up: a strangely comical face — ugly, sinister even, but definitely comical.

There was a wave of muffled laughter from the Spectrum audience.

"I see you have taken an instant liking to our dear friend Hog-Trotter," said LB. "Not as funny as he looks, I'm afraid."

"Is he as *stupid* as he looks?" said a young man in the front row.

"Oh, never underestimate this portrait of crime — where Hog-Trotter is concerned it's always wise to bear in mind the cliché "never judge a villain by his face"—however ugly that face may be. He is strangely good at second-guessing people and quite the intellectual. I wouldn't rule him out."

LB clicked the button again.

"Wow, *he* doesn't look like the criminal kind," whispered Ruby, peering at the green-eyed, sweet-looking man who filled the screen.

"Ah yes, Baby Face Marshall — now he *always* surprises everybody," replied Blacker.

"He's dangerous?" said Ruby doubtfully.

"Quite the cold-blooded killer," hissed Blacker. "You see Baby Face, don't bother calling for Mommy — run!"

Ruby gulped. She was used to the baddies she saw on TV. There the murderers always seemed to have a hump, or a hooked hand, or half a dozen gold teeth, something to give them away, but this guy looked like he might run the local pet store. The projector clicked again, and up came the face of a woman.

"Valerie Capaldi, also known as Nine Lives," said LB.

"Wow, she's pretty," said the same mouthy young man.

"Not as pretty now," replied LB. "A couple of years back she got into a nasty tangle escaping one of our agents — I would imagine she has a fairly ugly scar across her left eye. Be kind of hard to miss. They call her Nine Lives because she has cheated death as many times as any cat."

The woman on the screen didn't look the type, Ruby thought — in fact she looked like someone her parents might know.

"She's a decadent sort and pretty stylish," continued LB. "Though I would be surprised if she were involved in a gold heist—jewels and precious stones are more her style. She was trained by *this* gentleman." *Click.* "Fenton Oswald—he loves planning a good robbery, enjoys the challenge, but he is, strictly speaking, more of a jewel thief—spends most of his time in Europe."

He looked ordinary enough—the picture showed him exiting a jewelers in Berlin. He was wearing tinted glasses, a tweed suit, and carried a rolled umbrella.

Then came a very different sort of face, the *kind* of face you might expect to appear in an old movie, very melodramatic looking with slicked gray hair and pointed sideburns. The nose was long and elegant, which gave the face a dignified look, but the chiseled cheekbones were those of a gothic villain. His clothes were different too, long black coat and pointed black shoes polished to a high shine. The slide was aged, and the picture black-and-white. LB clicked past him without explanation.

"Who was *that* guy?" asked Ruby.

"Oh, him?" said Blacker. "That was the Count."

"The Count of what?"

"The Count von Viscount. If you think he looks like something from some old B-movie then that's because he is."

"He used to be an actor?" asked Ruby.

"Not an actor but a director—there's a theory that he turned to crime when all his movies were trashed by the critics. Some say he was a little ahead of his time—the moviegoing world wasn't ready for him back then. Still isn't—too dark, too strange, too dangerous. Unfortunately, he became a much more successful criminal than he ever was a filmmaker—only one of our agents ever met him and lived to tell the tale."

"Who was that?" asked Ruby.

"Oh no one," said Agent Blacker quickly. "No one you would know."

Bradley Baker? wondered Ruby.

"It's been a long time since we heard from the Count," said Blacker.

"But he's a contender?" asked Ruby.

"Oh, he's been off our radar so long we are wondering if he isn't pushing up daisies—that, or he retired."

"How would you know if you *had* heard from him?" asked Ruby.

"You can recognize a Count von Viscount crime because it is always bizarrely melodramatic. You can be sure if someone is dangling you over a bubbling volcano rather than just dropping you in it then it is almost bound to be the Count."

"That's a comfort," said Ruby.

"Of course, I've never had the pleasure of meeting him myself but they say he was always very charming—right up until the moment he decided your time was up."

Ruby shivered.

Suddenly the lights came on—the briefing was over. Ruby managed to slip out, hidden amongst the crowd; in the corridor she adopted the pose of someone who was fed up of waiting.

A short while later Hitch stuck his head out of the door. "You're up, kid."

When Ruby walked in, LB didn't waste time with hellos.

"So, Redfort, anything to report?"

Ruby tried to look confident, even if she didn't sound confident. *Here goes everything.* She cleared her throat. "Um, not quite but almost."

"What does that mean?" said LB.

"I think I have almost figured something out but I kinda need, well, I sort of wondered if I could, you know . . ."

"Spit it out, Redfort."

"Take a look at Lopez's stuff." The words hung stupidly in the air; LB didn't say anything but Ruby could gauge what she was thinking by the scowl on her face.

"What 'stuff'?"

"The stuff she had with her when she died in that avalanche."

"And why would you need to look through Lopez's backpack? What does it have to do with anything?"

"I just thought maybe she could have had the missing code with her," said Ruby.

LB looked at her as if she hadn't heard quite right.

"Lopez was a *professional*. Do you even know what that means? She wouldn't dream of removing classified evidence from Spectrum and take it with her on vacation—up a *mountain!*"

It did sound kind of preposterous when put like that, but Ruby persevered. "But the thing is, I've been thinking, what if everything isn't quite as it seems? What if Lopez found something but she didn't tell anyone that she had found that something but instead decided to check it out herself?"

"You're talking crazy, kid—why would she not tell anyone?"

"Because she was bored?" suggested Ruby.

"Because she was *bored*?" LB clearly couldn't believe her ears. "This isn't an installment of Nancy Drew, this is the real world, and in the real world Spectrum code breakers don't just run around playing hero because they get *bored*."

"But you see I think that's what coulda happened and I think she found something and someone saw her find that something — someone who didn't want her to find it — so they bumped her off."

"Redfort! She died in an avalanche — let's not let our imagination run away with us. It was an accident! Lopez was a desk agent, not some action hero."

"But you see," said Ruby, "the code isn't anywhere in the files so Lopez must have had it with her."

"What you mean is that because *you* can't find it, then it can't be there."

"No, I *know* it isn't there because . . ."

Ruby tailed off, she could hardly tell LB *how* she knew it wasn't there. Instead she simply had to stand there looking like some dumb kid until LB, exasperated, waved for her to go. When Ruby got to the door LB said, "By the way, you're out of here — you failed and that's all there is to it."

CHAPTER 26
The Little Brown Box

BEING DROPPED BY SPECTRUM was humiliating but Ruby wasn't going to take it lying down. If she could only get some proof—get her hands on that piece of paper.

By the time Hitch dropped her back home it was already early evening. Her parents were out and she wasn't in the mood to sit eating her supper alone so she headed off in the direction of the Double Donut. When she arrived she settled on one of the high stools at the counter and was about to order when a thought occurred to her. She slipped off the stool and went straight to the phone booth next to the restroom.

"Hey, Clance, meet me at the Double, as soon as."

"I'm not really hungry, Rube," replied Clancy.

"Good, 'cause I wasn't planning on eating." She put the phone down.

Fifteen minutes later a very out of breath Clancy stumbled through the door.

"What kept you?" said Ruby.

"Give me a break! I ran the whole way. So what am I doing here exactly?"

"I'll tell you in the cab," said Ruby.

"Oh brother, not again!"

Soon enough they were in a car heading east.

"So," said Clancy, "what's going on?"

"So LB wouldn't listen. I told her my hunch. I told her that Lopez was most probably bumped off by the Fool's Gold Gang. It makes sense — she wasn't trained as a spy and as a consequence she got spotted."

"Do you think the Fool's Gold Gang know who she was working for?"

"Nah, I figure they don't — I think they think she's just some nosey parker who happened to be looking in their direction, and they don't like people looking in their direction."

"They sure don't," said Clancy with a shiver.

"My guess is they tailed her to see what she was up to and when she ended up mountain climbing, they came to the conclusion that she was just some woman who had accidentally seen something suspicious but to be on the safe side they decided to rub her out. Only they're smart — they make it look like an accident by starting an avalanche."

"Do you think they mighta spotted *you*? This Fool's Gold Gang?" Clancy was beginning to feel queasy again. Danger did that to him — he had a weak stomach when it came to life-and-death situations.

"I certainly hope not, not now I have seen some of the likely suspects — one of them looked like Dracula."

"What, you saw the actual gang?"

"No, not the gang, just some possible suspects — in a slide show." Ruby hadn't meant to tell him about that. She was telling him far too much — knowing too much about a bunch of ruthless killers wasn't going to do his health any favors at all.

"So who were they?"

"Look, we're here now, Clance — I'll tell you some other time, OK? It was no big deal — just a few faces."

"Tomorrow?" said Clancy.

Minutes later the cab pulled up on Maverick Street. The two of them stepped out on to the sidewalk; there was no one around, it wasn't a residential neighborhood and being Friday evening the shops and offices were deserted.

"This place gives me the creeps," said Clancy.

"Well, I'm not planning on staying the night — we'll take a look in the box and then go home."

"Box? What box?"

"Just a box of Lopez's stuff."

"What stuff?" said Clancy.

"The stuff she had on her when she died."

Clancy shivered — he wasn't feeling so good. "I'm not sure about this, Rube — can't you just ask LB about it again tomorrow?"

"Look, you don't get it, Clancy — there is no tomorrow. LB fired me, OK?" She hadn't wanted to tell him that.

He was suitably stunned.

"So do you see why I have to do this?"

Clancy nodded; he knew she had no choice.

"Look, Clance, we'll just break in to the office, take a look around, and then I promise I'll take you home."

"Break in to the office?" said Clancy, alarmed.

"Well, it's not technically a break-in. I have the key code. Blacker gave it to me. It's just we will probably be murdered by Spectrum if we get caught using it."

Clancy was speechless as he watched Ruby punch in the door code and turn the handle. "Well, come on, bozo. Don't hang around waiting to get caught."

Clancy was unimpressed by the Spectrum secret agency office.

"What a dump!" he marveled. "I think someone has been pulling your leg. I don't think these people are secret agents at all."

But Ruby wasn't listening, she was busy climbing up the high file shelves that spanned the back of the office.

"What are you doing?" said Clancy.

Ruby pointed at the box on the very top shelf; it was wrapped and ready for mailing. "I can't reach. I am going to have to stand on your shoulders."

"Oh, man, you owe me. You really owe me."

It was a little perilous but somehow Ruby was able to balance without either falling or injuring her friend; carefully she reached for the little brown box.

"You really owe me," repeated Clancy.

Once down, Ruby placed the package on the desk and carefully unwrapped it. She lifted the lid and one by one took each item out. There was a silver metal water bottle, some sunscreen, some gloves, a penknife, and a powder compact.

"How very strange," said Ruby lifting out the compact.

"What is it?" said Clancy peering over her shoulder.

"Why would Lopez take a powder compact up a mountain?"

"She *was* very into her appearance," suggested Clancy.

Ruby gave him a look. "She's dangling off a mountain, Clance, when exactly do ya figure she's gonna touch up her makeup?"

"I was just coming up with a possible explanation is all — perhaps it was her lucky powder compact."

Ruby rolled her eyes.

"OK, if you're so smart, you tell me."

"I think," said Ruby, holding up the compact. "I think she took this with her for a reason." Ruby clicked open the case. "I think this just might be where she hid the code!" But when Ruby looked inside she was dismayed to see nothing but a powder puff and some slightly tired-looking beige powder.

"Oh," she said.

Clancy chewed his lip. "Never mind, Rube — you *could* have been right, it's perfectly possible. I mean perhaps it was where she kept the code but someone already found it."

"Yeah, and perhaps I was just actually wrong, perhaps it's got nothing to do with anything."

Ruby sat down, deflated. "I guess we better put everything back just how we found it and get out of here."

"Look, I'll do it, Ruby. I'm good at leaving no tracks."

Clancy had just repacked the box and Ruby was just struggling to push it onto the topmost shelf when they thought they heard a car pull up — its lights illuminating the shabby office. They held their breath and waited — but the car drove on by.

"Can we maybe get outta here?" pleaded Clancy.

The whole way back Ruby said not one word. And she spent the weekend alone.

CHAPTER 27
A Formula for Murder

WELL, LOOK WHO IT IS — it's that Redfort kid."

"Ha-ha, very funny, Del," said Ruby.

"So how's your grandmother?" asked Mouse.

Ruby caught Clancy's eye. "She's as well as I've ever known her."

"That's great," said Red.

"Yeah, it would be if she wasn't dead," muttered Clancy under his breath — Ruby kicked him quite hard in the back of the leg. His squeal was drowned out by the sound of the school bell. The five of them made their way to class.

"Hey, Ruby," said Clancy when the others were out of earshot. "You said you were going to tell me what you saw in that slide show — did you see anyone really dreadful?"

"Oh, that, they were just having a beauty pageant of all the likely suspects."

"What do they look like?"

Ruby wanted to tell Clancy everything but the more he knew the more at risk he was, and for that matter the more at risk she was.

This is why you should only have dumb friends, thought Ruby.

"Catch you later, OK?" said Clancy.

At recess, Ruby tried to take charge. "Look, Clance, the thing you gotta remember is, you aren't meant to know *anything.* I would get practically torn limb from limb for telling you a zillionth of what you know."

But Clancy just replied by assuring her that he could be trusted. "You know me, Rube, they could feed my toes one by one to a hungry pack of vultures but I would never blab."

"Pack isn't right, Clancy."

"What?" said Clancy.

"Pack, it isn't a pack of vultures. It's something but it isn't a pack," replied Ruby.

"Pack, gang, gaggle, that isn't the point — what I am saying to you is that you can trust me. I don't blab, never have, never will."

"I know that, Clancy. Of course I know that but you gotta see . . ."

All the while Ruby was talking she was fiddling with something in her pocket, snapping it open and shut. She wasn't aware she was doing it until Clancy said, "What's that clicking noise? Are you fiddling with that key ring thing again? Because it's driving me crazy."

Ruby jerked her hand out of her pocket and Lopez's powder compact clattered onto the concrete of the schoolyard.

Ruby and Clancy stared down at it.

"You took it?" said Clancy.

"I didn't mean to," said Ruby. "I didn't even know I had — boy, am I ever in trouble now!" The mirror was broken and the powder had all spilled out in a dusty explosion, but as the powder settled it revealed a secret. The force of the fall had popped open a section of the compact that Ruby hadn't even realized was there, a tray designed to hold the powder puff. But instead of the puff, the tray contained a piece of folded paper.

"What is it?" whispered Clancy.

What it was, was a small piece of Fountain Hotel notepaper rubbed lightly with a pencil to reveal a series of negative lines through the graphite. Lines and in one corner, a word.

"The missing code," Ruby said in a hushed whisper. "It has to be — so, I was right all along, it never was in the files."

"Just looks like lines to me," said Clancy. "Lines and some kinda gobbledygook." He pointed to the strange code-like word within the mass of lines.

nAAlsi 206

Ruby sat on the bench thinking hard. What was it Lopez had said? *"I saw it in the mirror and it all made sense."* What if she hadn't meant the *Twinford Mirror* — what if she had meant an actual mirror? Slowly, Ruby picked up the compact from the ground and reflected the paper in the glass. The lines were the other way around and the letters in the left-hand corner now read:

nAAlsi 206

"Well, still doesn't make any sense to me," said Clancy.

"No, me either," said Ruby.

The bell sounded to signify the end of recess, and Ruby reluctantly headed to class. All she could think about was Lopez, how one day she had been sitting bored to death in a little brown office on Maverick Street and three days later she was dead. It was like LB had said, curiosity can get you killed.

Ruby opened the door to classroom 14B and sat down.

"Remind me," Mr. Singh was saying, "what's the formula for sulfuric acid?"

"H_2SO_4," said Ruby without looking up.

"Correct answer, Ms. Redfort, but incorrect classroom. If memory serves, I see you for chemistry on Tuesdays."

Ruby glanced around her. "Oh, I see what you mean, wrong room, wrong class." She picked up her bag and stumbled through the door and back downstairs to classroom 14A directly below.

Muttering apologies for her late appearance, Ruby made her way to her desk and sat down.

"As I was saying," said Mrs. Schneiderman, "Khotan was a Buddhist region up until the eleventh century when it came under the ruler Yusuf Qadr Khan and the religion changed. The famous explorer Marco Polo visited Khotan in 1274 — he had heard the stories about the famous Jade Buddha and wanted to see it for himself but discovered that it had long since been smuggled out of the country — no one knows when or by whom."

"What's the big deal, Mrs. Schneiderman," said Vapona. "It's just jade, right? My mom has jade."

"Well, where to start, Vapona . . . " Mrs. Schneiderman was flustered; to say that she found Vapona Begwell very difficult to teach was an understatement.

"Apart from the beauty and significance of the Buddha itself, it is important to remember that this isn't just any jade, this is translucent jadeite jade — many people regard it as the most valuable kind. Though not the people of Khotan: *they* prized the milky-white nephrite jade found in the region—considered it more precious than gold. And that's what makes it such a mystery—what was a jadeite jade Buddha doing in Khotan in the first place? How did it get there? Jade is found all over the world, but jadeite jade is not found in China."

Vapona was yawning rudely. Red Monroe hated to see Mrs. Schneiderman's feelings get hurt and so she did what Red did best, she pretended to take an interest. "So, Mrs. Schneiderman, where does jadeite come from?"

"Oh, good question, Red. It's found in places as far away as New Zealand, and as local as California. It's also found in Alaska, Guatemala . . . and of course Burma, which is the most likely place for the Buddha to have come from. You can tell the difference between jadeite and nephrite not only from their appearance but also because of course they have different chemical compositions."

Vapona was by now resting her head on her desk and doing her utmost to look supremely bored.

Mrs. Schneiderman looked defeated.

But Ruby Redfort's brain was working overtime. *Of course,* she thought . . .

"So, Mrs. Schneiderman," continued Red brightly, "you say jadeite has a different chemical composition from nephrite jade—what might that be exactly?"

"Well now, let me think," said Mrs. Schneiderman. "I believe it's . . . sodium, oxygen, silicon, and what's the other one . . . oh yes, aluminum."

As she spoke, she picked up her chalk and began to write on the board but Ruby already knew.

$NaAlSi_2O6$

Not a word, a formula.

Ruby's hand shot up. "Mrs. Schneiderman, could I possibly be excused? I just remembered something really, really urgent that I must do."

Mrs. Schneiderman looked bewildered. "But, Ruby, this is history. You are in class. How can I excuse you without a note?"

"Good point," said Ruby, and she began to scribble something on a piece of Redfort headed notepaper. Then she handed it to Mrs. Schneiderman.

"But Ruby, you just wrote this, the ink is still wet."

"Just wave it around a bit, it'll dry in no time." Ruby had already gathered up all her things and was heading to the door.

"But that's not what I meant, I mean it wasn't written by your mother."

"Don't worry, Mrs. Schneiderman, my mom would give you the big OK if she was here—look, it has her signature."

Mrs. Schneiderman looked at the note, and indeed it did.

My daughter Ruby is to be excused from history if she feels
an urgent need to be somewhere else.
Yours faithfully, S. Redfort.
P.S. thank you for teaching my daughter about the
Jade Buddha of Khotan, lord knows I've tried.

By the time Mrs. Schneiderman could form a word, Ruby had already skidded down the corridor and was very nearly out of the school gates.

She ran and ran until she reached the pay phone on the corner of the street. Her call was answered after two rings.

"Hey, Hitch, you wanna know what I know?"

"That depends on what you know, kid."

"Let me rephrase that," said Ruby. "You WANNA KNOW what I know?"

"OK, now I get it—what have you got?"

"Something I just saw in the mirror," said Ruby.

Silence.

"You still there, Hitch?"

"I'll pick you up, kid."

"Then I better tell you where I am."

"I know where you are, kid, you're on the corner of Lime and Culver."

"How'd ya know that?" asked Ruby, genuinely amazed.

"I have this little device that tells me which pay phone you are on and exactly where it is," replied Hitch.

"Creepy but cool — I must remember never to lie to *you* about my whereabouts. Better be quick, I just ditched school and there could be consequences."

"I'll handle that. Be with you in ten."

Eight minutes later Hitch's car pulled up.

"You're early," said Ruby.

"Watch must be fast," replied Hitch. "So what's this all about?"

"Buy me a soda and I'll tell you."

Hitch shrugged. "You drive a hard bargain, kid."

When they reached Blinky's Corner Café they sat down at one of the lemon-yellow booths at the far end where it was quiet.

"OK," said Ruby in a low whisper. "You know how I thought Lopez might have taken the code with her up that mountain?"

Hitch frowned.

"Well, now I got proof, the only thing is you're not gonna be too happy about how I got it."

Hitch raised an eyebrow.

"I know, I know, LB's gonna be mad as a snake but you can just tell her I cracked the code. 'I saw it in the mirror and it all made sense.'"

"You're telling me you cracked the Lopez code?" said Hitch.

"I sure am," Ruby nodded.

"And how did you do that, kid?"

"OK, well, you gotta promise not to freak out."

"I don't like the sound of that," said Hitch.

"Well, it gets worse; the thing is, I know Lopez worked out the fountain was the Fountain Hotel, and I know she went there herself, and what's more I know she was spying on a woman in a hat with a veil — the same one from the bank, I think — and that she picked up a piece of paper she wasn't meant to pick up. I also know that she got caught doing it."

Hitch's eyebrow was working overtime. "And how do you know all this?"

Ruby shrugged. "Let's just say I did some research. You see I began to wonder if this avalanche was really an accident — I mean, maybe someone wanted her dead."

"I'm beginning to see your point of view," said Hitch.

"Now for the tricky part," said Ruby.

"The tricky part? I thought you playing at detective was the tricky part."

"No, you'll see — it gets worse. I needed to find the piece of paper and I had a feeling that Lopez might have had it with her when she died, and thinking about Lopez and how smart she was made me think she would never have left it just lying around in her hotel room — she had to have it on her."

"Kid, I don't like where this is going — please don't tell me you took a look through her things."

"It was the only way to know for sure," said Ruby. "And it's not like I didn't ask."

Hitch frowned. "Go on."

"Well, I found one thing that didn't make sense — why would she take a powder compact mountain climbing?"

"And why would she?" asked Hitch.

"Because she used it to hide this." Ruby placed the ratty piece of notepaper on the table. Hitch looked at it.

"Looks like a lot of lines to me — like a maze puzzle ... some kind of plan or map?"

"Yep, that's what I think it is — I'll bet it's a map of the Twinford City Bank vaults."

"So? We knew they had that," Hitch said, shrugging.

"But," continued Ruby, "when you look at it in the mirror like . . . *so*, it becomes a map of the City Museum basement — Jeremiah Stiles designed the two buildings as mirror images of each other."

Hitch said nothing — just waited for her to continue.

"And you see this writing in the far corner here — *NaAIsi 2O6*?"

Hitch nodded. "Is it a storage room number? A code number for one of the antiquities?"

"Not exactly — it's a formula," said Ruby.

"A formula for what?" said Hitch.

"A formula for something that the people of ancient China considered *more* precious than gold."

"Jade?" whispered Hitch.

"Those creeps aren't coming for the gold," said Ruby. "They're coming to steal the Jade Buddha of Khotan."

"Well, I'll be darned," said Hitch.

"Lopez got confused — got the whole thing the wrong way around. She was sorta right but wrong — until she saw it in the mirror."

"I think it's time you explained all this to LB," said Hitch, dropping some bills onto the table. He patted her on the back. "Kid, you're a genius — a soon to be dead genius, of course, but a genius nonetheless."

CHAPTER 28
Secretly Super

LB GAVE RUBY QUITE A DRESSING-DOWN about breaking in to the Maverick Street office.

"You had no right to break in to a Spectrum department," she said.

"It wasn't *technically* a break-in," Ruby had countered. "I mean technically you did give me the key code — I just let myself in is all."

"If you want to get *technical*, Redfort, you took something that wasn't yours, and *technically* that's stealing."

LB wasn't too happy about the trip to the Fountain Hotel either. "Why in the name of good sense didn't you tell Agent Blacker about your hunch and let him handle it?" Of course Ruby had her reasons, reasons that involved not ratting on Lopez, reasons that involved wanting a piece of the action, but she couldn't see a whole lot of point in going into them.

All in all, Ruby got quite an earful, but despite the rap on the knuckles, she thought she could see something different in LB's eyes, something approaching respect perhaps. But all she said was, "Nice going, Redfort."

Then she turned, picked up her phone, and started issuing a million orders.

Ruby guessed she had been dismissed.

It was strange for Ruby returning to Twinford Junior High the very next day. She felt a sense of elation as she biked the short distance to school, but once she walked into her homeroom and sat down at her desk, she felt a steady lowering of her spirits. She had a lurking sense that whatever thrill had come her way was most probably over. Yesterday she still had something, something she had to solve to convince Spectrum she was worth the trouble, but now that she had, what was there?

"'Nice going'? That's all she said?"

Clancy had been pretty indignant when Ruby met up with him that evening. He couldn't believe that his pal, the smartest person he had met in his whole entire life, Ruby Redfort, was being treated like a nobody.

"You have to remember, Clance, it isn't like normal life. LB does this kinda thing every day — for her it's probably no biggie."

"No biggie!" said Clance. "You save the Jade Buddha of Khotan and it's 'no biggie'?"

"Well, my folks will be pleased, anyway," said Ruby. "Not that they will ever know, of course."

"Yeah," said Clancy, "that's the problem with being a superhero, no one ever knows how super you are."

When Ruby got home she went to find Hitch. He was packing up his room.

"Leaving already?"

"Not right away but soon — just waiting to get my orders."

Ruby looked around — there wasn't a lot to pack up, yet somehow, as he moved his things into boxes and trunks, the soul seemed to disappear from the room.

"So what's happening at Spectrum? You must be lining up some heavy-duty security for this whole museum launch."

"Apart from the laser lockdown system we are about to install, we also have the whole security team that *was* assigned to the bank, *and* of course Spectrum agents will infiltrate the guests — oh yes, and Ambassador Crew has generously loaned the museum his personal security staff."

"Clancy's dad is lending his security staff? Wow, this Buddha must be important."

"Well, kid," said Hitch, lightly punching her on the arm, "I don't know if you've heard, but it is the *Jade Buddha of Khotan*."

"Oh yeah, now that you come to mention it, I think my folks might have said something about that."

He winked and continued to slip shirts from hangers.

"Anything you need me to do?" asked Ruby hopefully.

"I think you can consider yourself off the payroll, kid. You did what needed doing, somewhat unconventionally it must be acknowledged, but we folks at Spectrum are grateful to you. Now you can go back to what you do best."

"Yeah, and what's that?"

"Bugging the heck out of poor Mrs. Drisco."

"Oh, sure. That's what I live for."

Ruby went upstairs to the kitchen and whistled — from nowhere Bug was by her side, wagging his tail.

"At least I still have my old pal Bug. I don't suppose you'll ever dump me, right? At least, not while there's food in the refrigerator." Bug licked her on the cheek.

"Your breath could be fresher but thanks anyway." She scratched him behind the ears.

Ruby and the dog made their way down the back stairs and left the yard by the back gate. It was a beautiful evening. The sun was getting ready to set and the breeze that touched her face was warm — but for Ruby it might as well have been thunder and hail, for she felt nothing but cold stinging disappointment, a feeling Ruby Redfort was simply not used to.

Just like that, Ruby's life in the fast lane had hit a dead end.

CHAPTER 29
A Regular Girl

RUBY WAS GLOOMIER STILL when she arrived at school the next day only to find Clancy out sick.

"Toothache," said Red.

"But they extracted it. How can he have a toothache?"

"Infected," said Mouse. "That's what I heard Mrs. Bexenheath saying to Mrs. Drisco."

"Tooth decay: one of the top-ten reasons for all absent days," said Del.

"So what, now you're some kind of tooth statistics expert, Del?"

Del put her hands on her hips and looked hard at Ruby. "Redfort, what's your problem? You've been acting sorta weird for a while and now you seem to have a bug in your behind."

Del liked to use last names when she was making a point.

Ruby was annoyed. She was annoyed with Del and she was annoyed with Clancy. No one was saying that was fair, 'cause it wasn't, but that didn't stop her from being annoyed. As far as Ruby Redfort was concerned it wasn't fair that she had managed to work out what eight top undercover agents hadn't been able to work out—yet where had it gotten her? Back in junior high, where every day was the same.

After class Ruby walked out of the gates and saw her mom parked across the street. *Why is she here? Darn it!* Ruby had planned to head over to Clancy's.

"Hey, Mom, what's going on?"

"I thought we could go shopping—I want you looking pretty at the museum do," said her mother. "And it wouldn't hurt to get something for *our* party tonight—heaven knows what you are planning on wearing."

"What are you saying? What's wrong with my clothes?" said Ruby indignantly.

Sabina looked at Ruby's attire. "Where to start?"

"What's that supposed to mean?"

"Oh honey, do you *have* to wear those T-shirts? You could look like a regular girl if you tried." Today Ruby's T-shirt bore the words, *a bozo says what.*

Ruby got into the car.

"*What?*" said her mother, staring hard at the words on Ruby's shirt.

"Exactly," said Ruby.

"What does that even mean?" Sabina sighed as she pulled away from the curb and into the traffic. "I have the prettiest daughter in town and all she wants is to look 'different.'"

"Why would I wanna be the same?" said Ruby.

"I'm not saying exactly the *same*—just a bit the same."

"A *bit* the same?"

"More normal, like other people want to look," said Sabina firmly.

"You want me to look more like her?" said Ruby, pointing out Vapona Bugwart's best friend and sidekick, Gemma Melamare, a glossy girl with shiny blond hair and more makeup than a department store cosmetics counter.

Sabina shivered. "No siree, Bob."

They drove in silence for about fifteen seconds, before her mother perked up again. "Oh yes, Ruby, I have to tell you—turns out there is a rumor going around that there was a big conspiracy to steal the Jade Buddha of Khotan. Can you believe it?"

"Are you kidding?" said Ruby.

"Yes, it wasn't the bank at all."

"So, what, will they be bringing in some top security staff?"

"Oh, yes! Only Ambassador Crew's top expert people, that's how important this —"

"Yikes, Mom!" screamed Ruby as a maroon car overtook them at great speed and swerved into the gap in front of them.

"Jeepers!" screeched Sabina. "Some people's driving! What was the point of that?" She honked the horn to show her displeasure. "Anyway, as I was saying, it is absolutely impossible to break in to the museum now they have all these lasers and the lockdown system. Isn't that something?"

"Yeah," said Ruby.

"I'm so excited! Your father's going to bid for a chance to look the Buddha in the eye at the stroke of midnight. It's the chance of a lifetime — imagine, not only the opportunity to halve his age but the chance to double his wisdom. What do you think, Rube?"

"Will we even notice?" said Ruby.

Sabina looked in the mirror — there was a black car edging closer and closer to their bumper. "What's that nut behind me doing? She'll end up in our trunk if she gets any closer!"

The black car started honking.

"Heavens!" exclaimed Sabina. "The standard of some people's driving is just criminal!"

"You can say that again," said Ruby.

Suddenly they felt their car jerk forward as the black car rammed into them.

"I've got nowhere to go, lady!" shouted Sabina loudly. The maroon car had them boxed in.

"Mom! We're gonna end up inside that parked truck if you don't get us outta here fast!"

It was true: they were heading straight for the open back of a large green truck. It looked like it was deliberately waiting to swallow them up.

Ruby grabbed the wheel and screamed, "Step on it!"

Her mother floored the gas pedal and they shot through a gap in the traffic — her eyes closed, expecting the worst, as the car careered across the freeway, tires screeching, vehicles honking, and . . .

. . . somehow they made it safely off at the next exit.

"I would suggest that crazy redhead remove her enormous shades and take a proper look where she is going!" said Sabina, gulping in air.

Ruby glanced in the mirror, but the black car was nowhere to be seen. Yet she had a strong feeling the woman's poor driving had nothing to do with her eyesight.

"So now they're dropping you?" Clancy was having a hard time taking this news in stride. He had come over as soon as he got Ruby's message. "First of all they *barely* thank you, and now they drop you?"

"They haven't *dropped me*, they just needed me to figure something out and now that I have that's that." Ruby was trying to put a brave face on it but Clancy wasn't giving up.

"Oh fine, so you work out the whole thing and they just give you your marching orders like they never needed you in the first place."

"No, Clance, you got it all backwards . . ." argued Ruby, but Clancy was just warming up.

"I can't believe they would just use you like this, pick your brains and kick you out."

"Clance, it's not really like that."

"You must feel terrible, Rube, all wrung out like an old dishrag."

"Clance . . ."

"Dumped in the trash with all the rotting garbage."

"Thanks, Clance," said Ruby. "I feel a whole lot better talking to you."

"Sorry, Rube, I wasn't trying to make you feel bad, it's just I hate to see this happen to you."

"I know," said Ruby. "I guess I thought they might keep me on, get me to do other things . . . it woulda been fun." She sighed. "Look, let's forget about it — let's just hang out, OK?"

"OK, but how about we get some pizza?"

"I thought you had a tooth infection?"

"Nah, I was faking it. I haven't done my French assignment, so I skipped school. My dad's gonna kill me if I flunk again."

"Clance! Why didn't you say? Look, I can help you with that this week sometime."

"Really?"

"Sure I can — do it in my sleep."

"Thanks, Rube, let's go find Ray's Pizza Van — I'll even pay."

"Friend, you got yourself a deal," said Ruby.

CHAPTER 30
Room Service

CLANCY CREW AND RUBY REDFORT were hanging out in Twinford Square eating two slices of sausage, anchovy, and cauliflower pizza they had just purchased from Ray's Roving Pizza Van.

"Good combination, Clance, weird but yet, somehow, good," mumbled Ruby through a mouthful of pizza.

"Yeah, well, you know, I thought the crunch of the cauliflower would perfectly complement the saltiness of the anchovy, and the sausage would give it a sort of sausagey flavor."

"And you're not wrong, my friend," said Ruby. These highbrow pizza discussions could go on for some time, but today something else had caught Clancy's attention. As he ate he was watching a red-haired woman taking photographs of the square. It was a nice spring evening and the square was looking particularly pretty, but this woman was taking *a lot* of photographs and they weren't just of the trees and the flowers. She had a camera with a long lens and she was slowly moving around photographing every single building in the square — almost like she was documenting them.

"Hey, Rube, that lady with the red hair — the one taking pictures — I swear I've seen her somewhere before."

"Yeah, you could have seen her anywhere, lot a people in Twinford, Clance."

"Yeah but, Rube, this is different. I've seen her before but not in Twinford."

"So? You saw her somewhere else." Ruby was concentrating on getting a piece of stringy melted cheese into her mouth.

Clancy didn't take his eyes off the woman. "She's taking an awful lot of pictures."

"No law against it," said Ruby.

"I've seen her with a camera before — I know I have. There's something about her that's giving me a funny feeling."

Ruby gave him one of her sideways stares. "You sure, Clance?"

"Yeah, I got one of my hunches, Rube, trust me on this."

"I trust you, Clance — never doubt the Clancy Crew funny feeling is what I always say."

Clancy nodded. "You think we should follow her?"

"Why not?" said Ruby, flicking crumbs from her jeans.

They waited until the woman had gotten halfway across the

tree-filled square before they began to tail her. It wasn't difficult because it was a sunny day and there were lots of people out strolling with their dogs, and this provided good cover.

They followed the woman until she disappeared into the revolving doors of the Grand Twin Hotel, and sneaked in behind a young couple and their four arguing children. Ruby noticed the concierge give the redhead a key to room 524 and watched as she made her way to the elevators. As she disappeared from view, Ruby spied an unattended room-service trolley in the corridor — it looked like it was on its way to someone's suite, though the waiter was nowhere to be seen. Without saying a word Ruby walked over to it and pushed it toward an open elevator. Clancy followed nervously.

"Stop twitching, Clance, you'll get us caught — confidence is everything." She pressed the button for the fifth floor.

"Now what?" said Clancy.

"Now, take off your sweater."

"Why?" asked Clancy.

"Because you got a white shirt on, that's why. And if you wrap this tablecloth around your waist you'll look like a waiter — see?"

"I'm thirteen years old, Ruby, and skinny as a string bean. Nobody's gonna mistake me for a hotel waiter."

"Will you just believe me!" hissed Ruby.

"OK, I'll believe you, Rube, but I don't think anyone else will."

They wheeled the trolley along the fifth-floor corridor until they got to room 524, at which point Ruby crawled under the trolley and hid herself beneath the tablecloth.

"Now what?" whispered Clancy.

"Knock," hissed Ruby.

"I was afraid you were gonna say that," said Clancy, before knocking so quietly that it was a wonder anyone heard.

The door was opened by the redhead, holding a telephone and deep in conversation with the person on the other end.

"Sorry, Bobby — someone's at the door," she said into the receiver. "Yes?" She was looking hard at Clancy.

"Room service," said Clancy doubtfully.

"I didn't order room service," said the woman, fumbling for her glasses.

Clancy didn't say anything until he felt a sharp pinch to his right leg.

"Compliments of the hotel," he blurted.

"OK, put it over there," the woman said, gesturing over to the far side of the room. She squinted. "Pretty young for a waiter, aren't you?"

"I'm older than I look," Clancy assured her.

"You better be because you look about nine."

Clancy decided he did not like this woman.

She resumed her telephone conversation. "Look, I'm going to have to go in a minute, Bobby, I need to wash this tint out before my hair turns scarlet."

While Clancy was pretending he knew how to set up a room service trolley, the woman disappeared into the bathroom. Ruby, hearing the door close and the sound of the shower being turned on, stuck her nose out from under the tablecloth.

"All clear," said Clancy.

Ruby looked around. "So what are we searching for?" asked Clancy.

"I don't know, evidence."

"Of what?"

"How should I know, Clance, you're the one with the hunch — would you stop asking questions and get looking."

Ruby was by now rifling through papers and notebooks while Clancy tried on some overly large tinted glasses he had found lying on the table. There were several pairs, all equally huge but in different shapes and colors.

"Cool," said Clancy.

After about five and a half minutes Ruby came to a pile of photographs scattered on the desk — they looked pretty boring and appeared to have been taken in some sort of airport bar or lounge.

She flicked through them quickly until she came to a picture of some people she recognized standing in a crowd at the bar — even though it was a back view and even though you could only see part of their heads, there was no mistaking that the people in the photograph were her parents.

It was perfectly obvious that the photographer had not intended to snap the Redforts; they had just gotten in the way. No, the subject was someone else some distance away from the photographer. A small man with a huge gray mustache was staring straight into the camera, and when Ruby looked into his eyes she felt a cold shiver shoot up her spine — she had no idea who the man was but the look on his face was one of pure terror. The following pictures showed the man turning, pushing through the crowd, knocking into a woman — her mother? Making for the doors, disappearing from view — and two men in dark suits — were they tailing him?

"Look at this, Clance." Ruby was holding the photo, the one of her parents. "Recognize anyone you know?"

Clancy stared at the picture for a full thirty seconds before saying, "Well, yes, I do actually — that man in the background, the one with the huge mustache, I saw him the other night."

"What do you mean you saw him the other night?" exclaimed Ruby.

"It was when I came over—while you were making fruit drinks in the kitchen. Your mom and dad were going through their slides—boy, were you ever right, it was super boring. Remind me not to do that again.... I mean maybe I'm wrong, but to me, one picture of snow looks very much like another?"

"Clance, would you just get on with it."

"Well, this guy with the mustache was in one of the slides— he's the guy who spilled that drink all over your mom's jacket."

"But why would this woman in the shower have pictures of a funny-looking guy like that?" said Ruby.

"That's the other thing," said Clancy. "The woman—I've remembered where I saw her before, she's in the background of one of your mom and dad's pictures."

Ruby said nothing. She was staring hard at the photograph. "So what you are saying is that the man with the mustache, my mom, my dad, and the redhead were all at the same airport together."

"I didn't say they were together," said Clancy, walking over to the sideboard.

"No, that's right, they weren't *together* but they are connected somehow, so what's the connection?" said Ruby.

"They were all flying to Twinford?"

"Well, we don't know that for sure, we know my Mom and

Dad were, and we know the redhead lady is here, but the mustache guy, well, he could be in Hong Kong for all we know."

"Hey, Rube, look at this!" Clancy held a small diamond-encrusted revolver in his hands.

"What are you doing! Will you put that down!"

Clancy went to put the gun back where he had found it but it slipped from his fingers and clattered noisily onto the floor.

"Hey, what's going on out there?" shouted the woman.

Ruby jumped, the photos tumbling out of her hands. "Let's get outta here," she hissed.

"Sorry, ma'am!" called Clancy, grappling to replace the gun. "All done! Just leaving!"

The two of them made a dash for the door. Once in the corridor they ran like crazy. They took the back stairs, which led them out into a narrow alley, which joined Derwent Street. Then they ran through Twinford Square, and all the way along Chance; they ran and ran until they turned the corner of Amster Street and collapsed, out of breath, outside the Double Donut Diner.

"Oh, boy . . . that was . . . close," said Clancy barely able to get the words out. "Remind me never . . . to get involved in one of your . . . hair-brained schemes . . . again."

"You should talk — it was your hunch, and if you hadn't been so clumsy then —" she stopped midsentence.

"Clancy, where did you get those glasses?"

Clancy looked at his reflection in the window of the Double Donut Diner. "Whoops," he said, "I forgot to put them back on the table—I guess they belong to that lady. It's OK, though, she will probably think I picked them up by accident, thinking they were mine."

"Oh yeah, Clance, that's highly likely, they are after all exactly as big as your whole entire face—I'm sure she will think it's a simple mistake. Some spy you are, I would recognize those glasses anywhere . . . a-n-y-w-h-e-r-e . . ." Ruby broke off. "I take it back. You're a genius, Clance my old pal. A genius!"

"What? What did I do?" stammered Clancy.

"I just realized where I saw those glasses before—this woman today, she practically ran my mom off the road. Well, she was wearing those glasses."

"But why would she try to run your mom off the road?" asked Clancy.

"That's what I gotta figure out," said Ruby. "Hey, look, I gotta go, I need to do some thinking—there's a lot I've been missing, Clance, A LOT."

CHAPTER 31
When You're Out, You're Out

WHEN RUBY FORCED HER WAY THROUGH the gate and hurtled up the path she saw the back door was standing open. She bolted through and up the kitchen stairs. "Where's Hitch?"

Consuela just looked at her and said, "Why is everyone in such a big hurry?"

Ruby didn't have the breath to answer questions. "Hitch . . . where?" she repeated.

"He's loading the car," said Consuela sulkily.

"What?"

"He's leaving — good-bye — *adiós!*"

Ruby turned and ran back down the stairs and out to the garage. She found Hitch pushing his case into the trunk of the silver convertible.

"Where you going?"

"That's confidential, kid."

"What? I read every one of Lopez's files, spent some time in her brain, but now everything's *confidential*?"

"That's about it, kid. When you're in, you're in; when you're out, you're out."

"OK, well, you might change your mind when you hear this," said Ruby.

"What is it? I got a plane to catch in less than"—Hitch looked at his watch—"seventeen minutes."

"OK," said Ruby, "it all started this evening when I was eating pizza with Clancy."

Hitch rolled his eyes heavenward and pulled on his jacket. "Save it, kid. It will be a nice story for when I get back."

"Nice story? You have to be kidding—this isn't some fairy tale, you know."

"Kid, I've got work to do."

"Look, buster, are you gonna listen for seventy-five seconds?" There was something in Ruby's voice that made Hitch stop short.

"OK, I'll listen if you can talk fast—but I've only got about sixty now, so when I say fast, I mean fast."

"OK," said Ruby. "As I was saying, it all started this evening when I was eating pizza. Although I guess it all really started before that when my parents' luggage went missing and then we got robbed and then there's this maniac in big glasses who bumped into our car on the highway."

Hitch looked at her like she had gone stark raving mad. "What?" he said.

"The redhead," said Ruby. "She keeps sorta appearing . . ."

"What on earth are you talking about, kid? You aren't even half making sense."

"Well, this redhead walked by and Clancy was sorta intrigued because she was acting a bit suspicious and he thought he had seen her before somewhere strange but he couldn't put his finger on where, and so I say 'let's tail her'—so we did. She went back to the Grand Twin Hotel and Clancy kinda dressed up like a waiter and we got into her room and kinda checked it out."

"You *kinda* checked it out?" repeated Hitch, incredulous.

"It was just a hunch. Clancy gets these hunches and I have learned it is often wise to follow them up."

"OK, kid, so you find yourself in a complete stranger's hotel room. What do you do next? I'm all ears."

"When she's in the shower we go through her stuff."

"You go through her *stuff*?" said Hitch, appalled.

"Well, Clance doesn't, he just tries on her glasses. Boy, did he look a sight."

"You break into a woman's hotel room and Clancy tries on her glasses?"

"What, is there an echo out here? Look we didn't *break in,* we *conned* our way in."

"Oh, that makes it so much *better.* So Clancy gets a hunch, and *cons* his way into an innocent woman's hotel room; she takes a shower while you ransack the joint."

"Look that's what I'm getting at, she ain't so *innocent.* I think she is somehow involved."

"Involved in what?" asked Hitch, who was very near the end of his rope.

"I'm not exactly sure, but involved in something," said Ruby.

"*Involved in something.* What does that mean?" Just then Hitch's watch beeped. He looked at the flashing dial, pressed the *Speak* button, and extended the antenna. "Yes, I'm on my way. Over."

"What? You can't go! Clancy and me think this has everything to do with the Jade Buddha. Don't you see?"

Hitch turned and looked hard into Ruby's eyes. "What I see is some schoolkid who's in way over her head, *way* over. This is not an episode of *Crazy Cops!* You are not an agent, this is not some game. And what the heck are you doing talking about a Spectrum case with your pal Clancy? You were told to keep your mouth shut!"

Ruby had never seen Hitch angry like this. She shouldn't have told him about Clancy. That was a mistake.

By now Hitch was in the car, turning the key in the ignition.

"What about tonight? My folks are expecting you to serve drinks at their party. It's important to them, they're gonna be real mad — you can't just go!" Ruby was getting desperate, trying to find anything that might stop him from leaving.

"It's covered," he said angrily.

"What about the redhead?" shouted Ruby.

But her voice was drowned out by the sound of the car engine.

As he drove, Hitch thought about Ruby. He was about as angry as he had ever been.

What on earth had gotten into the kid?

She might be brilliant but she was way out of control, living out some secret agent spy fantasy.

As much as he wanted to strangle her, he really should get someone to keep her safely under lock and key while he was away — he could strangle her when he got back.

He pushed a button on the dash and was put straight through to HQ.

"LB, look, maybe it's nothing but Ruby's got it into her head that she's some kind of action agent. I think she could get herself into some real trouble if someone doesn't keep an eye on her."

"You want to tell me what's happened?"

"Well, today she was breaking into some woman's hotel room with her school pal Clancy."

LB gave a heavy sigh. "I never should have used the kid, shoulda learned my lesson by now."

"You're gonna have to watch her, she could get into some serious trouble," said Hitch.

"OK, I'll put Froghorn on it."

"Froghorn?" blurted Hitch. "I'm not sure that's such a good idea, the kid and Froghorn didn't exactly hit it off—can't you assign someone else?"

"We only *have* Froghorn, all our other agents are tied up on bigger things."

"I'm not sure he can handle it."

"Don't worry about Froghorn, I'll tell him to play nice."

True to his word, Hitch did have it covered—at seven o'clock a young woman in an elegant cocktail dress arrived at the Redfort home.

"Hitch sent me—the name's Christie. I'm going to be making and serving your cocktails this evening. I believe you have approximately sixty guests tonight?"

Brant Redford smiled. "Very nice to meet you, Christie. I'm Brant, but where's . . ."

"Hitch? Oh, he had a personal emergency, I'm his cover. Where should I set up the bar?"

Consuela scowled and pointed Christie in the direction of the living room.

By the time Sabina made her way upstairs, Christie looked well into her stride.

The phone in the hall rang. Ruby picked up and said angrily, "Redfort household, shaken and quite possibly stirred."

"So what did he say? Does he know this redhead and why she might be after some man with a mustache or what?" It was Clancy, but he wasn't bothering with hellos.

"I never got a chance to find out — he was in kind of a hurry," said Ruby.

"What? You gotta tell Spectrum, Rube, this could be important — it could be to do with the Jade Buddha."

"You think I don't know that?" said Ruby. "But what can I do if they won't hear me out?"

"Make 'em," said Clancy firmly. "Go there and make them listen — people could be in danger. Remember what happened to Lopez."

He's right, thought Ruby. Clancy could be stubborn and sometimes a royal pain but he was seldom wrong.

Unnoticed, she slipped away from the party and upstairs to

her room. She pulled on a pair of jeans underneath her dress, popped on a pair of sneakers, and climbed out of the window and down the side of the house. Once in the yard she whistled to Bug. She biked through town, up Mountain Road to the Lucky Eight gas station, the dog easily keeping up with her. The manhole cover was still there but when she tried to lift the lid, no matter how hard she heaved it just wouldn't budge.

Now what?

She rode down to Twinford Bridge, climbed over the rail and on to the iron supports, inched her way along until she got exactly halfway but the rusty door was no longer there and it was impossible to see that it ever had been. Then she rode into town as far as Maverick Street, got off her bike, and walked to the shabby brown door next to the Laundromat. The buzzer was still there but the keypad was gone, and no matter how much she buzzed and knocked, there was no answer and it didn't seem like there ever would be.

She was out of ideas. *Guess we might as well rejoin the party, Bug.*

As they walked through the front gate of the Redfort residence, a voice said, "And just what have you been up to, little girl?"

Ruby spun around and came face-to-face with Froghorn.

"Why is it your business, bozo?"

"Babysitting duty *again* — Spectrum wants me to keep you out of trouble." He looked smug.

"What? That's all I need, some duh brain checking up on me."

"I can assure you I don't *want* to be here — and I am not sure what crime I committed to end up on this detail."

"Maybe it was the suit," suggested Ruby.

Froghorn clenched his teeth. "I'll be watching the back gate, little girl — you won't find it so easy next time. Oh, and don't go breaking into any more hotel rooms with your little friend, inch-high private eye!" He smiled his sour smile, evidently pleased with *that* one.

When everyone had gone and the house was quiet, Ruby tiptoed into the kitchen and sat staring at the toaster. She even put in some bread, but when it popped up there was no secret message — it was just toast.

Upstairs, she checked her personal answering machine in the vain hope that there might be a call from Hitch, but the only message was from Red explaining that she had had a *"small accident"* with Ruby's violin but that it was *"definitely fixable, although it was going to take a lot of glue."*

Ruby sat down on the beanbag. Sure, it was furnished, but

without any of her personal stuff, it didn't feel right. Nothing about *anything* felt right. Life without Mrs. Digby certainly didn't feel *right,* and she had a horrible feeling that things were only going to get a whole lot *less* right. But for now Ruby Redfort would do as Hitch had told her and "sit tight"—what choice did she have?

The next day passed without sight nor sound of the Redfort butler.

When Ruby asked her parents if they had heard from him, they simply said, "He sent us a telegram to say he had personal business but would be back for the museum party and after that he would be moving on."

"That's it?" said Ruby.

"I hear you, Rube, we miss him too," said her father. "He is so organized."

"I'll say," said her mother. "Never forgets anything."

"Banana milk," said Ruby.

"What?" said her father.

"Banana milk, he forgot to order the banana milk."

"Well, let's hope the next guy is *twice* as good, huh honey?" said Brant.

"I'll be happy if he is *half* as handsome," said her mother, laughing stupidly.

But Ruby wasn't even listening; she was longing for someone else to come home.

Mrs. Digby would never forget banana milk.

Mrs. Digby, where are you?

Mrs. Digby was sure
she could hear something,
a sort of scraping sound
coming from behind
the wall. . . .

Rats, she thought.

Mrs. Digby didn't like rats. She especially didn't like being *alone* with rats. The thieves, whoever they were, had left her in the warehouse with only the TV for company, but at least they hadn't bothered to tie her up. "Where's she gonna go?" the thuggish man had said.

OK, so she might not be able to escape, but Mrs. Digby wasn't about to put up with any rats.

They might be one of God's many creatures but I'll be darned if I'm going to share my dinner with them. She was fond of saying this whenever she saw a rat, whether it be up close and personal or on some TV show.

She listened harder and picked up an oriental lamp. *You come through here, Mr. Rat, and you are going to be mincemeat I'm telling you.*

The scraping sound stopped.

Mrs. Digby stood stock still.

Was it listening?

Get a grip on yourself, old lady.

CHAPTER 32
The Advantage

THE DAY BEFORE THE MUSEUM PARTY, Ruby's mother walked into the living room, threw her keys on the table, and said, "My goodness, am I ever tired! It's been a long day at the gallery, and I had to come back from lunch early because my assistant was out sick."

Ruby didn't feel too sorry for her since she was aware that her mother usually took *two hour* lunch breaks.

"*Oh*, I bought you these *divine* shoes!" Sabina opened a shoe box and produced a pair of sparkly red clogs. "You can wear them to the museum party. Aren't they cute."

Ruby looked at them. She wasn't so sure. "I guess," she said.

"Well, try them on."

Ruby knew she would get no peace until she did, so she slipped them onto her feet — they were surprisingly comfortable and sort of cool in an uncool way.

"The soles are real wood," said her mother. "Adorable! Do you love them?"

"Love 'em," said Ruby, who was hoping to get back to the TV show she was watching.

But her mother wasn't finished. "I'm late home because just as I was leaving work, this woman came into the gallery, oh my, was she pretty — tall, elegant, nicely dressed — and she was chatting to me about the new paintings we are showing; she really liked them too."

"Oh, yeah?" said Ruby.

"Did she ever! I think she really might buy one — two even." sighed Sabina happily.

"Oh, that's nice," said Ruby. Why did her mother always have to strike up a conversation when she was in the middle of one of her favorite shows? It was the new season of *Crazy Cops* — she had been looking forward to it for a long time.

Drat!

"We got on terribly well. She was charming. She was admiring my suit and she said, 'You should get a powder blue one because it would look great with your coloring,' and I said, 'It's funny you should say that because I have a beautiful powder blue Oscar Birdet suit,' and she said, 'Oh do you? I love that designer.'"

"That's nice," yawned Ruby.

"She asked me if I ever wear it to work because she'd love to see it, and I said, 'Oh yes, ordinarily I would but I had a little accident with it the last time I was wearing it and it's still at the dry cleaners."

"Boy! Sounds like you two really had a fascinating chat." Ruby was staring at the screen, trying to work out what it was that Detective Despo had discovered — he was looking pensive, and when Detective Despo looked pensive it always meant he was on to something.

Darn it!

"Yes, we did," continued her mother. "And she asked me where my dry cleaner was because she was looking for a good one — good dry-cleaning can be such a problem. I said I would look it up — and she said, 'As soon as you find out, could you be sure and let me know?'"

Detective Despo was getting in his car and was radioing for backup but Ruby had no idea why. "Mom, could you just move a little to the right? You are blocking my view." She hoped her mother would get the hint. Her mother moved but continued to talk.

"I told her, '*You* should really get a little powder-blue Oscar Birdet suit yourself, redheads always look beautiful in blue.'"

Ruby's ears pricked up; many, tall, pretty, elegantly dressed women in the world had red hair, but her mother seemed to be bumping into a lot of them lately.

"By the way," her mother continued. "It's nice to see you wearing your contact lenses for a change. I don't understand this fashion for glasses. This woman I'm telling you about, she was wearing the hugest tinted glasses you've ever seen. Such a shame, one could hardly see her face."

Bingo! It had to be. It could only be! The woman from the hotel, from the square, the woman in the car, and of course the woman at the airport—there were coincidences and there was bad luck and her mom was certainly running into a lot of one or the other. Her mother carried on talking, but Ruby heard none of what she said—she was too busy thinking about the little man with the huge mustache. What did he have to do with all this?

And then, suddenly, she knew.

"So, Mom, you remember when you bumped into the guy at the airport, the guy with the mustache?"

"How could I forget? That suit will never be the same," Sabina said, sighing.

"Well, he didn't give you something, did he?"

"Whatever do you mean, Ruby? Why would he give me something?"

"Well, I don't know, but could he have slipped something into your pocket, without you knowing?"

"Why would he *slip* something into my pocket, why not just give it to me like a normal human person?"

Ruby took a deep breath. "Well, you see, it happens all the time in *Crazy Cops*, someone who's being tailed by the cops or even tailed by the bad guys, purposely bumps into a complete stranger and slips something into their pocket — a secret code, or potion, or valuable thing. Maybe the thing is stolen!"

"I can assure you I would know it — that suit is very fitted, the pockets aren't made for putting things in, it would ruin the shape," said her mother firmly.

"But what about," ventured Ruby, "if it was something really tiny, like a note, or something small but valuable, like for example a ring or a key?"

"If it were a ring or a key then the metal detectors would go off — I had to go through metal detectors to board the plane. Besides if there was anything in the pockets the dry cleaner would have phoned to let me know — they always do. By the way they found a watch in your jacket."

"Oh, did they?" said Ruby. "I was missing that . . . but they didn't find anything in yours?"

Sabina looked at her daughter, bewildered, and said, "Just what are you getting at, Ruby?"

Ruby saw that look in her mother's eyes and knew there was no point trying to persuade her that a small man with a mustache, for whatever reason, had almost certainly planted something on her. Something that other people—ruthless killers, in fact—badly wanted. That it was not a coincidence that her parents' luggage was lost, and the very next day the house robbed. That Mrs. Digby was not sulking but was most probably stolen along with the furniture. And that her mom was very lucky not to have been kidnapped herself—someone had certainly tried. At best her mother simply wouldn't believe her, and at worst she would panic.

Ruby took a deep breath and said, "Oh, nothing. Guess I've been watching too much TV is all."

"I'll say," said Sabina, patting her daughter on the head. "Your father is always saying so."

She left the room, and Ruby thought about what her mother had said. It was true, a ring or a key or something like it would have set off the metal detectors, but there had to be a reason everyone was after that jacket—Oscar Birdet wasn't *that* good a designer.

She took out her notebook and made a list of what she knew, and just as important, what she didn't know.

WHAT SHE KNEW

1. That a mustachioed man had most probably
slipped something into her mother's pocket,
back in the Geneva airport.

. . . .

2. That an elegant woman with big glasses
and red hair was prepared to commit numerous
crimes to get it. Steal, kidnap, or maybe
even kill; she had a gun after all.

. . . .

3. That whatever the something was, it was
still in the jacket.

. . . .

4. That her mother's life might well be in
danger.

. . . .

5. That this was no time for sitting tight.

WHAT SHE DIDN'T KNOW

1. Who the man with the mustache was, good or
bad.

. . . .

2. What he had slipped into her mother's
pocket.

. . . .

3. Why the redhead wanted it.

. . . .

4. Why anyone wanted it.

. . . .

5. Which dry cleaner had the jacket.

. . . .

6. What any of this had to do with anything.

"But wait a minute," said Ruby out loud—maybe she did
know something else after all. Ruby thought back—it was

Hitch who had taken the jacket to the dry cleaners. It was likely he would have kept a ticket, and it was more than likely that he would have stuck it on the refrigerator door — she'd seen him do that several times with other things. Ruby got up and went into the kitchen. She scanned the refrigerator — it was covered in receipts and lists, postcards and coupons, all stuck in place with magnets.

There it was:

Crisp'n Clean
for all your
dry-cleaning
needs

Ph: KLondike 5-1212
REQUEST NO STARCH

She crossed off number 5 from her list of unknowns — she had the advantage.

CHAPTER 33
Crisp 'n Lean

SHE WAS PRETTY SURE SHE KNEW where Crisp 'n Clean was located — she had seen their sign, which had neon lettering and a neon laundry-detergent box that spilled neon bubbles. It was somewhere on the east side of town. She rarely went to that particular district but she had passed it once or twice and the brightly colored sign had lodged in her mind. The *C* of *Clean* was broken so it read *Crisp 'n lean.*

Ruby felt there was no time to lose, not if she was right about the woman who had visited her mother's gallery earlier that day — and she was sure that she was. She grabbed her schoolbag and called out, "Hey Mom, just popping over to see Clancy. I promised him some help with his French assignment."

This wasn't an actual lie; she *was* going to pop in on Clance. She had promised, and Ruby Redfort always made a point of keeping her promises.

"OK, honey! Your father and I will be at the very last and

final museum meeting before the big launch — we can't wait, it is so exciting. I am wondering, mmm, what do you think? Should I wear the yellow dress or the silver? I look fabulous in yellow but then again silver is a statement, don't you agree? Oh my, of course! I should wear jade, it would be perfect! Only thing is I don't have a jade dress . . ."

Her mother's voice drifted away as Ruby slipped out of the door.

Ruby could see Froghorn: his car was parked across the street and he was watching the house. Or at least he s*hould* have been watching the house, but instead seemed to be involved in some chitchat with Consuela.

He was leaning, his hand on the hood, trying to look cool. *What a potato head,* thought Ruby. Unnoticed, she climbed on her bike and set off for the east district. She almost instantly regretted that she hadn't swapped the sparkly red clogs for some practical sneakers — they made pedaling difficult.

A few miles from home, she found herself in the industrial district, and after riding up and down several wrong streets she finally came upon the one she was looking for. The light in the window of Crisp 'n Clean was on, but the back of the shop was dark and after several minutes of knocking it became obvious that everyone had gone home for the night.

Drat!

Ruby parked her bike in the alley that ran alongside the building, and looked for a way to get in. About ten feet above her head was a little window. It was small, but then so was Ruby; if she could *reach* it there was a good chance of her wriggling through.

She looked around and saw at the far end of the alley a mass of old crates and cardboard boxes — she began to drag them underneath the window. It wasn't long before she had constructed a sort of cardboard tower. But was it going to take her weight?

Lucky I skipped dinner.

Ruby took a deep breath. The box construction was very unstable, but strong enough for her to climb; however, as she pushed herself through the opening, the makeshift staircase gave way and toppled back into the alley.

Don't worry about that now, thought Ruby as she tumbled onto the hard linoleum floor. *Just find that dumb jacket and get outta here.* The room was full of sewing machines and reels of cotton, clothes piled up waiting to be mended. It seemed likely that the cleaned items would be downstairs near the front of the shop. It wasn't easy to see; the lights were off and she didn't want to alert anyone by switching them on. She did, however, have her mini flashlight — it would have to do. She would need to be careful — she didn't want to draw a crowd.

Ruby trawled through the racks of clothes. There were quite a few powder-blue ladies jackets. *Must be a fashionable color.* She had to look at the label in the back of each one before finding her mother's—the Oscar Birdet.

This is what all the fuss is about?

She slipped it from its hanger and peered into the tiny fitted pockets. Empty? But there had to be something; surely she hadn't been wrong about this.

She slipped her fingers into the left-hand pocket—nothing—and then the right.

Something.

Something cold and flat.

She drew it out.

And almost invisible.

She could scarcely feel its weight in her palm. *So that's what they've been looking for—no wonder no one found it.* It looked like a letter *K*, a *K* with holes punched through it. What was it? And where to put it? She instinctively felt like she should keep it with her—not in her bag. And not in her jeans pocket: it looked delicate, made of glass.

Ruby thought for a moment, then, taking the barrette from her hair, she slipped the glass *K* on to it and clipped it back in place. It was barely visible in her thick dark hair. She had always felt that the most obvious place was often the safest place to hide something. **RULE 3: PEOPLE SO OFTEN DON'T SEE WHAT IS RIGHT IN FRONT OF THEIR EYES.**

Then she folded the jacket and stuffed it into her bag. *Might as well make my mother happy. Now, better get outta here.*

She looked at the back door — it would be a lot easier to leave that way than by the tiny upstairs window. She turned to go and then she remembered the watch. She didn't want to leave it here, not when she was so close.

Better be quick. The mending room was upstairs — she headed back up to the second floor and let the flashlight dance around the room. It wasn't obvious where to start looking. She thought for a moment. The cleaners were bound to have a drawer for found items.

What was that?

Ruby froze.

Was that a car pulling up at the back of the building? No, it was nothing. *Boy, Ruby, get yourself out of here before you have a heart attack. Just get the watch and get out!*

There was a desk in the corner — maybe there. She tiptoed over to it and began opening the drawers. And there it was, a brown envelope with *Redfort* scrawled on it. She opened it and took out the watch.

"*Got ya,*" she whispered, fastening it around her wrist. Suddenly, Ruby heard the sound of breaking glass. She stood stock-still—and then she heard a door opening. Someone was coming in and it was high time she got out.

She slung her bag over her shoulder, then pushed herself back out through the small window. She leaped headlong into the pile of cardboard boxes. She was glad she had watched all those episodes of *Crazy Cops*—they had taught her how to land. Now her adrenaline was really pumping—the fall had dislodged her left contact lens, and her right eye had begun to stream. For a few seconds she found herself practically blind. Why wasn't she wearing her glasses? Somehow, she stumbled into her bike, got on, and pointed it in the direction of town. She rode fast, not wanting to tempt fate by looking behind her.

Just pedal, Ruby!

As she rode, her right eye began to clear and she could see enough to know she wasn't far from home. She began to laugh, the slightly hysterical laugh of one who is both relieved and a little surprised to be alive. No one had seen her, and she had gotten away free as a bird—luck was on her side.

Ruby had many hiding places, all of them good ones. As soon as she got back she would choose the best . . .

But she had forgotten something. *Clancy!* She had promised she would help with his assignment.

Drat! OK, Clance my old pal, I'm coming. She made a detour at Rose and turned left up Birchwood.

It would be nice to see Clancy — although she wasn't in the mood for French. However, she wouldn't say no to a tall, cool glass of lemonade. She was just turning the corner onto Ambassador Row when she saw a dark silver car pass by. She watched as it drove a little beyond the Crews' house and came to a stop just in front of the neighboring wall, its engine idling. She wasn't sure but wasn't that...

Hitch? She smiled. *Just in the nick of time too!*

She pedaled fast up the road toward the car. Boy, was Hitch going to feel pretty stupid for ignoring her now! Maybe she would confess about blabbing to Clancy — how she had *had* to tell him all about Spectrum. After all, Hitch was going to be so impressed by her detective work, he probably wouldn't even get mad. She had her line all worked out, as soon as that butler guy opened the car door she was going to deliver her smart remark.

Ruby hopped off her bike and propped it against the huge brick wall, skipping toward the car. She had her hand on the door and was about to open it when she noticed something strange.

This car that looked silver in the moonlight was *not* silver, it was gray.

It was not a convertible.

And the man who had just wound down the window was not Hitch.

Ruby froze as she looked into the friendly green eyes of Baby Face Marshall.

And the words of Agent Blacker came shooting back to her.

If you see Baby Face, don't bother calling for Mommy — run!

What Clancy saw . . .

Clancy watched as Ruby rode toward a silver car parked in front of the Smithsons' luxury home. He saw her jump off her bike and lean it against their wall.

What are you doing, Ruby?

He saw her skip over to the driver's side as whoever it was wound down the window. *Hitch!* thought Clancy. Then Ruby got in a little awkwardly and the car zoomed off into the darkness.

"Darn it, Ruby, you promised!" said Clancy, slamming his bedroom window. "Now I'm really in trouble!"

He sank back onto his chair and stared at the blank piece of paper in front of him. Now the only thing to look forward to was getting an F from Madame Loup.

CHAPTER 34
They Could Feed My Toes to a Pack of Vultures but I Would Never Blab

THE NEXT MORNING Hitch walked into the kitchen.

"Well, hello there, stranger," said Sabina warmly.

"Nice to have you back on board," said Brant. "Things haven't been the same without you."

"Glad to hear it," said Hitch. "Now where's that short kid? She not bothering to get up these days?"

"Oh, you know how it is," said Sabina, rolling her eyes. "Trying to get Ruby out of bed early on a Saturday morning is next to impossible."

"I'll offer her French toast," said Hitch. "She'll be down those stairs before you can say 'maple syrup.'"

Hitch knocked on Ruby's door and was not surprised to be met with silence.

He knocked again, a lot louder, and when there was still no answer he opened the door a crack and let Bug bound over to her bed.

"Hey, kiddo, rise and shine, it's a big day for . . ." his voice trailed off.

It was clear to anyone who knew Ruby that she had not slept in her bed—it being perfectly made and Ruby being no maker of beds. *That's strange*, he thought. He picked up Ruby's donut phone and dialed the Crews' number. The maid answered and put him through to Clancy, who was brushing his teeth.

"Clancy, it's Hitch—I don't suppose Ruby is with you, is she?"

"No," replied Clancy. "And the weasel can collect her own bike—thanks to her I'm sure to be getting a big fat F."

"Her bike?" asked Hitch. "She didn't ride her bike home last night?"

"You *know* she didn't. She left it leaning against the wall—didn't lock it or anything."

"Why would I know that?"

"You picked her up in the car, *remember*?"

"No, I didn't."

"Yeah, you did—I saw you with my own two eyes."

"It wasn't me, kid."

"Look," said Clancy Crew, "one thing I know about Ruby is she wouldn't have just gotten into some stranger's car, and one thing I know about me, I got pretty good eyesight." But there was no answer from Hitch because Hitch had already hung up.

He pressed the tiny button on his wristwatch phone and was instantly connected to LB.

"We have a situation."

LB took a deep breath, "What kind of situation?"

"I think Ruby has gotten into the wrong hands."

"The wrong hands? What do you mean by that?" asked LB.

"Someone has taken her."

"But why? How would anyone have caught on to the kid? No one knows she's been working for us — I made sure of that."

"I think it could have something to do with the redhead she was talking about. We knew the kid was smart, but I think she might have even better instincts than we credited her with — I think she found something out and I think she got clocked doing it," said Hitch.

"Where was Froghorn when all this was happening? I specifically asked him to keep Ruby safe."

"Beats me, but wherever it was, he certainly wasn't keeping an eye on the kid." Hitch was feeling horrible — the kind of guilt that causes nausea. *Why didn't I listen? I never should have let LB assign that numbskull.*

"Get ahold of him," said LB. "And tell him to get his wretched behind in here before I start thinking about using him as shark bait."

"I think shark bait should be *my* fate," said Hitch. "I'm the one who should have been looking after her."

"You're being too hard on yourself—it was Froghorn's responsibility. He was assigned to keep her out of trouble."

But Hitch couldn't agree.

"Please tell me Klaus Gustav is safely in Twinford?" said LB.

"He is—Blacker flew him in yesterday. I hear he's not exactly all things nice—no wonder he's a recluse. But at least he *is* secure and all tucked up at the Grand Twin."

"And you?"

"I've been working with the security squad and everything looks as locked down as it's ever going to be," replied Hitch.

"Well, that's something," said LB. "So this kid Clancy—do you think Ruby might have confided in him, told him everything?"

"There's a good chance," said Hitch. "Ruby can keep a secret, no doubt about that. But Clancy *is* her closest friend; if she's going to tell anyone it's going to be him."

"Speak to the kid, find out everything he knows." With that she was gone.

Hitch got in his car and drove the short distance to Ambassador Crew's elegant residence.

He swung the car through the main gates and parked. As

he climbed the carved stone steps he smelled the fresh scent of blossom and felt the warm sun on his back; it was hard to believe anyone was in peril on a morning like this. The housekeeper answered the door and asked him to sit in the hall while she went to fetch Clancy.

Hitch perched uncomfortably on a delicate French chair and gazed around at the imposing portraits of ambassadors and dignitaries — they all looked back at him with accusing eyes. He was feeling bad. OK, so it wasn't his fault that Froghorn was an incompetent idiot and had let Ruby slip through his fingers, but the truth was he should never have left her with him in the first place.

Should have listened to her. Someone else could have gone to brief the security staff. And it had to be said that as far as working with thirteen-year-old kids went, you could do worse than Ruby. . . She was one cool customer, funny too. But now she was gone and he could only blame himself.

Kid, if you're still out there, I'm gonna find you. You can count on it.

Hitch was pulled out of his circular thoughts by the appearance of Clancy, his face displaying considerable mistrust.

Hitch stood up. "Shall we go outside?"

The two of them sat down on the warm stone steps facing the twisty gates, Ruby's bike visible through the bars.

Hitch looked at Clancy. "So what do you know?"

"What I *know* is that Ruby was meant to be coming over last night. She arrived OK but then *you* showed up and now I am wondering *where* she is."

"You don't believe me when I say that didn't happen?"

"I got no reason *to* believe you — a lot of weird things have been happening since you showed up."

Hitch shrugged. "So what do you know about HQ?"

"I know HQ stands for headquarters," said Clancy.

"OK, let's try another one. How about Spectrum, you know anything about that?"

"Well I know about the color spectrum: red, orange, yellow, green . . ."

"Smart, very smart — how about the Jade Buddha?"

"Well," said Clancy, "I know that the Museum is having a big launch because the Jade Buddha of Khotan is coming to Twinford, everyone's talking about it."

"Kid, cut the choirboy act would you and just tell me what you know."

"I'm sorry," said Clancy, shrugging, "but I am not sure what you are getting at."

"What I am *getting* at, is what do you know about this case, about Ruby's undercover work?"

"I guess we have our wires crossed because I don't have a clue what you want me to say and I don't know anything about any undercover stuff."

The boy's face was a mask. It was hard to believe that Clancy knew more than he was letting on. "You got a problem with me, kid?" asked Hitch.

But Clancy said nothing.

Hitch looked the boy square in the eye. "Your dad has security cameras trained at the house and the road in front. Why don't we take a look at the tape — see if that car was mine?"

Clancy Crew got up slowly and led the way into the office where the security monitor was kept. He clicked the tape and rewound to about eight o'clock the previous night. The image was grainy but it was easy to see the figure of Ruby riding into the frame, and seconds later Hitch's car pull up. He saw Ruby happily walking toward it, saw the window wind down and a hand appear. He couldn't see the driver, nor could he make out Ruby's expression, but . . . was that a little step back she took?

Clancy paused the tape and looked hard at the car.

"Does that look like my car? Look closely," said Hitch.

Clancy looked closely; the car was parked at an angle and the vehicle plates were not in the shot but even so there were things about it that did not seem very "Hitch-like."

"Do you honestly think that I would drive a car with *those* hub caps?" said Hitch. It was true, they were a little flashy, and now that he came to look closely, Clancy could see this car was no convertible.

Suddenly he felt very cold and very unsure.

Hitch turned to go. "When you're ready to talk, kid, call this number." He placed a card on the table and walked out of the house. All Hitch came away with was the knowledge that as far as Clancy Crew was concerned, Ruby had told the truth — the boy would take a secret to the grave.

CHAPTER 35
Nine Lives

AS SOON AS HE HEARD HITCH'S CAR drive away, Clancy grabbed his sweatshirt and the card and ran toward the front door. Then he turned and shouted, "Just off to meet Ruby, OK?"

"Make sure you are back in good time for the museum party!" called his mother. But Clancy was already out of the house. Climbing on Ruby's bike, he rode off toward Amster.

He made a right at Everglade until he got to the little green opposite the Double Donut Diner. He propped the bike against a fence and walked over to the oak tree. Clancy hadn't checked it for a while but today he just had a feeling — call it a hunch.

He looked around — no one was about, so he swung himself up onto the first branch and then climbed high into the tree. He reached into one of the hollows and felt around — something was there. When he withdrew his hand he was holding a little paper crane. It was the symbol for loyalty, and when he unfolded it the note translated as:

If anything happens to me,

blab to the butler.

It was hard to know whether Ruby had written this as a joke or if she had actually had some premonition that something dark was coming her way.

But it was all he needed.

Clancy ran to the nearest phone booth and dialed the number on the card — his call was answered after the first ring.

"She told me about her work with you and Spectrum, she didn't want to but I wouldn't let it go, she had to."

"It doesn't matter about that, not anymore," said Hitch. "Just tell me what you know — Ruby said something about a redhead, you saw this woman, right?"

"Yes," said Clancy, "I did, we both did."

"Meet me at one hundred and one Maverick Street," said Hitch. "Can you do that?"

"I think I can find it," said Clancy.

Clancy arrived at the Spectrum office twenty-five minutes later. He was out of breath and thirsty but when Hitch answered the door Clancy forgot all about that.

"It was me who spotted her," said Clancy.

"We're talking about the redhead?" said Hitch.

Clancy nodded. "When I spotted her in Twinford Square, I knew I had seen her some place before but I couldn't think where."

"So you followed her?"

"Yeah, we followed her to the Grand Twin Hotel and we managed to get into her room."

"What did you do then?"

"Well, Ruby started going through a stack of photos she found on the desk."

"And you?"

"Well, I noticed that the woman had all these glasses, huge glasses, tinted, sorta like sunglasses but not, 'cause you could wear them indoors."

"So?"

"So," continued Clancy, "Ruby pulls out this photo from the stack of pictures and I remember where I'd seen the redhead — she was in the Redforts' slide show, in the background of one of their vacation pictures."

"They didn't know her?" asked Hitch.

"No, they didn't. Anyway, then when we are outside the Double Donut, I see Ruby is staring at me because you see I have forgotten to take off the lady's glasses."

"And Ruby recognizes them?" suggested Hitch.

"Yeah," replied Clancy, "but she didn't say why."

Hitch reached behind the file shelf and the bookcase slid to one side, revealing a passageway. "Come with me, kid."

"Hey, that's kinda corny!" said Clancy.

"Corny it may be, but Ruby never found it," replied Hitch.

Hitch led Clancy down to the cinema room deep underneath the office. He switched on the projector and clicked through the slides until he got to one of a woman stepping out of a jewelry store.

"I know the picture's black-and-white but could this be the woman?"

Clancy looked up at the image: the woman in the photograph had the same elegance, the same style, the same mean look about her. The main difference was that this woman wasn't wearing huge tinted glasses, so you could clearly see her heavily-lashed eyes.

"It does sorta look like her," ventured Clancy, "but the woman I saw had a big scar across her left eye — I only saw it for a couple of seconds but you couldn't miss it."

Hitch felt his blood run cold: now he was sure. It was Nine Lives Capaldi who had taken Ruby, and he knew there was not much chance of finding her alive.

"What is it?" said Clancy.

"This is Valerie Capaldi—we call her Nine Lives. The last time she crossed my path we got into a fight—I left with a torn-up leg and she left with a nasty gash to her left eye. I haven't seen her for a couple of years," added Hitch, staring at the screen, "but if Nine Lives is involved then Ruby is in a lot more trouble than I had thought."

Sabina heard the front door open and the heavy footsteps as Hitch climbed the stairs to the living room.

"So where's Ruby?" she called, adjusting her dress.

"Don't worry about Ruby, I'll make sure she is there on time."

Brant breezed into the room, smiling. "That daughter of mine around? I hope she's not going to be late—she has a terrible problem with punctuality."

"She'll make it, I promise you that—everything is going to be all right," said Hitch. "You can count on it."

Sabina looked at him. "Darling Hitch, no need to be so dramatic." She laughed. "You're almost worrying *me*—she's not going to wear one of her awful T-shirts is she? I'm not saying I wouldn't mind because you know I would—but nothing can ruin tonight for me—nothing."

CHAPTER 36
A Colony of Vultures

RUBY SAT UNCOMFORTABLY IN A LARGE SHABBY CHAIR. A chair that might well have belonged to Dracula himself, with its dragon feet and bloodred fabric. Her wrists and ankles were bound and her mouth gagged, a blindfold across her eyes. She could hear sounds, mutterings, heavy objects being dragged across a stone floor. She could sense that something — several somethings — were in the room even if she couldn't see them. She felt as if she were surrounded by vultures . . . *a colony of vultures! That was the collective term for them — fine time to remember that.*

Then, suddenly, light.

Someone removed the silk scarf and Ruby found herself once again staring into the pretty eyes of Baby Face Marshall. He really did have a very sweet face. It was hard to believe what Agent Blacker had said about this clean-cut guy with his tidy features and straight teeth.

"Got something to say, cutie?"

Baby Face ripped the tape from her mouth. Her eyes began to water.

"Oh, now don't cry—tell me what I need to know and you can run along back to Mommy and Daddy."

"Look, first of all I don't cry—least not because some schmuck with a face like a baby is giving me grief, and *second* of all, as I was saying to those cronies of yours before they stuck packaging tape over my mouth, I don't *know* anything."

Baby Face didn't like the line about his having a face like a baby, Ruby could tell—his voice got a whole lot harsher.

"What were you doing at Crisp 'n Clean dry cleaners?" He leaned very close when he said this—his breath warm against her face.

"I was picking up a dress for tonight, for the museum shindig, you know the one, everyone's talking about it, the old Buddha thing? You see I forgot to collect my outfit and my mother will be mad as a bear if I don't wear it this evening. You know how mad bears can get, don't ya?"

"Yeah, I hear bears are capable of knocking a person's head off."

Ruby regretted bringing up the subject of bears—she didn't want to be giving him any ideas. The one thing Ruby Redfort knew about bears was **RULE 79: WHAT TO DO IF YOU MEET A BEAR — WISH YOU HADN'T!**

Baby Face picked up Ruby's backpack and pulled out the blue jacket. "This your outfit?" He was looking in the pockets.

"No! I don't believe it! What the . . . I guess I must have picked up my mom's dry cleaning instead of my own, how could I be so dumb?"

"Yes, that is a question I am asking myself," said Baby Face in a sinister tone.

"Look, mister, just what is it you want from me? You can have the jacket if it is such a big deal — my mom will kill me but I would rather deal with her than have you all unhappy."

"Oh, I'm not unhappy, Ms. Redfort, but I know someone who might be."

He turned toward the door.

"Hey come on, look at me, buster. I'm just a schoolkid you know."

"Tell it to my boss," hissed Baby Face as he closed the door behind him.

Hitch pulled up outside the museum entrance, and Mr. and Mrs. Redfort stepped out of the car. LB had insisted that he be assigned the job of securing the safety of Brant and Sabina Redfort. When he had argued with her she had countered, saying, *"You're too close to this thing, Hitch. Let someone else search for the kid — you're feeling guilty and guilt never did anyone any good. You're more use to us here. You've got to keep perspective."*

Chinese lanterns were strung along above the steps, and music drifted out across the square. The cherry trees had scattered blossoms across the path and all in all it was a very beautiful scene. A gentle breeze, a mild night — a perfect evening for a party. Fairy-tale perfect.

Hitch however, noted nothing of this. All he registered were security guards, cameras, and agents. He switched on his watch transmitter and spoke into its speaker. "Any sign of the kid?"

"I'm afraid not, Hitch. We've been looking all over Twinford and a ways beyond too, but it's like she just disappeared into the night."

Hitch sighed heavily and took the incoming call from Agent Blacker. "Do you want the good news or the bad news?" asked Blacker.

Hitch groaned.

"Well, the bad news is Mr. Klaus Gustav has yet to emerge from his hotel room so we haven't had a chance to brief him on our security — Dr. Gonzales is beginning to wonder if he is ever going to show."

"And the good news?" asked Hitch.

"I'll call you when I've got some."

❋ ❋ ❋

Ruby listened.

She heard the determined clack of expensive leather-soled shoes making their way along the stone corridor. The footsteps were far away but steadily getting nearer. Even the sound of them — so regular they reminded Ruby of a ticking clock — seemed to be announcing something awful. By the time they came to a stop outside the huge wooden door Ruby's heart was beating so hard her whole body could feel it.

As the door creaked slowly open, Ruby felt perspiration trickle down her face, though it was deathly cold inside the room. The figure that stood there cast a long and eerie shadow, a shadow almost independent of the man it belonged to. It was impossible to see more than that, but then Ruby, with just the one contact lens, stood very little chance of seeing anything very clearly.

However, she understood something without looking, without seeing — her sixth sense was telling her that this man was not a good man.

This is the sort of man, thought Ruby, *who might indeed dangle one over a bubbling volcano . . . just because . . . why not?*

CHAPTER 37
Time Waits for No Man

SHOULD HAVE WORN THE YELLOW, thought Sabina, *I'm a knockout in yellow.*

Sabina Redfort hadn't quite recovered from the disappointment of discovering she wasn't the only one to have thought of wearing a jade-colored dress; most of the women at the party were attired in varying shades of green. Still, her iced canapés were a triumph and the green martinis were a masterstroke. All in all the party was a glittering success.

She was roused from her self-appreciation by the voice of Freddie Humbert.

"And where is that clever daughter of yours, Sabina?"

"She might be clever, Freddie, but it seems she still hasn't learned to tell the time. If there is one thing Brant and I tried to teach her, it's punctuality, but it's a losing battle with Ruby."

"Ah, she's a great kid though," said Brant. "Easily diverted, but a great kid."

"Diverted!" Sabina frowned. "The clock will strike midnight before she appears and it will all be over."

"It's true," said Freddie Humbert. "Kids nowadays have got no ability to listen to simple instructions."

"Here you go, Dad," said Quent, returning with a tray of drinks. "Two martinis, one with extra olives, one with no olives, one mineral water, ice, and a twist of lime, and a jade juice, no fruit."

"I blame that old devil, the TV," asserted Marjorie Humbert. "Quent's usually glued to it."

"Having a proper conversation is impossible," said Freddie.

"Maybe Hitch knows where Ruby might have gotten to," said Sabina distractedly.

Hitch, meanwhile, was scanning the room. *Just where are you, Nine Lives, and who in all the underworld are you working for?* Who would be insane enough to believe that they could outwit Spectrum, dodge a whole security team, and steal what was considered "more precious than gold?"

The shadowy man walked toward the chair. He seemed to be studying her.

"So, *you* are Ms. Redfort . . . Ms. Ruby Redfort." The man pondered her name as if placing it in some invisible title sequence.

"I am sorry for your discomfort — did Mr. Marshall bind you too tightly? He can be very thoughtless."

He had a disconcertingly kind voice — soothing, calm, at times barely audible.

"It's a shame about the temperature. It does seem to stay icy cold in this tower, yet such a mild evening."

Ruby searched his eyes but saw only blackness: no pupils, no iris. *Shark's eyes*, she thought — impossible to fathom. He moved over to a table and poured a glass of water from a jug.

"Did Mr. Marshall even offer you a drink? I imagine not, and yet manners, they say, make the man — without them, what are we? Monsters?"

Ruby thought of her father. How often she had heard him say "Manners maketh man." He was clearly wrong.

"A little consideration goes a long way, does it not, dear Ms. Redfort?"

Ruby wondered when the torture was to begin.

He raised the glass as if in a toast. "You're sure I can't tempt you?"

Ruby cleared her throat and tried to gulp back her fear. "Who are you?" she asked.

Why she asked she did not know; she knew the answer and she had no desire to hear it spoken out loud.

"Forgive me, here I am talking of manners and I have forgotten my own, but then I imagined an intelligent girl such as yourself would already know." The man smiled and his white teeth glistened. "They call me the Count," he said calmly, reassuringly even.

But Ruby's blood had already run ice-cold, her limbs felt all at once very heavy. For she was face-to-face with the archenemy of all archenemies. Perhaps *only* the mysterious Bradley Baker had ever escaped the Count's chilling clutches — was there really any chance for a thirteen-year-old schoolgirl from Twinford?

She felt for the key ring still clipped to the chain on the back of her jeans — it was a comfort to hold it in her hands. She slid the tiles around nervously, and, without knowing it made a word.

HELP

Hitch looked at his watch, and the little light that was once again flashing; this time, red.

It was beginning to spook him — Bradley Baker was long gone, yet it was as if the *young* Bradley was trying to make contact across time and space. The giant clock on the museum wall was ticking, its huge hands clicking steadily toward midnight and still no sign of anything to lead him to either Ruby or Ruby's captors.

"Let's talk about Spectrum," said the Count.

Ruby didn't so much as blink.

"You're going to have to spill the beans sooner or later, Ms. Redfort. I would urge you to do it sooner — I find waiting such agony, don't you?" He smiled.

But Ruby said nothing.

The Count just laughed. "A bit late for keeping your mouth shut, isn't it? If only you could have been less *chatty* the other day, then you wouldn't be in this"— he waved his hand carelessly —"little situation.

Ruby tried to think back. When had she blabbed about Spectrum?

The Count shook his head. "I must say, on the whole you are very discreet — we would never have known you were involved at all if it hadn't been for that one call to your friend, Master Crew."

The conversation with Clancy! One stupid phone call had her all tied up and about to die! Why couldn't she keep her big mouth shut? It was just *one* little rule after all. Why couldn't she just *keep it zipped.*

"You bugged the phones?" whispered Ruby.

She had imagined she was invisible just because she was a kid, but a spy should always assume that someone might be there watching through the keyhole, or listening at the door —

it didn't matter what age you were. **RULE 9: THERE IS ALWAYS A CHANCE THAT SOMEONE, SOMEWHERE IS WATCHING YOU.**

"You robbed the house? You took everything but left the phones?" It was all beginning to make sense: those hang-up calls, no one on the line . . . just the bad guys, checking to see who was there.

The Count nodded. "Not me personally, you understand. As a rule I don't go in for heavy lifting." He chuckled at that one, but Ruby wasn't laughing.

"And you stole my parents' luggage . . . and tried to kidnap my mom?"

"Well, there, my dear, I must confess to being quite deceived by your mother. We have been watching her all these weeks, thinking that she was in some way masterminding the museum security—that she had cunningly met with that mustachioed fellow in Switzerland, thus foiling our plans to silently break in to the museum and take the Buddha of Khotan by stealth." He paused. "So tell me, how did such a clever girl come up with such—how do you put it? Such dumb parents?"

The little red dot was still flashing. Hitch flicked the watch to radar mode and sure enough it gave a coordinate—the signal was coming from the east wing of the museum, the tower in fact. Should he check it out? He couldn't, not now.

Don't get distracted, keep your eye on the ball.

Count Von Viscount was pacing around and around the room; he seemed to be enjoying himself. "So tell me, why has Spectrum once again resorted to using such young agents?"

Ruby was puzzled. *What is he talking about? Young agents?*

"Why, surely they have told you about the wonder kid — the *ex*-wonder kid, I should say."

Ruby stared into his black eyes. *Is he telling the truth?*

"Ah, I see from your expression that they omitted to mention the astonishing talent that *was* Bradley Baker."

"Bradley Baker? He's a kid?" gasped Ruby.

"*Was.* Many, many light-years ago. He was recruited at seven and grew up to be Spectrum's finest. I believe I first encountered him when he was around about your age, and what a talent. . . . The only agent to ever make a return visit. Careless of me? Or clever of him? Who can say? But I'm afraid Spectrum lost him in the end."

"You killed him?" whispered Ruby.

"Oh, goodness me, no. Haven't you heard? Bradley Baker died

in a plane crash while flying over a mountain range—I saw it with my very eyes. Plane burned to a cinder, his handsome face never to be seen again. Poor LB, how she mourned him."

"So LB and Baker were close?" Ruby's curiosity outwitted her fear for a moment.

"Oh, more than that. They were engaged—in love I believe." The Count said this with some distaste. "It was all very unfortunate—to see Spectrum's most talented code breaker and daring agent go up in flames."

"So that's why Lopez wasn't allowed to go on missions?"

"Lopez? Ah yes, Lopez. We weren't exactly sure where she fit in, she covered her tracks well—no link to Spectrum at all, until we heard *you* blabbing about her. Not that it made a difference to her fate."

Ruby winced.

"So Spectrum keeps its code breakers indoors these days. Foolish. There is no such thing as safe. Better to be prepared for danger than to close our eyes to the possibility of it."

Ruby could see that he was right. She was just about living proof of it.

"My friend Madame Erhling," he continued, "spotted Ms. Lopez at the Fountain Hotel."

Madame Erhling—the woman in the veiled hat, thought Ruby.

"But of course we had no idea she was involved with such a prestigious spy agency. She was no more than a rank amateur. If they had only trained dear Lopez," he continued with a theatrical flourish, "perhaps *she* would be sitting here today—instead . . . of . . ." The Count laughed. "Well . . . you."

Ruby shivered.

"But avalanches are such unpredictable things. And loud noises—dynamite for example—do tend to set them off. What a shame. Such a smart lady: I think her brain was almost equal to mine, and I am considered *quite* the genius."

Ruby rolled her eyes. "Some genius. You left her with the code, which is the reason we caught on to you," she said. "You gotta learn to look—check, check, check."

The Count narrowed his eyes. "Talking of which, let's cut to the chase, shall we?"

Ruby gulped.

"Just tell me where it is and I'll leave you in peace."

"Where what is?"

"Ms. Redfort, let's not play games, not you and me. We are above all that surely."

"But look at me, what could I possibly have that you could want?" But Ruby's heart wasn't in the lie—**RULE 26: NEVER KID A KIDDER,** she thought.

He stared at her with his cold black eyes.

"OK," she ventured. "I give you the key, you let me go?"

The Count shook his head sadly. "I'm afraid that's just not how it works. You see you are in the worst possible position to make a bargain."

Ruby swallowed — her mouth was very dry and beads of sweat were forming on her brow.

"Speak up, Ms. Redfort."

But Ruby said nothing.

He stamped his foot. Ruby jumped and felt a heavy lock of hair fall across her right eye. And her barrette — her barrette slipped slowly, very slowly past her nose. She held her breath.

Will he see? Of course he will.

The Count reached his long elegant hand out, slipped the barrette from her hair, and just like that . . . the glass *K* was his.

"Good, no need for torture today — you see how pleasant things can be?" he said. "Poor little Dorothy, doesn't look like you are going to make it to the Emerald City after all." He looked at her clogs. "Not even your ruby slippers can save you now."

"Never mind, I'm not really dressed for a party," said Ruby with a weary smile.

The Count looked at Ruby's T-shirt, which read, *in deep trouble.*

"No, I dare say you are right, though the sentiment is perfect for the occasion," said the Count with a wink.

"What now?" Ruby's voice was almost a croak.

"Quite right, let's move on, no more chatter," said the Count. "I have devised something rather splendid for you — it's straight out of *The Wizard of Oz*. What a wonderful film *that* could have been, if only someone with a little *imagination* had directed it. My favorite scene is the one where the witch turns over the hourglass — Dorothy will die when all the sand has fallen. What a shame, I always thought, not to put little Dorothy *inside* the hourglass. So much more dramatic, far less chance for error . . . So consider this a remake, the version Hollywood would not dare to screen!"

Ruby's eyes grew very big and she could no longer be sure that her heart was still beating.

"Well, now my pretty," said the Count, adopting the Wicked Witch of the West's mocking tone. "When the clock strikes half past eleven, the tower you are sitting in will begin to fill with jade-green sand like a giant hourglass."

Ruby winced — she had never liked sand in her hair, but to be buried alive in it was gruesome beyond anything she had seen in any of Mrs. Digby's thrillers.

"You can kill me if you want," said Ruby, her voice beginning to crack, "but that won't help you get past all the museum security, all the alarms, all the guards. You haven't a chance of getting anywhere near the Jade Buddha of Khotan."

"It's sweet of you to show your concern but I have it all beautifully choreographed, and I have the perfect little distraction for the good folk of Twinford — a power cut and an explosion all in one. It really will be very exciting. Total blackout, so dramatic. Blow up the bank and watch all those pretty green dollars float up into the sky. And of course once the power is cut they can forget about all their clever little lasers — they will look like they are activated but I can assure you, they won't be!"

Count Von Viscount looked at his watch — it was an old-fashioned timepiece, kept in his pocket, secured by a chain. "Time marches on, however, and now I regret I must leave you. I am glad we had a chance to meet, too bad I will not have the pleasure again."

And with that, he was gone.

Ruby couldn't be sure, but as the door closed, she thought she heard the sound of a woman's voice — one she almost recognized. But before she had a chance to search her mind, she heard another.

Is that singing?

Ruby looked up, and there perched on a ledge was a reel-to-reel tape player, playing a tune she knew very well. *Mr. Sandman* — her father sometimes whistled it before bedtime. She shivered. Would this be the last time she ever heard that song?

Think like that, Ruby, and you're already dead.

CHAPTER 38
The Sands of Time

HITCH WATCHED AS A TALL MAN in a rather old-fashioned suit walked into the imposing museum hall, followed by a relieved-looking Agent Blacker.

The clock struck eleven thirty. *Just in the nick of time,* thought Hitch. Herr Gustav had been expected at least three hours ago.

He radioed the search team again. "The kid?"

"Nothing," came the reply.

On the other side of the room, Clancy had spotted his parents — they were talking to Mr. and Mrs. Redfort and an elegant man who Clancy didn't recognize.

"I just don't know where that daughter of ours has gotten to — I was so hoping to introduce you," said Brant, shaking the man's hand.

The man smiled reassuringly. "I am sure she is somewhere

nearby . . . buried up to her ears in something. I remember myself as a child," said the man. "I used to wish I could lock myself away and listen to music undisturbed."

"That sounds like our girl," said Brant.

"No doubt she'll be wearing something utterly inappropriate for the evening," said Sabina, plucking a long red hair from the man's jacket. "Forgive me, force of habit," she said, laughing.

The man smiled again. "She sounds like an intelligent girl, Mrs. Redfort. I am sure she will have chosen an outfit that befits the occasion." He turned. "And who is this?" He was looking at Clancy, who by now was standing next to him.

"Oh, I'm sorry, Herr Gustav, this is our son Clancy," said Ambassador Crew.

Clancy shook the man's hand. "Pleased to meet you, Herr Gustav — I had a hunch you would be much shorter."

Herr Gustav laughed. "Sorry to disappoint you, Master Crew."

Meanwhile, locked in a tower someplace, who only knew where, a schoolgirl was watching as the sands of time fell about her.

Oh boy, thought Ruby, *how did I get into this mess?*

She was in what amounted to a giant egg timer, and it was clear that no one was going to rescue her before her three and a half minutes were up. What was the time, she wondered. Had the museum launch even begun? And that's when she remembered something very important.

The escape watch. Although both her hands were tied, her fingers were free and so, patiently and with great care, she started to feel each of the twisting winders and tiny knobs and switches. There had to be a cutting device on this thing — every spy surely required a laser? Watch any Hollywood spy movie and it was only a matter of seconds before the hero made use of the laser gadget.

First thing I shoulda done when I took that darned watch was look for that old laser feature.

She could have kicked herself — indeed would have, had her legs not been tied together. She twisted and turned every possible button on the watch but nothing happened — not a thing. The sand was falling fast, and although the chair was raised up on a platform, her shoes were nearly buried.

And then she felt something warm on her wrist — no, not warm, hot.

"Ouch," shrieked Ruby. She had found the laser.

With a little more *ow*-ing and a lot of cursing, Ruby finally directed the cutting device at the ropes binding her wrists.

Once her arms were free she set about releasing her feet.

She was stiff and her limbs were aching but what was the point of thinking about that, she hadn't even *begun* to get out of this little mess.

"I am just about bursting to see the Buddha rise from the floor — I understand it does so in the blink of an eye! Am I right?" Sabina could barely contain herself.

"Quite right," agreed Herr Gustav. "The clock strikes midnight, the lights go out, and a second later there it will be."

"On the absolute stroke of midnight someone is going to get a chance to look into the eyes of the Jade Buddha of Khotan! Isn't it thrilling?" she said.

"Thrilling," agreed Klaus Gustav.

"And you are the only person who can make that happen, since you are the one who holds the key."

"Indeed," nodded Klaus Gustav. "I hold the key to the secret of the Jade Buddha of Khotan."

"Will you unlock the case yourself, Herr Gustav?" asked Marjorie Humbert.

"You can count on it," he said, patting his breast pocket.

"I heard you were Swiss?" said Clancy.

"Indeed," replied the man.

"Is that a Swiss accent you have?" asked Clancy.

The man nodded.

"Because it sounds sorta, not Swiss, more like—"

"Clancy! It's not polite to ask questions like that," said Mrs. Crew, her embarrassment evident. This was not the behavior of an ambassador's son. "I'm sorry, Herr Gustav, our son rarely knows when to stop."

"I was just asking," said Clancy.

"Well, don't," said his father.

Ruby stood on the chair and, holding her wrist very steady, aimed the watch at a metal hook just above the window and pressed down on the winder button.

Out shot the titanium cable. The grabber claw reached out, missed the hook, and the cable slid down the wall.

Ruby quickly retracted it and tried again. *Come on, I don't have time for this.* This was true: the sand had already reached the seat of the chair. Ruby took aim again, and—*bingo!*—the claw closed around the hook. Ruby closed her eyes, pressed the retractor, bracing herself to be whisked at lightning speed through the air ... and nothing happened.

No, no, no! You are a rescue gadget and you rescue, that's what you do!

The sand was covering her feet and the tower was filling up fast. *You can't jam! Spy gadgets don't jam!* She pressed again — still nothing.

OK, you can jam but not now! She pressed the button again — nothing for one split second . . .

And then quite suddenly Ruby was wrenched from the chair and carried away high above the sand and onto the window ledge.

Take your time, why don't you!

She released the grabber and assessed the situation. The window, it seemed, was boarded shut from the outside, and she didn't have enough space to give it a good hard kick. She looked around. Right in the middle of the ceiling hung an iron chandelier. If she could just grab on to that, she could swing herself at the blocked window and dislodge the boards — how she was going to get down from the window was a whole different problem. Several times she pressed the cable button, but to no avail — it really had given up.

OK, Rube, you still have time, don't panic. She looked at the tape machine with its big spools turning around and around — and she had an idea. *Sorry, buster, but you are beginning to get on my nerves.*

Ruby took off one of the reels and pulled at the yards of song tape, then she took the key ring from her jeans and tied it to the tape, making a weight. Using this as a sort of lasso, she was able to hook and pull the chandelier toward her until she was able to grab hold of it. Then, hanging from it like a trapeze artist, she swung back and forth until she had gathered enough momentum to break through the wooden boards.

Only thing was, she had gathered a little too much momentum; she crashed through the window and was flung into the night sky.

By now Klaus Gustav was surrounded by all the glittering folk of Twinford.

"To make a completely unbreakable glass display case is quite a feat, Herr Gustav. Just how was it done?" asked Ambassador Crew.

"That was easy," said Klaus Gustav. "It was the key that was the tricky part."

"Might we see it, Mr. Gustav, I have been just dying to know what it looks like," implored Sabina.

But Klaus Gustav just tapped his nose. "Secrets, all secrets."

Clancy looked at Herr Gustav, the Swiss man with the accent that reminded him of . . . *who was it?*

"Well, we are very proud to welcome you to Twinford and our city museum," said Ambassador Crew.

Herr Gustav smiled and his black eyes glistened.

Dracula! thought Clancy.

The scrabbling sound
had gotten louder.
It was definitely coming
from behind the
bookcase. . . .

Mrs. Digby gripped the lamp. *I'm ready for ya, the Digbys' have never been afraid of anything.* (Well, except rats, of course).

"Ach," came a voice, "Ich habe auf meine Brille getreten!"

Mrs. Digby was surprised to hear a rat talk, a foreign one at that. "What language is that you're speaking?" she asked.

"Oh, so someone *is* there," came the voice again, this time in English. "Who are you?"

"I'm the one holding the heavy lamp, ready to knock you out, is who I am. Who are *you*?"

"I'm being held captive. Could you help me?"

"How do I know you're not one of them?"

"Because if I were, I wouldn't be stuck in here."

Mrs. Digby thought for a moment — he didn't *sound* particularly dangerous, and seeing as they were in the same situation she thought she might as well get along with him. She set about pulling all the books off the bookcase until it was light enough to move.

"OK, you ought to be able to squeeze through the gap, unless you are very fat, which I don't s'pose you are if they have been feeding you the kind of rations they have been feeding me."

Gradually, one limb at a time, a little old man appeared.

A little old man with a huge mustache.

"Klaus Gustav," he said, offering her his hand.

CHAPTER 39
Lucky Twice

CLANCY WAS TRYING TO GET HITCH'S ATTENTION but Hitch was on the far side of the room, his eyes scanning the crowd, and he wasn't noticing Clancy's subtle hand gestures.

Would you just look over here!

Clancy didn't know what to do — he didn't want to leave the man in case he disappeared but he couldn't do anything about anything without Hitch. He began to wave and Hitch waved back, awkwardly — the way people wave when they don't know why they are waving.

Clancy tried again, this time more wildly, like a drowning person.

"What are you doing?" said his mother through clenched teeth.

"Waving," muttered Clancy.

"Well, would you please stop it," she hissed. "It's embarrassing your father."

But Clancy couldn't stop — he had to make Hitch see that something very terrible might be going on. This man who claimed to be Klaus Gustav was not Klaus Gustav. Clancy was sure of it.

Lucky for Ruby, she hadn't actually fallen the one hundred and two feet to the ground below, but instead found herself clinging to a branch of a very rotten tree, dangling a mere *sixty* feet above the ground.

What now?

This was Ruby's last thought before a huge thunder-like boom shook the building. It came from Twinford City Bank. It was a deafening noise, an explosion.

Inside the museum, for one half of a split second all the guests went quiet — only the party music played on.

And then — pandemonium.

Martini glasses dropped and shattered on the marble floor, a hubbub of noise rose up, some folks screamed, and fear sparked like electricity. A sea of people rushed toward the doors. An alarm went off and sirens screeched — it was panic and chaos.

But Clancy Crew was desperately trying to find a way back through the crowds — people were pushing and shoving, trying to get out into the square, and he was the only person headed in the other direction. He felt himself being forced backward, and then all of a sudden, a hand grabbed him and pulled him free.

"Where are you going, Clancy Crew?" It was Hitch.

Clancy's eyes were wild with panic. "That man, Klaus Gustav — I think he's a fake. I think he's meant to be a small man with a mustache — the man from the airport. I think *this* guy is the one who took Ruby."

"You know what, kid," replied Hitch, "I've got a hunch you might just be right."

"So now what? The man, he's disappeared — how are we going to find Ruby without him?"

Hitch looked at Clancy. He really wasn't sure about this, but it was his only hope. "Your pal Ruby, do you happen to know if she might have taken something from Spectrum? A gadget?"

"Nothing she told *me* about," said Clancy.

"You haven't happened to see her with a key ring — one with little colored letter tiles that you can slide around?"

"That? Yeah, but it's not from Spectrum — it's just some dumb old key ring she said she found."

Hitch smiled. "That's no dumb old key ring — that's a very sophisticated piece of Spectrum gadgetry," he said, pulling Clancy out from the scrum and toward the rear staircase.

"What do you mean?" called Clancy.

"It's a mini locator," shouted Hitch. "Used to belong to one of the smartest agents who ever lived. Slide the tiles, form a word, and it sends me a signal." He tapped his watch. "I got a hunch that I just might know where to find our friend Ruby."

Clancy looked at the little red light flashing on the dial. And then suddenly everything went dark.

Outside the museum, dangling sixty feet above the ground, Ruby was beginning to lose her grip.

Yikes, she thought, *this is not a good situation.*

She wasn't sure how long her fingers could hold on, but it was the branch that gave up first, crumbling in her hands.

And she felt herself once more, tumbling through the air.

By now the bank was crawling with security staff. Everyone from inside the museum was outside watching the bank. There were police cars everywhere, screaming sirens, and alarms setting off other alarms.

But Hitch hardly heard them. All he could hear was the pounding of his heart as he ran down stone corridors, up steep stairways, all the way to the tower. He ran like a man possessed, he ran like his life depended on it.

By the time Clancy Crew arrived at the heavy oak door, Hitch had already levered it open. Clancy Crew watched as green sand spilled out into the corridor and he watched as Hitch sank slowly to the floor. His head was in his hands, and the light on the little watch radar had gone out.

"Rube?" whispered Clancy, crumpling to his knees.

"I'm sorry, kid," was all that Hitch could say.

But Ruby Redfort was lucky: in fact she was lucky twice.

First, because the power lines broke her fall, and second, because the explosion at the bank had extinguished the power.

After she had checked that she was still alive, Ruby inched along the cables until she was dangling over a large, leafy shrub. She let go — not a cushy landing exactly but she was at least all in one piece, although she seemed to be missing a shoe.

Nice going, Rube! A super great time to lose footwear.

She couldn't see a thing, let alone a small size 5 lost in a thicket.

Having gotten her bearings, she picked herself up, then half ran, half limped toward the building. The place was totally deserted and all she could hear as she made her way down to the museum vaults was the commotion outside. Every last person was watching things unfold at the bank.

Ruby wasn't greatly surprised to find the basement door

unlocked. It was just as the Count had promised — the lasers securing the entrance looked like they were active but the locks had failed and no doubt someone was already inside. Carefully, she pushed open the door and stepped into the dimly lit passage.

Bang!

Another explosion. More alarms. More sirens.

And then the emergency lighting in the museum basement went out.

Hitch was trying to pull himself together. It wasn't easy. He was also trying to pull Clancy together, which was harder.

"Clancy, listen to me. I have to get to the museum basement — to the vault. You go alert your dad's security team — tell them it's all about the Buddha. You have to convince them that the bank is a decoy — I know it doesn't look that way but it is."

But Clancy wasn't moving.

Hitch clicked his fingers in front of Clancy's face. "You hearing me, kid? I need your help."

Still nothing.

Hitch slid over to the broken figure that was Ruby Redford's closest friend and put his hands on his shoulders. "Kid, this shouldn't have happened. It's my fault, I realize that, but I think I know who did this and I think I know where to find him. I want to make sure he pays for what he's done to Ruby — and I need your help."

Clancy looked up, his face gray and his eyes hollow.

"Can I count on you, kid?"

The boy nodded and got to his feet.

"Here," said Hitch. "Take my lucky lighter, it's never let me down."

Trying to navigate the dark passageways was not easy — not without a flashlight. Ruby had memorized the basement plans, she knew them inside out, but the blackness was disorienting and she had little idea where she was or where she was going.

But she hoped that *wherever it was,* she was going to make it in time.

She felt a wave of panic as claustrophobia swept over her.

Deep breaths, Rube — it's just a little darkness, nothing else . . .

Darkness and some crazy count who just tried to bury you alive.

She moved as silently as she could. *Don't warn him. You have the advantage — he thinks you are dead.* **RULE 43: IF YOU'VE GOT THE ADVANTAGE — MAKE SURE YOU KEEP IT.**

She rounded the corner and there, bathed in a dim but beautiful light, sat the Jade Buddha of Khotan. More precious than gold. Even from where she crouched she could see that the carving was exquisite, the jade itself perfect translucent stone. She felt drawn to move closer but she resisted, knowing the Count couldn't be far away. She was right — seconds later he appeared like magic from the pitch black, holding the glass key.

Carefully, he pushed the key into a slot in the glass cylinder and the door slid open. In his left hand he held a silver metal tube. *What was that?* Then suddenly she saw a tiny beam of light shoot out. He seemed to be studying something — *was it the eyes of the Buddha that interested him? Was he just marveling at the beauty of it or was there something else he was looking for?*

He reached into his breast pocket and pulled out a notebook and fountain pen.

He was writing something down.

Why?

"Well, well if it isn't little Ruby slippers, the snoopiest kid on the block."

Without even turning around, Ruby recognized the sweet voice of Baby Face Marshall.

"Oh cripes! Not you again."

By now Hitch was standing outside the museum basement door. He pushed the transmitter button on his watch. "Blacker, you there? Blacker, are you receiving me?"

Nothing. It was the same with the other agents. *OK, one last try — you better be there, LB.*

Five seconds later LB came on the line. "Speak."

"The explosion at the bank — it's a bluff, a distraction. They are after the Jade Buddha, and I'm pretty sure we are dealing with the Count. It has all the hallmarks of his work. He's got his hands on the key. He's the one who took Ruby, I just know it."

"Where is she now?" said LB.

Hitch paused. "I'm afraid the kid . . ." His voice faltered. "She didn't have a chance."

LB took a sharp breath as if she had something to say, but no words came out.

"Look, I'm going after him — find me some backup." His transmitter cut out.

Clancy meanwhile was lost. Galleries stretched in every direction and with only the flame from Hitch's lighter it was difficult to work out where the nearest exit might be. Every door seemed to lead him to another. For all he knew he could be running in spirals — destined never to find a way out, like a fly trapped in a jar.

Hitch switched on his agent-issue flashlight. It had a powerful directional beam and he was able to sweep light across the main corridor — passageways zigzagged every which way.

He recognized the various twists and turns from the museum plans he had studied. It was no trouble navigating; he was trained to find his way in impossible conditions. The tricky thing was second-guessing any surprises that might come along the way. In the maze of passageways it had been deathly quiet but as he moved farther and farther into the museum vaults he thought he heard a voice — or rather voices.

Two of them.

Clancy flicked on the lighter. There it was:

EXIT TO MUSEUM GARDEN.

About time, he muttered as he leaned hard on the door and fell out into the warm night air. He was now at the back of the building. He would have to run around the north side to get to the square. He held the flame up and looked for the path. Something glinted. It was red and seemed to sparkle. He walked over to take a closer look. A red shoe, a very small red shoe. He smiled.

Rube, I got a funny feeling you're not dead. And I have a hunch I know exactly where to find you.

The Count carefully locked the glass case, slipped the key into his jacket pocket, and walked slowly over to where Ruby stood. "Ms. Redfort, you do surprise me. I am not sure whether I should be delighted or disappointed that you escaped the tower. Am I getting sloppy, or are you remarkable?"

"Mm, that's a hard one to call. I'd hate to hurt your feelings, so let's just go with me being remarkable."

The Count nodded. "What courage you have for someone so small and defenseless — quite admirable."

Ruby had her eyes trained on the Count's pocket.

"Yeah, well you know, I've grown quite fond of you too."

The Count laughed. He couldn't help liking this gutsy schoolgirl from Twinford — it was only a shame to see such talent wasted. "So what can I do for you?"

"Back there in the tower, I felt we really hit it off — and you are such good company," said Ruby, giving the Count a little dig with her elbow.

"Understandable, I'm sure," the Count replied. "Your stupid parents must be quite a burden to you."

Ruby felt the glass object in her palm. "Speaking of stupid, you really shouldn't leave your valuables lying around — they can so easily get into the wrong hands." She held the key up in front of his face.

For a second the Count was thrown. "How did you . . .?" Then he made a grab for it. Ruby tossed the glass key high into the air and it made a tiny tinkling sound as it hit the stone floor somewhere in the pitch-blackness of the vault.

The Count laughed. "Oh, dear Ms. Redfort — you think because the key is glass that it will therefore break? I'm afraid you are mistaken."

This unfortunately was true. Ruby had indeed assumed that a key made of glass would certainly shatter into a hundred pieces.

"Well, good luck finding it before the clock strikes twelve," she said, trying to hold on to her bravado.

Baby Face was gripping Ruby by the hair. "What do you suggest I do now?"

The Count smiled. "Oh, you know — kill her."

CHAPTER 40
Look Into My Eyes

THE MUTTERINGS WERE GETTING LOUDER; Hitch knew he was getting near. He switched off the flashlight and followed the voices. Were there three now? A dim green light was filtering out from under a door — suddenly it opened and Hitch's heart leaped as he watched Ruby being half dragged, half marched across the passageway by none other than Baby Face Marshall.

Not dead, thought Hitch, *just furious.*

Ruby wasn't taking it lying down. "I don't like people messing with my hair, buster!"

"*You tell him, kid,*" hissed Hitch, his hand reaching for his revolver.

Clancy was standing by the basement door. Unlike Hitch and Ruby he had not studied any plans, and was unlikely to make it through the maze of corridors. What to do? Should he go in or get help?

As it turned out he didn't have to make a choice. An elegant hand reached around and took him by the throat.

"Hello, waiter boy, you looking for something?"

Hitch had his gun trained on Baby Face and was waiting for him to relax his hold on Ruby. No, too risky. He would have to creep up behind him, take him by surprise.

Baby Face was enjoying the moment.

"So you think you are pretty smart, huh? Clever enough to outwit me?"

"It wasn't so hard," said Ruby. "You see, Baby Face, you aren't a good checker — you left me with a very handy gadget, a lifesaver as it turns out. *Always* check the prisoner for lifesaving gadgets. Don't they teach you that in creep school?"

Baby Face didn't like that, he didn't like it at all. He wasn't going to be told his job by some teenage brat. He reached into his back pocket to pull out his knife and as he did, Hitch ran out of the shadows, karate chopped him in the back of the neck, and Baby Face Marshall slumped to the floor.

"Nice to see you, kid."

"About time you showed up," said Ruby. "Thought you must have been busy stuffing yourself with canapés."

"Canapés? Nah, they give me indigestion." He took a good look at her. "You OK, Ruby?"

"Never felt better," said Ruby, smoothing her hair and dusting herself off.

There was a buzz and suddenly light as the power came back on, and there was Valerie Capaldi standing in the doorway, holding a diamond revolver to Clancy Crew's temple.

"Well, well, well, if it isn't the secret agent extraordinaire and his little pet."

"Hello, Nine Lives," said Hitch. "I almost didn't recognize you — something about you is different, more distinguished somehow. . . . It could be the red hair, or perhaps it's the scar. You know it suits you — adds character."

Valerie Capaldi scowled. "You're going to regret that you disfigured me. I'm going to kill you and I'm going to kill the boy and when I'm done I'm going to kill the girl. How about that?"

She wasn't lying, anyone could see that.

Nine Lives raised the little gun and pointed it at Hitch. "Any last words?" she said.

"Let me think," said Hitch, "I'm sure I can come up with something."

Ruby felt for the dog whistle still around her neck.

Nine Lives took aim. "Too bad I'm gonna mess up that nice suit of yours."

Ruby brought the whistle to her lips and gently inhaled.

"Well I guess it's time to say *adiós*," laughed Nine Lives. "Look into my eyes — they'll be the last you see."

"Not quite!" shouted Ruby.

Her voice appeared to be coming from just behind Capaldi, who spun around in confusion — just enough time for Hitch to lunge toward her and grab hold of the diamond revolver.

Only Nine Lives Capaldi wasn't letting go. They struggled, Nine Lives lashing out with her claw-like nails, scratching at Hitch's face. Blood everywhere. Clancy was finding it hard to breathe, his throat caught in her grasp.

Then there was a shot.

Valerie Capaldi's smile twisted into an expression of surprise. Her hand released its grip on Clancy and moved to clutch her heart. She looked up at Hitch. "You killed me?" she said as she slid to the floor. In her left hand the diamond revolver glittered, a pool of crimson forming where she lay.

For just a second the three figures were frozen. Hitch had so many times fought Nine Lives only to watch her somehow leap to her escape — wounded but always alive. Could it really be over?

Suddenly there was a roar of anger from Baby Face Marshall

as he flung himself at Hitch, sending him sprawling across the room.

The key! The Count!

Ruby seized the moment. "See you in one minute, Clance. I gotta do something."

"Ruby, don't go!" he yelled.

Hitch called out something but Ruby couldn't make out what it was. She didn't have time to wait—her watch said one minute to midnight. With the lights back on, the Count would surely have found the glass key—the Buddha might already be gone.

She sped across to the inner vault just in time to watch as the Count reached his hands into the glass cylinder. He looked up in surprise as Ruby plucked off her remaining shoe and flung it hard at his head. It hit him square in the face and he lost his balance—just for a second, but it was enough. At that moment the clock struck midnight, there was a whirring sound, and in the blink of an eye, the glass cylinder shot up through the ceiling.

The Count cried out in fury as the Buddha disappeared from view. The vault was plunged into blackness for just a second and when the lights flickered back on, the vault was empty—he was gone. All that was left was the glass key glinting on the stone floor.

Where is he? Ruby was dumbfounded. *He's got to be in here somewhere — there's no way he could have gotten past me.*

But it was if the Count had simply dissolved away.

Suddenly the passageways were swarming with agents and security guards. When Ruby walked outside she saw Baby Face Marshall being led toward a waiting police car, his hands cuffed, his nose bloody. *Not such a pretty sight now.*

"I'll get you, brat. You see if I don't," he growled.

"Tell it to the judge, Baby Face," shouted Ruby.

"Hey, Rube!" Clancy came running toward her, flapping his arms Clancy-style and sort of hopping up and down. "Boy, am I ever glad to see you, I thought maybe . . . you know . . . you'd . . ."

"Gone to a better place?" replied Ruby. "Nah, not me, Clance my friend — it takes more than an evil genius to get me popping my clogs."

"Which reminds me," said Clancy, "I found your shoe!"

"Gee thanks, I wondered where that had gotten to — turns out these just might be Dorothy's ruby slippers after all. Don't s'pose you got my glasses there too? These contact lenses suck."

A hand ruffled her hair. "Hey there, Ruby, long time no see."

Ruby looked up to see the friendly face of Agent Blacker.

"Thought you might possibly want a jelly donut," he said,

handing her a brown paper bag. "Nothing like a near death experience to give you an appetite."

"Hey, you read my mind," said Ruby.

Hitch, meanwhile, was talking into his watch transmitter. He looked disheveled, perhaps even tired, but his easy cool was back. "Yes, Baby Face has been apprehended. He's being taken away right now."

"And the others?" said LB.

"Capaldi just ran out of lives. But I am afraid the Count, well, he got lucky — slipped right through our fingers."

"He always does," said LB, with a sigh.

"Just a minute," said Hitch. "I got someone who wants to say hello." He held his watch to Ruby's mouth.

"Hey there, LB. I got a complaint. Those gadgets of yours — you know some of them are faulty? I coulda been toast, you know what I'm saying? Lucky for you I don't die so easy."

The kid's alive? For one heartbeat LB was speechless — but *only* for one heartbeat. A second later and she had regained her composure. "I presume you are talking about the Bradley Baker gadgets you stole? They are vintage, Redfort — what do you expect?"

"Bradley Baker's gadgets? How did you know I even had them?"

"I like to think I know most things."

LB disconnected the call, let out a deep breath and smiled. *That's some kid,* she thought.

Crowds of people were gathered in the square: fire trucks, TV crews, and all the citizens of Twinford. While no one was looking, Ruby slipped under the police tape and up the museum steps. The place was deserted and her footsteps echoed on the marble floor, but as she made her way into the great hall she could see the Jade Buddha of Khotan, radiating its mysterious green light, and there standing in front of it was Ruby's father.

"Dad?"

"Hey, Rube, do I look wiser?"

Ruby put her head on one side. "Nah, just greener." Brant Redfort, the lucky soul to look the Jade Buddha of Khotan in the eye at midnight — but then Brant Redfort was born lucky.

"Isn't it magnificent?" His voice had a faraway tone and he seemed almost hypnotized. "Just look into its eyes."

And Ruby did.

And she saw that the Jade Buddha of Khotan really was something.

They stood staring at it for a while longer before Ruby said,

"What are you doing in here anyway? I thought everyone was out looking at the bank not being robbed."

"I came to look for you, honey. Your mother and I were wondering where you had gone to. We have been searching all over — thought you might have gotten lost inside the museum."

"There you are, Ruby!" came Sabina's voice from across the hall. She was about to be alarmed by Ruby's appearance, particularly her T-shirt, which now bore the slogan *trouble,* the *in deep* bit somewhat obscured by mud, blood, and dirt. However, all that came out of her mouth was, "Oh, my! Isn't it just beautiful!"

And it was — too beautiful for words.

The tranquility wasn't to last, though; the Redforts were roused from their appreciation by the following sharply spoken statement.

"Ruby Redfort! I get kidnapped for a few weeks and look what happens — what in tarnation have you done to yourself?"

It was Mrs. Digby, who was looking pretty extraordinary herself, dressed in one of Mrs. Redfort's evening gowns, a mink stole around her shoulders. Standing by her side was a short man with a huge mustache.

"Mrs. Digby!" said Ruby, grinning. "You look like a million bucks."

Cat Woman

RUBY WAS STANDING OUTSIDE Mrs. Beesman's house with Clancy Crew.

He was peering over the fence, looking at the debris in her yard. Boy, was it ever a mess.

"We really have to do this?" said Clancy.

"You got me into this, Clance, telling my mom I was such a *super nice* kid, helping old Mrs. Beesman out. Now I guess I gotta *be* a super nice kid."

Clancy sighed. "I was only trying to cover for you, Rube."

"I know," said Ruby, giving him a friendly thump on the arm. "Just next time *think* before you open that big mouth of yours."

Clancy frowned. "You sure she wants us to clear her yard?"

"I had to talk her into it," said Ruby. "She took a lot of persuading."

They were about to push open the gate when they were surprised by a beeping sound coming from Ruby's coat.

"You're bleeping," said Clancy.

Ruby pushed up her sleeve to reveal Bradley Baker's watch, still fastened around her wrist. The fly was flashing blue. In all the chaos of last night Ruby had forgotten to hand it back to Hitch. With some trepidation she pushed the talk button and held the watch to her ear.

"Where are you!" demanded a gravelly voice.

Ruby gulped. She didn't really feel up to talking to an irate LB. "Look, sorry about the watch and the whistle — I promise I'll hand them to Hitch before he leaves."

"Too late for that, Redfort," said LB. "He's back at Spectrum."

Ruby's heart sank. *Just like old Mary Poppins,* she thought, *he's taken off without so much as an* adiós. "He could at least have said good-bye," muttered Ruby.

"Good-bye? What do you mean good-bye?" said LB. "I just wanted him to bring in that watch so we can have one of our technicians take a look at it. A faulty rescue device is no good to any agent."

Ruby's mind was working overtime but she couldn't make sense of what LB was saying.

"You can consider this your week off, Redfort, but I want to see you at six a.m. in exactly seven days' time, no excuses, no sick notes from your mom. Understand?"

Ruby did not. "My week off?" she stammered. "My week off from what?"

"You want to be an agent, don't you? Well, being an agent takes a lot of training. Hitch will be in charge of that so you had better listen to him." LB cleared her throat before saying, "The rescue watch you can keep, but look after it, it belonged to a friend of mine."

"You can count on me," said Ruby.

"I hope so," said LB. She paused. "Oh, and by the way, you did good, kid."

WHAT I KNOW AND WHAT I DON'T KNOW

· ·

OK so I bet you are wondering what happened
to Froghorn? Well, he got himself in some
very deep water "a good agent should never
take his eye of the ball" that's what LB
said. I believe he's on the coffee-and-donut
detail for the next six months. That's
Spectrum speak for stakeout duty.

Why Buzz is called Buzz? It's simple:

What I <u>can't</u> tell you is what the Count was
looking at with that little laser light
thing—who knows if we'll ever find out but
I'll bet he wasn't trying to discover the
secret to world peace. Clancy's got a hunch I
haven't seen the last of that fellow. I think
he could be right.

Ruby Redfort

CLUE 3:
IF YOU ARE HAVING TROUBLE WITH
RUBY AND CLANCY'S CODE, GO TO
WWW.RUBYREDFORT.COM
FOR HELP.

SOLUTIONS

(1) Solution: First take Trunch across the river. Asimov and Carlucci are safe together. Then take Asimov across but since you can't leave Asimov and Trunch together you must bring Trunch back. Then take Carlucci across the river. Finally come back for Trunch. Everyone is safely on the other side.

(2) Solution: Put three bars on each side of the scales. If they balance then the gold bar you didn't put on the scales is the counterfeit. Otherwise take the three bars that are lightest on the scales. Take two of these bars and put them on either side of the scales. If they balance, then the bar you didn't put on the scales is the counterfeit. Otherwise, the lighter of the two bars is the counterfeit.

(3) Solution: 42

Acknowledgments

Special thanks to my publisher and editor, Ann-Janine Murtagh, for all her help and support during the many years of thinking about writing and actually writing this book. Few editors can be tougher than her and I am grateful for it. I am also very grateful to Adrian Darbishire and Rachel Folder for reading and rereading the text and talking through countless plot options and coming up with some really good ideas along the way. Thanks to Pete Lambert, Lucy Mackay, and John Perella for discussing Ruby Redfort ad nauseam. Thank you to David Mackintosh for his beautiful and clever design work and to Nick Lake for his thorough and thoughtful editing. Last of all, thanks a whole heap to Trisha Krauss and Lucy Vanderbilt for advice on American-speak.